About the Author

...orn Linn B. Halton lives in the Forest of Dean, in the
...her lovely husband and Bengal cat, Ziggy.

...peless romantic, self-confessed chocaholic and lover
...coffee. For me, life is all about family, friends and

...weekend, I can be found either in the garden weeding,
...a paint brush in my hand - house renovation and
...ng furniture is another passion of mine! Oh, and I do
...he occasional glass of White Grenache ...'

...novels have been short-listed in the UK's Festival of
...ce and the eFestival of Words Book Awards. Linn won
...13 UK Festival of Romance: Innovation in Romantic
...award.
...n writes chick lit, cosy mystery/romances, romcoms and
...n's contemporary fiction– *written from the heart, for the*

🐦 @LinnBHalton
f facebook.com/LinnBHaltonAuthor
www.linnbhalton.co.uk

D1579896

Also by Linn B. Halton

Falling: The Complete Angels Among Us
A Cottage in the Country
The Secrets of Villa Rosso

LINN B. HALTON

A division of HarperCollins*Publishers*
www.harpercollins.co.uk

Harper*Impulse* an imprint of
HarperCollins*Publishers*
The News Building
1 London Bridge Street
London SE1 9GF

www.harpercollins.co.uk

This paperback edition 2017

First published in Great Britain in ebook format by
HarperCollins*Publishers* 2017

A catalogue record for this book
is available from the British Library

ISBN: 9780008261290

Typeset in Birka by Palimpsest Book Production Ltd,
Falkirk, Stirlingshire

Printed and bound in Great Britain

My Christmases have been, for the most part, wonderful times creating memories I will always cherish and for which I am so very grateful.

But, as is true for lots of people, there have been occasions when my heart has been heavy. When you lose a loved one it's a bitter-sweet time, but as a new generation starts to fill the empty seats around the table, you know you are truly blessed.

Seeing Christmas once more through the eyes of the children around you isn't just special, it's magical and the best Christmas present I could ever ask for.

So I'm dedicating *Christmas at Bay Tree Cottage* to Billy, Lily, Joe and Maddie.

The Christmas table is growing and even though Mum and Dad can't take their seats, their presence is keenly felt.

Merry Christmas to everyone and hugs to those whose Christmas this year will be tinged with sadness. Remember that love never dies because we carry it with us in our hearts, always.

Linn x

Prologue

'Daddy, you've been gone a while. I was worried you wouldn't make it back in time for Christmas!'

Maya's sweet little voice rose up in the darkness, reflecting a real sense of relief, closely followed by the love and joy bubbling up inside of her.

'I know, Princess, it's complicated. Some journeys take longer than others. Have you been a good girl?'

'Yes, Daddy. Well, mostly. It's still dark outside, is it snowing?'

'No, no snow today.' Maya wriggled down the bed, snuggling in as Niall tugged the duvet a little higher, tucking it in around her.

'It's still early, baby, you need to go back to sleep now.'

'Will you stay with me?' Her voice was a whisper, sleep beginning to wrap itself around her once more. 'You won't go away?'

'I'll be here when you need me, Maya. Daddy's always here.'

Niall lay down next to his daughter and within seconds her breathing settled into a slow, rhythmic pattern.

'I've missed you, baby, and I'm sorry.' His words seemed to echo around the room, even though his voice was barely audible. In his head all he could hear was the haunting strains of Maya's favourite Christmas song by the infamous Wizzard. The words seemed to overtake his thoughts as he began to relax. *When the snowman brings the snow—*

Chapter 1

Elana

Christmas is Coming

It's not that I'm a Christmas grouch, or anything, but this back-to-back festive cheer with the first of December still a week away is beginning to grate just the teensiest bit. Admittedly, a few of the oldies do get my foot tapping, but the last thing I need until I meet this deadline is to be distracted. The clock is ticking and that awful, cold-sweat panic is beginning to set in. There are bills to be paid and having to do Christmas on a tight budget is yet another pressure.

'Maya, can you turn that music down just a little bit, please? Mummy's trying to work.'

'Okay, sorreee.' The sound of her lilting voice drifting into the study makes my heart squish up with love, tinged with that now all-too-familiar sadness. The volume reduces by a few decibels, only to be replaced by shrieks of laughter as Maya and her best friend, Amelie, continue stringing beads for the Christmas tree. The tradition she's always known still has to be upheld. At the moment it's all about Christmas magic, until the year that she's ready to face the dreaded truth – that Santa isn't real. And this could be the last one, assuming we make it to the twenty-fifth without her caving in to the rumours. Even at the tender age of six and a half, some kids are so *knowing* these days and want to grow up much too quickly. Others, like Maya, are content to hang onto their childhood as long as they can and choose to ignore the rumours they hear at school. I guess it's all about that inner desire to believe it's a time when wonderful things can truly happen, no matter how old we are.

Oh, Santa, what would I wish for? To turn back the clock, but then what would be the point? I give myself a shake, this isn't helping at all.

Once again my concentration is shattered beyond redemption and all it took was one line from a stupid Christmas song. The oldies are the best, but not when all they serve to do is to bring back painful memories. My head tells me firmly not to go there. I refuse to get maudlin as we approach the second Christmas without Niall. He would be disappointed in me. I thought I was doing much better this time around and avoiding the slippery slope that always seems to be one step away. It's a ride I've taken so many times since the funeral, but wallowing is a luxury I can't afford. Maya not only needs me to be strong, but to be in the moment with her. We missed too many moments in those early months after Niall was taken from us. The therapist I'd been seeing helped me to understand that when a loss occurs without warning the adjustment is always going to be difficult. Niall was strong

4

and healthy, and ... amazing. So full of life. But I wasn't there with him when he took his last breath, crushed in a tangle of torn metal wedged beneath a barrier on the motorway. My stomach does an involuntary somersault as I try to push the horror away, realising no good comes of re-living the worst moment of our lives. The investigation concluded that one of the tyres had a blowout and his efforts to avoid careering into a lorry had actually caused the car to roll. In my heart I wondered if his reactions weren't as sharp as normal, because he was over-tired and he paid the ultimate price in his haste to hurry home to us. He'd been working long hours to keep the money coming in to pay for the renovation work on our dream cottage on the edge of the Forest of Dean. Anything we could do ourselves, to save paying someone, we did, and that meant spending evenings and weekends stripping walls, filling and painting. He kept saying it wouldn't be forever, but it turned out that for us it was *our* forever.

Reaching out for the coffee mug, I take a large gulp. It's cold, but I need the caffeine hit. The funny thing is that even now I still find myself listening for his key in the door, as if what's happened is nothing more than a nightmare from which I'm going to awaken. Tears these days are few and far between. There are none left to shed and I'm glad about that, at least. But the last thing I need now is to be using up energy I don't have trying to be bright and breezy for Maya if I let myself regress. We're at that sensitive time in her life when she's changing in so many ways. At the moment she claims with a fierce determination that she believes in Santa, but I'm not sure whether it's more about the desire to hold onto that belief, rather than the innocent, wide-eyed acceptance of the fairytale. Losing her dad was loss enough; perhaps this is one step too far and she feels as if the life she knew is slipping away from her.

I turn back to the flashing cursor in front of me, switch screens and begin typing.

Diary Log – day 481 since Niall left us. We're doing okay. 10 days to hit my deadline and 29 days to Christmas. When did life become all about numbers?

I glance back at the entries above, reflecting that my therapist, Catherine Treadwell, would be proud. Gone is the anger once reflected in my daily entry, but gone also is any real sense of commitment to moving on. I'm in limbo. Reality now is worrying about money first and everything else second. Niall's life insurance policy paid off the mortgage on this place but with only one salary coming in now, I'm living from month to month. Every penny of our nest egg went towards the renovation work, but we weren't worried when the money ran out. We thought we had time on our side to turn Bay Tree Cottage into the perfect home. Except that, even if all the work is eventually carried out, it never will be *perfect* now, will it? How can it be, without Niall?

***

'Mum, can we light the log fire tonight?' Maya looks up at me with eager eyes.

'I think we should wait until the weekend, darling. There isn't really time to appreciate it on a school night, is there? Besides, I'm not even sure whether there are any logs left in the store. I promise to get it sorted as soon as I can.'

It was Niall's job, sorting the fire. He would have booked the chimney sweep in early autumn and had the logs all ready and waiting, stacked neatly against the back wall of the garage. Ironically, last year I was much more organised. I suppose it was one of my coping mechanisms during those raw, early weeks and months. Keep going; keep doing something – anything, so I didn't have to listen to what was in my head. But I feel bad. Maya will remember that this time last year we spent every evening huddled together on the sofa in front of the fire, reading. Hour upon hour we escaped into alternative worlds inspired by some wonderful authors. Roald Dahl's *Matilda*, E. B. White's *Charlotte's Web*, and Maya's favourite, Jill Murphy's *The Worst Witch*, a story of tenderness and triumph.

It was the very worst of times, but I focused on getting us through it one day at a time. My gut instinct, immediately after the accident, had been to sell the cottage, just to escape that prevailing sense that something was missing. Niall was no longer here and it would never, ever be the same again. But soon realisation dawned that Maya needed a sense of continuity; the memories trapped within these walls were a lifeline for her, although a cruelly painful reminder for me. In a way she feels her dad is still here and I can't take that away from her.

In a strange, surreal way, last winter brought us even closer together on a level that wasn't really about the mother-daughter relationship. It was the bond of loss and of adjustment. I enjoyed the tales we read together just as much as Maya had done, desperate to escape our stark reality. Watching TV wasn't even an option, as I couldn't connect with the images flickering in front of me long enough to stop my mind from taking over. But reading a book out aloud, well, it wrapped us both in a cocoon.

Before heading into the kitchen to think about our evening meal I add chimney sweep, logs and fire-lighters to my to-do list. Clearly, it's important to Maya for her to mention it and maybe it's something we both need at the moment. Guilt starts to creep into my head, a niggling worry that seems to be there at every turn these days. I'm conscious that what she needs is more time from me and I wish there was a magic wand I could wave to solve my money worries. Pride won't let me take the money Mum and Dad offered and, besides, what I need is a permanent solution. Unless work picks up, either I look for a job that pays more money but still allows me to work from home, or we move to a place that's cheaper to run. The latter option would break Maya's heart because she isn't ready to let go.

Everyone understands that coping with the death of a spouse is heart-breakingly tough, but the reality is so much more complicated. It's the problems that those around you don't even give thought to, which threaten to steal away the ground beneath your feet.

I switch screens again, noting that it's three days since my last entry.

Diary Log – day 484. Christmas is coming. Will it be our last one here? Quality time with Maya v holding onto memories. It's a decision I still can't make. So for now we stay.

Chapter 2

Elana

All Work and No Play

'How are you doing with that deadline, Elana?' Eve busies herself making us both a coffee as I settle myself down on the sofa.

Looking around, what I feel is a sense of calm. I love popping into Hillside View as it reminds me how wonderful it's going to be once Bay Tree Cottage is finished. Both semi-detached cottages stand alone on an outcrop of rock, with almost surreal views across to the river, and with the Forest of Dean as a backdrop. Ironically it was the one thing that originally spoilt it for us, the fact that it wasn't detached. Now, I'm thankful to have Eve, Rick and little Amelie, who is Maya's best friend, on the doorstep.

Both cottages had been empty for quite a long time, owned by an eccentric local farmer, who was in his eighties and seemed oblivious to the decay as the buildings deteriorated. Hillside was already sold when we first came to view Bay

Tree and the moment we drew up outside we knew this was going to be our home. We looked at it longingly for what it could be, rather than with the cold appraisal needed when taking on a project of this scale. It's the reason we didn't hold up our hands in horror at the amount of work that was going to be required, imagining the cosy place it would eventually be. Now what I have is a cottage that is half-renovated and no idea when, or if, I'll ever be able to afford to get it finished.

'It's coming along, albeit slowly. I seem to have a client who is driving the publisher mad at the moment. He's hardly ever around and has missed our last three Skype meetings. How on earth I'm supposed to pull together his biography, goodness knows! If this job falls through I'm in big trouble.'

Eve shoots me a sympathetic look and holds out a coffee mug.

'Thanks. It's my third cup already and Maya's only been at school an hour. Anyway, what was it you wanted to talk about?'

Eve shifts from foot to foot, her face colouring slightly as she settles herself in the armchair opposite me.

'It's not good news, I'm afraid. The builders have now fixed the leak and given the roof a once-over. Surprisingly it's in pretty good condition. Their boss, Matthew, says both cottages were re-roofed some time in the last eight to ten years. However, unfortunately, the chimney needs re-pointing urgently. He's not sure it's safe, so he's going to arrange for scaffolding to be erected and his son, Luke, will be here next week to work on it. The bad news is that yours is in the same state.'

I put the coffee mug down on the side table and push

myself further back into the sofa, trying hard to keep my face composed. More money I don't have.

'Look,' Eve leans forward to touch my arm, 'we can get him to do the work and you can pay us when you can. I know this is the last thing you need at the moment, so don't worry about it. Let us handle it as we're going to incur the cost of the scaffolding anyway, so it will only be the labour costs and a few materials. It's best to get it sorted and there's no hurry with regard to the money.'

I can see that she's embarrassed, but with our girls playing outside whenever they can, and living in a windy position on the side of a hill, this is a health-and-safety issue. It's not something that can be ignored, or postponed, just because I can't afford to have it done. And I don't accept charity, even when it's well-meant. I try not to let a sigh escape, because I know it would quickly turn into a sob. I swallow determinedly – no point in panicking until I know what's involved.

'That's so kind, Eve, and please do thank Rick, too. I'm sure I can stretch to it, though. If you can get Matthew to give me a quote that would be great and, of course, it needs to be sorted quickly.'

We exchange glances and I can see by her frown how troubled she is for me.

'Hey, don't worry. I'm doing okay, really.' I give her a reassuring smile.

Eve eases herself out of the chair and walks around to sit next to me on the sofa. She places her arms around my shoulders and gives me a warm hug. This isn't about money, or a chimney. This is about being weary; so tired of thinking that

I want to switch off my brain and wishing I could spirit myself back two years in time. Golden days that I didn't realise were so very, very precious.

'Time heals, my lovely friend. But there will be setbacks. Sometimes you need to just let it all out, there's no shame in that.'

It's comforting, not least because there aren't many people who understand the frustrations that are still a part of my daily life. My parents would be horrified to know that, because they believe this strong front I'm presenting to the world. They are proud of me because of the way I'm coping and wouldn't know what to do if they thought for one moment I was so fragile I'm in danger of ... what?

'Thank you, Eve. It helps, you know. Just once in a while I need to drop my guard. And the chimney, just get Matthew to pop in to see me. It's kind of him to have checked it out and I'm happy to pay half of the cost of the scaffolding.'

'Don't you even go there! I feel awful having to raise it and wish we could have simply told him to get on with both jobs. But he needs your permission, of course. And you can't light the fire until he gives you the all-clear. Oh, life, eh?'

The sigh that escapes her lips is one of empathy and concern. With our girls being only six months apart in age, Niall's death also affected Eve in a very real way. It was a reminder that you can't take anything for granted, even the fact that there will be a tomorrow. In some ways I hope that it has brought Eve and Rick closer together, allowing them to appreciate how lucky they are to have each other.

'Actually, I also have a problem with a leak in the spare

bedroom, so maybe he could take a look at that, too. The last thing I want is to risk it getting worse over the Christmas holidays. It's on my to-do list but until I have the draft outline of this biography done I can't turn my attention to anything else.'

'You never said who it was you're writing about. Is it anyone interesting?'

'Aiden Cruise.'

Eve rolls her eyes and laughs out loud.

'Ha! Good luck pinning down that bad boy! Is it going to be X-rated?'

'Well, if I don't get at least one more lengthy Skype session in with him, all I can say is that at the moment it all seems rather tame. But then we've only covered his early years and rebellious teens; we didn't get as far as his front-page, post-fame antics.'

'Ooh, the best bit is yet to come, then. Will you get to meet him face to face?'

That's something I've been wondering myself, but mainly because it's difficult with regard to babysitting for Maya. I'm pretty confident that I can get the overview of the book finished if Aiden will honour just one more session, but when it comes to fleshing out the story I'm going to have to really pin him down. I'll have until May next year to get the first draft to the publishers, so for the moment that's a worry for the future.

'To be honest, he's so hard to contact that I think I'll probably end up having to follow him around for a few days to get him talking. I've been liaising with his manager, Seth, and he's promised me that Aiden will be there for my next call, so we can wrap up the outline. He's sympathetic, understanding the problem I have and he suggested I see Aiden on tour some time. If I spend January doing all of the preparation and research work, I'm hoping to have a list of questions for him to focus on when we finally meet up. Fortunately, I have quite a lot of information already, but I have to sift through it and once that's done, it will just be a case of filling in the gaps with the really personal stuff.'

'It's not an easy job you do, is it? Are biographies the hardest to do?'

'Well, to be honest, I prefer straightforward editing jobs but this pays really well. It's easier when it's someone the public adore. Aiden's book will be a best-seller simply because people love reading an exposé about a bad boy. But if he doesn't open up and give me the really interesting stuff, then the publishers won't be happy. On paper what I seem to have so far is a picture of a rock god and each person I talk to seems to be describing a very different man. It's all very confusing. I get a fixed fee from the publisher for the job, but they're more likely to use me again in the future if I can really get to the heart of this story. The problem is that if Aiden keeps avoiding me, then I'm never going to gain his trust and get his side of things. I've interviewed two members of the group, his ex-manager and a few celebrities whose paths he's crossed over the years. What's missing now is the detail only he can give me to bring the story alive. The other project I'm working on in between the biography is editing a set of children's books. Although it's the eight years and up age range,

I've read the first one to Maya and she seemed to love it, so I can't wait to work on the second and third books.'

Eve reaches across for her coffee and then sits back snugly into the corner of the sofa.

'Well, when it comes to your little jaunt with Aiden, Maya is very welcome to stay with us. The girls would love having a couple of days together.'

The sad thing is that I constantly sense the awkwardness Eve feels about my situation and it has affected our friendship. As if all the good things in her life might somehow be a reminder of how awful my life has turned out to be. Rick is an investment and mortgage adviser, well-regarded and with a growing clientele. Money has never been a problem for them and they are the perfect family unit. We all got on so well because it seemed we had mirror lives and so many shared interests, not least, turning a pair of neglected cottages into comfortable homes. I don't envy her, or the wonderful life they have, but I will admit there are moments when I catch myself wondering where we'd be now if Niall hadn't died. Would Bay Tree Cottage be finished and we'd be looking forward to a magical Christmas?

'Thanks, if Mum and Dad aren't available to look after her I might take you up on that offer. I appreciate it, Eve, what you've done. You're a good friend and I know I'm truly blessed. In fact, I have no idea how I would have coped without you on the doorstep. And Maya, too. Amelie has been a tremendous friend, she's a very special little girl.'

I mean every word of it. I've often heard the girls chattering away and Amelie is definitely an old head on young shoulders.

'They never go away,' I'd heard her tell Maya once. 'Your dad would never leave you. You just need to talk to him.'

I was watching them through a crack in the door, just to reassure myself that Maya really did want to play that day. She hadn't been sleeping well and her little face was so pale. Eve and I were encouraging the girls to spend more time together, as my therapist had advised me to keep things as normal as possible. Normal? I nearly screamed at the top of my voice when she'd said that. 'What's normal?', but then that was in the early days.

So they played and each day was a little easier than the one before. Without Eve, Rick and Amelie I don't know how we would have got through it. It's a debt that money can't repay.

Chapter 3

Elana

I Need to Get My Act Together

'Mrs James? I'm Matthew's son, Luke Stevenson.' The guy on my doorstep sticks out his hand in a friendly manner. The first thing that pops into my head is that, up close, he's younger than I expected. From ground level, the few times I've seen him he looked older, somehow, but then he was always the height of a cottage away as he clambered over next door's roof. I suppose roofing work does require a good level of fitness and agility. And he has that in spadefuls. His hair is dark, short around the sides and longer on top. He has a boyish look that doesn't really go with his body, which is strong and athletic. Clearly he doesn't bother to shave every day, but it suits him. His father, who is probably in his fifties, seems to do just about everything aside from roof work, from what I've seen. Guess that makes a lot of sense; why would he when he has such a fit son to do it for him?

I offer my hand and we shake, then I invite him inside. He seems a little hesitant, but I'm conscious of the heat drifting out of the open door as it's such a chilly day. I can almost feel the oil flooding out of the tank to keep the boiler going.

He glances down at the floor, seemingly looking for a mat on which to wipe his muddy boots. At the moment the down-stairs floor is still bare concrete and I've given up worrying about it. His eyes scan the little line of shoes and boots neatly standing to attention along one wall. He seems rather surprised, probably assuming he was going to walk into a beautifully renovated cottage, like Hillside View.

'I didn't mean to stop you; your neighbour mentioned you work from home. I was just wondering if you were happy with the quote my father dropped in and whether you wanted me to start work on the chimney. I'm almost done working on Hillside's repairs, so I could start tomorrow if you like.'

Thankfully, Aiden Cruise came through with that Skype meeting yesterday and I'm now on target to get the outline submitted. This means that in ten days' time the first payment should be hitting my bank account, just sixteen shopping days before Christmas. And, if I shop wisely, there should be enough to cover the work required on the chimney.

'Yes, that would be fine, thank you. It's been a worry, you know, since Eve mentioned it. The girls play outside all the time and we've had some really strong winds this winter. Actually, while you're here, I have a small leak in the corner of the bedroom ceiling. I wonder if you could take a quick look in case it's something you can remedy while you're up on the roof.'

I had hoped that Matthew Stevenson himself would call in with the quote, but I was out on the school run yesterday and came back to find an envelope lying on the hallway floor. It's reasonable enough, but my other little problem is a real concern, too, and I'm not sure whether Luke is the right one to ask.

'Sure.' He's already bent over, tugging at the knots in his boot laces. I find myself looking down at his feet as he eases them out, staring at his socks. They're black and one toe on his left foot is poking through a rather large hole. My gaze moves up to his face and he gives me an apologetic, and rather embarrassed, smile.

'I'm a bit behind on the washing,' he informs me. 'All the good socks were dirty.'

I'm tempted to laugh and don't know why on earth he would share that information with me, but instead I nod in acknowledgement and turn on my heels.

'It's this way,' I call over my shoulder.

I lead him from the rather dusty hallway across the open-plan dining room/study and kitchen, to the staircase. Upstairs is carpeted, but downstairs I've merely covered the concrete as best I can with large rugs. It helps to detract from the unfinished state and we're used to it now.

'You've done a nice job on the kitchen,' he remarks, probably thinking it's the polite thing to say.

'Thank you. Upstairs is virtually finished, which is why the leak is so annoying.'

We continue in silence, until we walk into the spare bedroom and he immediately lets out an ominous 'Oh'.

'Is it bad?'

The damp patch on the ceiling extends out about twelve inches from the corner and already the wallpaper at the top of both walls is beginning to peel away. It's a horrible blot on an otherwise perfect, country-cottage bedroom.

'Well, it's not good, let's put it that way. I'll take a look up top and see what's going on. Pity you didn't get this looked at a bit sooner, to save you redecorating. It could be a guttering problem, or maybe a few slates have slipped.'

For a moment my attention wanders and I'm transported back to the weekend we'd spent wallpapering this room. I can visualise Niall up the ladder as I passed him a pasted sheet of paper folded back on itself in loops. He'd taken it from my hands, but within moments it began to slither down to the floor and as I grabbed it the paper tore. It wasn't a good day, we'd both been tetchy and ended up having a row. We were tired and our patience was wearing thin. A day that was wasted with needless upset in the grand scheme of things because we had no idea the clock was ticking.

'Mrs James?'

Luke's voice brings me back into the moment and I try to shrug off the wave of sadness and regret.

'Sorry. Yes, I realise I should have looked into this sooner. It's been a busy time, I'm afraid.'

'I was thinking of the cost, that's all. These things are always cheaper to fix if they are caught early. If the water has blown the plaster, then it won't be a case of just replacing a couple of pieces of wallpaper. Anyway, I'll let you know what I find.'

As I follow him back down the stairs I give myself a mental

kick. I have to get a better grip on things, because he's right and I know that. He doesn't understand my situation, of course, but I have no excuse and it's a relief to know he'll begin work in the morning.

As I close the door behind Luke, I wonder if there's a bill I can avoid paying this month to cover the extra work. I know there isn't and reality hits that I'm probably going to have to take that loan from Mum and Dad.

The sigh that echoes around the stark hallway seems to grow in intensity, enveloping me with a sense of loneliness that is bone-chilling. Can I do this on my own? I used to think of myself as a strong person, but as time passes each little hurdle is beginning to feel like yet another mountain to climb.

***

Diary Log – day 486. 24 days to Christmas. 5 days to my deadline for the Aiden Cruise book outline and I'm on target. Christmas will happen and, fingers crossed, we will be lighting the fire. It seems almost as important to Maya this year as hanging onto the idea of Santa.

The remedial work to the roof is going to cost as much as the work on the chimney. It's with a heavy heart that I ring Mum to break the news, although she's clearly delighted to help out.

'You know, Elana, everything we have will be yours one day. So don't talk about loans, dear, it's only money.'

Her words make me feel even more miserable. I've just lost Niall, or that's how it feels still, and the thought of losing someone else is one I can't bear to think about.

'It's a loan, Mum, and I will pay it back once this book is finished. You and Dad must enjoy your retirement and I'm not going to rob you of that. Hopefully it will be a long and enjoyable one. You've both earned this time to do whatever you please. It's your time, Mum – remember that, because I don't want you living just through us.'

There are a few seconds of silence on the other end of the line.

'Darling, if you are hurting, then we are hurting. You and Maya are our world; we love you both to bits. We've had a wonderful life and we are so proud of you and how well you are coping. But we know you only choose to show us that brave face. We're always here for you if ... if things ever get too much.'

Her voice is strained and I know her eyes are filling with tears, as are my own.

I can't share this with you, Mum. I just can't. I shake my head, as if it's that easy to shake away my thoughts.

'That's life and we just have to get on with it. We're fine, really. And thanks for the loan, I appreciate it. Give Dad a hug from us!'

Almost as soon as I put the phone down, Maya rushes into the room.

'Was that Grandma Tricia?'

Her little face shows disappointment and, rather guiltily, I realise I should have called her in, even for a brief 'hello'.

24

'We'll see Grandma very soon, Maya, I promise. It was only a quick call today. Have you finished your homework?'

Her bottom lip wavers a little, telling me that she hasn't even started it.

'Can we light the fire, Mum?'

My heart sinks into my stomach.

'I'm afraid we can't, Maya. The builder has to sort the problem with the roof before he can move on to fix the chimney. If we light the fire now it wouldn't be safe. We want to be safe, don't we?'

She considers that for a few moments and then nods her head in agreement.

'How about tonight we cuddle up on the sofa and read anyway, we can light some candles instead of having the fire.'

'But it won't be the same, Mum. And if the chimney isn't safe how will Santa manage to come down it?'

'Well, I hope it will be all fixed by then. So don't worry about that now. Go and sort your homework, then after tea we can have a reading fest. Promise.'

She saunters out of the room without saying another word. I notice that there's no Christmas music, either. Guess we are both having a down day, so I'll finish up and get started on dinner. I don't know who needs this most tonight, Maya or me. As I put the PC into sleep mode, Niall's face stares back at me. One day soon I'll find the strength to take the photo off, but I'm still not quite ready.

Chapter 4

Luke

Some People Don't Appreciate How Lucky They Are

It's milder today and hard to believe it's December. This time last week it was blowing a gale and the rain was driving across the valley in almost vertical sheets, hitting the ground like bullets. Talk about changeable, but at least this is good weather for roofing.

I hate being the bearer of bad news for a customer, but whoever replaced this roof was either very sloppy or wasn't an experienced roofing contractor. Not only had a few slates slipped, resulting in a lot of water damage, but the lead flashing around the chimney is a mess. A quick check in the loft confirmed that the visual damage to the bedroom below only hinted at how much water was getting in. It was only a matter of time and a couple more heavy storms, before the lady of the house had a major leak on her hands that would have brought down the ceiling.

My mobile kicks into life and I groan as I spot the caller ID.

'Yes, Anita. What's wrong?'

'Joe has an ear infection and I forgot to pick up some medicine. It's important.'

'Of course, I'm on my way.'

I hate not knowing when Joe is ill and the fact that Anita only tells me things when it suits her. It's hard enough when a family splits up, let alone putting up with an ex who doesn't feel the need for two-way communication. She's happy enough to share information when she wants me to fetch and carry, but other than that I rarely get to hear what's happening. As I slip the phone back into my pocket and straighten, I take a moment to draw a deep breath. My eyes scan the ridge on the opposite side of the valley. A small, light aircraft is taxi-ing along the airstrip on the hill and I watch as it appears to bounce a little. The noise from the engine carries on the breeze, sounding mechanical, as old planes tend to do. Life is such a contrast at times.

I clamber down the ladder, stopping only to knock on Mrs James door to let her know I won't be around for an hour.

'Sorry, Mrs James, I need to run an errand, but I'll get back here as quickly as I can.'

She blinks, as if slightly taken aback by my words and I kick myself, thinking I should have said I needed to pick up some supplies.

'Oh, that's ... um ... fine. And call me Elana, please.'

She's a good-looking woman, but she wears an almost constant frown. She's probably only in her mid-thirties at most, but that overly serious disposition is ageing. Take now, for instance. She only opened the door about a foot and is peering out at me from the tiny gap. I mean, who does that? I'm not some stranger, I'm her building contractor and yet, on the other hand, she's just asked me to call her by her Christian name. Talk about mixed signals – guess I'll never understand women.

'Okay. Thanks, Elana. I'll be back shortly.'

Eve did mention that her neighbour works from home and I was to keep the noise down whenever possible. Rather remarkably, I didn't laugh, but managed to keep a straight face. How can you not make a noise when you're working on a roof? I need to hammer and saw at the very least and there's no way to do that without making a fair bit of noise.

Anyway, I didn't know her name was Elana. Unusual, but it suits her. She's rather different, a little posh I'd say. She has this mop of curls, the sort of hair that won't be tamed and her little girl is like a mini version of her. It's quite a contrast to her general demeanour, which is rather serious, based on the little interaction we've had so far. Still, I've done the polite thing, now I'm off to sort out Anita.

***

I don't know why I fall for it every time. When I arrive at Anita's apartment with the medicine, Joe is running around in the background looking his usual boisterous self. His face breaks out into a big grin the moment he sees me but Anita doesn't invite me inside.

'That took you a long time.' She scowls as she takes the box from me.

'I was on the roof of a cottage, halfway up a hill on the edge of the forest. I left as soon as I received your call, but it was a thirty-five-minute drive. So what exactly is wrong with Joe?'

As I peer over her shoulder she continues to bar my way, making it clear I'm not going to grab a cuddle from the little fella.

'He seemed a bit hot and he was pulling his ear.'

'Well, he looks okay, now.'

'Yeah, but kids are like that. They bounce back quickly. See you at the weekend.'

With that Anita shuts the door. I hear a yell from inside as Joe protests, but I know there's no point in trying to grab a few minutes with him. The court order says Saturdays ten until four, and Anita has no intention of showing any sort of flexibility.

It's tough being the parent who isn't the primary carer, but I have to work. I'm not saying it's easy for Anita either, but if she could only relax and let me help out I could easily have him more often. The problem is that the system is more about one solicitor against another, rather than common sense coming into play. And, not wanting to sound sexist here, but it favours the mother. Now I don't disagree with that, the mother-child bond is unique, but Anita constantly complains about being a single parent. She is a mother coping on her own for seven nights and six days a week, but that's her choice. I've offered to have Joe at weekends, and weekday over-nighters, if she's in need of a rest. And yet, in court, all I ended up with was six hours on a Saturday.

Whatever I do is wrong and no one seems to understand

that it's not fair. Anita left me, disappointed when I gave up my lucrative career in software design to help Dad out with the business. It's a small operation with a total of five of us covering most of the skill sets, from our electrician, to myself, the general builder/roofer. Was I happy to be back in the profession I'd trained in when I left school? No, and Anita knows that, but this is all about family. The pride my dad now has seeing '& Son' on those letterheads, is priceless. More importantly, Mum doesn't have to worry quite so much about the effects of his high blood pressure. It's under control again at the moment, but a dizzy spell when you're thirty feet plus in the air is a real scare. It isn't just roofing work, but anything off a ladder, or scaffolding, now makes her worry about him, so it's my job to keep that to a minimum.

If the price I paid is that I gave up my dream to maintain his, then what choice did I have? The livelihood of five families is on the line here.

Besides, regrets are something I can't afford at the moment. Having to pay maintenance for both Anita and Joe until he goes to pre-school, and Anita can get a part-time job, is understandably costly. The mortgage on our old apartment is expensive, but Anita said it was unfair to expect her to move into something cheaper. Thankfully, the tiny bedsit I rent is a good price and my needs are modest. I enjoy my own company and, to be honest, when I'm not working or with Joe, then I'm on the computer. Jeez, that makes me sound like a saddo, if ever I heard a sob story. But at the moment I can't contemplate having anyone else in my life to complicate it even further.

Ironically, the guy Anita left me for wasn't in the picture

for long. It takes a special person to take on someone else's son and accept the situation; plus the fact that I had no intention of absenting myself from Joe's life didn't go down too well. Anita was appalled when he suggested she hand over Joe to me, so they could 'start afresh'. The wake-up call made her bitter, because I think she began to realise that my loyalty wasn't quite so boring after all. Maybe stability was actually a big positive over wanting to socialise and party all the time. But then, she's still only twenty-two years old and at twenty-four I've had a couple more of those so-called delightful party years. Personally, I thought it was all a bit over-rated, if I'm honest. Getting drunk and chatting up women just to be one of the lads was often mind-blowingly boring. And yet it was how I met Anita. She was out on a friend's hen party at the time.

Anyway, it is what it is. The truth is that we were simply too young when we had Joe, despite being delighted when we found out Anita was pregnant. But I guess I'd always wanted to be a part of a stable family unit of my own, because my parents are so happy together. I'm used to family life, whereas Anita feels she's been robbed of her freedom. She's torn between a mother's instinctive love for her child and the hopeless feeling of being tied down, with a level of responsibility she couldn't even comprehend in the beginning.

Now she takes her frustrations out on me and I have to be man enough to accept that, because no matter what happens, we created one great little kid.

***

'Would you like a cup of tea or coffee?'

I look down over the edge of the roof to see Elana James shouting up at me, hands cupped around her mouth. You can't shout quietly, lady, it's a long way up. Admittedly she's rather reserved and it's kind of her to make the offer, so I hold up one hand in acknowledgement and shout back, 'Thanks, tea, I'll be down in five.'

It's about time I finished, anyway, so I adjust the tarpaulin and check everything is watertight for the night. I found a lot of broken slates that also need replacing and the order will be delivered in the morning. By tomorrow night I'm hoping the roof repair will be in hand and then I can start thinking about the work on the chimney. A voice suddenly rises up out of thin air, startling me; well it's more of a mumble, really. I ease myself into a standing position and hold my breath, straining my ears to catch the direction it's coming from. There it is again. I move closer to the chimney and now I can make out actual words.

'... and you have to promise me that you won't forget, Santa. I don't want my daddy to think I've forgotten him. You can't send presents to people who are in heaven, even though you can speak to them, of course. So I need you to take him something special from Mummy and me. I'll let you know when the chimney is fixed. And I'll leave you some extra biscuits on Christmas Eve. Thank you.'

A lump rises in my throat as the voice trails off into silence. No wonder the lady is so reserved; she's not divorced, as I'd assumed, she's a widow. I wonder when exactly her husband died. Her daughter is a really cute kid, bright and very polite.

Christmas can't be easy for them; it's a hard time of year when you have to live with regrets. I'll be with my parents this year for the first time since I left home when I was eighteen. Never thought I'd find myself back there at Christmas, staying in my old bedroom as if being married and becoming a dad is merely a dream.

I wonder if Elana heard her daughter's plea, too. It's none of my business, but it's probably the saddest thing I've ever heard. Right, time to get off this roof and drink that tea before I set off home for the day.

Chapter 5

Luke

Keeping the Client Happy

'Everything alright, my son?' Dad's voice booms down the line. Mrs James let me know he'd called in shortly after I left to run my errand.

'Yep. You know what kids are like; Anita had run out of medicine and was worried Joe was getting an ear infection. He was fine when I saw him, briefly. I wasn't invited inside.'

Dad makes a sound like 'harrumph'.

'Just do what you can, when you can, Luke. The little dude might not be aware of it yet, but he's lucky to have a dad who cares so much.'

It matters to me that my dad thinks that, although I've failed to give Joe the stable family unit he deserves. Maybe if I'd made the effort to take Anita out more, rather than assuming she was happy enough with a life that centred around just the three of us, we'd have stayed together. I thought that was what we both wanted, and I sure got that wrong!

'Thanks. Is Ma there?'

I hear him call out, 'Sally, it's your favourite son on the phone.'

A few seconds later Mum picks up the receiver.

'Only because he's my only son,' she comments, laughing. 'How are you, Luke – and Joe?'

'I'm fine, really. I just wanted you to know that there's no panic. Just Anita doing the usual; maybe Joe has been a little off-colour, but she wanted to remind me that she's the one who takes the brunt. It was just a trip to the chemist, that's all. I knew you'd be worried. He was running around in the background and seemed fine.'

'She didn't let you talk to him, then?'

The disappointment in her voice is a killer. She simply can't understand Anita's actions and she hates to think of the hurt it's causing me.

'I'll have him on Saturday, as usual. He was fine, that's all that matters.'

'Yes, that's the main thing. And you are okay?'

'Yes, Ma. I'm doing fine and loving my work.'

I can almost see the smile on her face.

'You're a good son and one day you'll find someone very special.'

If only Anita had thought I was a good husband, then life would be sweet. Instead, it's a mess and I feel like a failure. I've given my parents a grandchild, but one they can only see briefly every Saturday afternoon.

***

The replacement slates for Bay Tree Cottage don't arrive until late morning. Fortunately, it's a dry, bright day and even the sun is putting in an appearance. I can only hope this weather continues into next week, as I can't start work on the repointing if there's any sign of a frost. It's a job I'd normally look to postpone until early spring, but like Hillside View, it's a job that has to be done sooner rather than later. One really strong gust of wind could do a lot of damage and the debris falling from a roof could potentially kill someone.

The bonus of working up here is that it's quiet for the most part. The drone of traffic is hardly noticeable in the distance, and the odd car driving down the hill is merely a reminder of the existence of other people. It's certainly a great place to live. It's just a pity for Elana that the inside still needs quite a lot of work to finish it off.

As I climb down the scaffolding, more than ready to demolish my packed lunch, the postman is at the door of Hillside View and Eve looks up.

'Luke, I have a cheque here for you. Step inside while I go and find it.'

I loiter inside the porch, making sure I don't step off the coir matting. My boots are mostly clean, but the light-cream carpet beyond it isn't exactly practical. I guess when you have money that's not a major consideration.

'Sorry to keep you waiting, Luke. Here you go. Please tell Matthew that we're thrilled with the work and ask if he can confirm when exactly in January he's able to make a start on the new conservatory.'

'No problem, and it's nice to get feedback. And thanks, too, for your recommendation to next door.'

'Oh, Elana. Yes, an unfortunate expense for her, I'm afraid, but in another way she's relieved to think it will all be fixed very soon.'

I turn to go, then hesitate.

'Um ... just so I don't put my foot in it, or anything. Do you mind if I ask when her husband died? I heard her daughter talking about it.'

'About sixteen months ago in a tragic accident. A tyre blowout on the motorway. It's considerate of you to ask. So easy to assume a husband is around and she's very fragile still, naturally.'

I nod my thanks, holding up the cheque in acknowledgement and head off to the van.

It's a bit chilly, but with the radio playing in the background I'm happy enough sitting here eating my sandwiches and looking out over the extensive views. If only I could stop my mind wandering and wondering 'what if'. If Anita wasn't so bitter, if I'd realised how trapped she'd end up feeling—

A movement in front of me makes me jerk my head up and I see Elana parking her car up by the garage. As she walks down the path it would be rude not to wave. She smiles and when she draws alongside the van I wind the window down, because she appears to be slowing her pace.

'I'm sorry to interrupt your lunch, Luke. When you've finished do you think you could pop in and take a look at something?'

'Will do, Mrs James – I mean, Elana. I'll be in shortly.'

Even when she smiles there's that little hint of sadness in those green eyes of hers. Something that she probably isn't even aware is there, or maybe it takes one to know one. People who have sadness in their lives often carry it inside, unseen, but the eyes are the windows of the soul. When a hurt runs deep there's no getting away from it. I wonder if that's what people see when they look at me – the disappointment and sense of failure I feel.

I straighten my back and stretch out my arms, my muscles beginning to ache a little from sitting in a cramped space. I can't wait to get to the gym tonight and have a really good workout. Then it's a takeaway pizza and a little software program to test out. One of these days, hopefully, I'll have something to sell that will take away all of my money worries. Until then, though, it's back to the job in hand.

As I walk up to the front door of Bay Tree Cottage, Elana is looking out for me and immediately opens the door.

'Thanks, Luke. Much appreciated. The problem is in the utility room, this way. Don't bother about your boots, it's hardly pristine in here.'

She sounds accepting of the situation and I feel for her, now I understand the position she's in. She appears to be quite a proud lady and it must hurt, being alone with a child and living in something that is only partially completed.

I follow her into the narrow utility room and she pulls open the doors to the sink unit, exposing a large bucket half-full of water. A constant drip that is running quite fast is like a low drumbeat.

'How long's it been leaking?'

I look across at her and she grimaces.

'A while. I have to empty the bucket several times a day. And it's getting worse.'

A quick glance isn't enough to discover what's causing the leak, although it's sufficient to establish that this probably wasn't done by the best plumber in the world. If her husband did it I have to be careful. In fairness, it's not a really bad job, but there's a lot of pipe work running off to service the washing machine and dishwasher. I would have configured it differently, flush against the back wall so that if there was a problem everything was easier to access. Quite simply, this is a pig of a job, because it's going to be difficult to get a wrench in there to tighten up whichever joint is leaking.

'It's not a problem. I'll go and grab some tools.'

She lets out a sharp breath, clearly relieved it's something I can fix.

'I was rather worried you'd say it was a major problem. I'm afraid the plumber we used wasn't the best. My husband wasn't here when the work was done and when he saw it he thought it was a bit of a mess.'

I smile and shrug, but she looks back at me rather flustered. I'm not sure she meant to share that, so I make a quick exit and when I return she's nowhere in sight. I throw a dust sheet on the floor and open the doors wide, then take out the shelf. Lying down on my back I ease myself into the cabinet and stare up at the maze of pipes. Isn't it always the way that the leak comes from the top? It's the cold tap that's leaking; the drip is almost constant. I can just about get my hand up between the pipes and get the wrench in place, but when it bites I can only twist it about a millimetre at a time. Even then, nothing seems to be happening. Then it dawns upon me that whoever installed this probably cross-threaded it when they tightened it up. Every time I move it slightly, it's just going around the same thread. Nothing I do seems to stem the dribble of water. I hear a cough and as I begin easing myself back out, I find myself looking up at Elana.

'It's not going to be an easy fix, is it?'

I guess she can tell from the look on my face.

'Hey, it's not as bad as that. Someone has over-tightened the nut at some point and it looks like the tap itself is crossed-threaded. That means when I try to do it up it's not making any difference.'

'There's an "and", isn't there?'

I nod.

'And that means a new tap. The problem with the layout underneath there is that the taps were put in first. All the extra pipe work was installed without any thought to accessing the taps. In all honesty I'm better off doing a quick re-design so that it's easier for the future. If I try to replace the tap as it is now, it will probably take me longer than sorting it out once and for all.'

She nods. 'Okay. Thanks. No point in cutting corners. To be honest, I'm getting a little sick of the word *leak*. Do you have any idea how much this is going to cost?'

'It's a couple of hours' work and a tap, that's all. It won't be a lot. As I'm here working anyway, it will just be a small add-on.'

'Thanks, I appreciate that. Can I make you a drink?'

'That's very kind, but I'll pop off now to pick up a replacement tap. I have everything else I need in the van. It going to take me a couple of hours, tops.'

'Sorry to have pulled you away from the roof. Oh, there's my phone – I'll leave you to it. I'll make a cuppa when you get back. And thanks for not making a drama out of my little crisis.' She gives me a warm smile and the little furrow in her forehead disappears for a second or two.

***

Elana opens the door and I step inside, slipping off my boots.

'You know, there's really no need. It's not as if the floor is clean, the concrete constantly throws up a white dust and I've given up on it.'

'It's a habit – we like to respect our customers' homes. I'm going to have to turn off the water for a while, so if you need to run a tap for anything let me know when you're done.'

'The kettle is full, so no problem. It's only me here during the day when Maya is at school, so you aren't disrupting anything. One sugar, white – right?'

'Thanks. I'll make a start, then.'

As Elana disappears into the kitchen, I head off to the utility room. Walking past the computer in the corner of the dining room, I can't help but notice the photo of a rather good-looking guy on the screen. It must be so hard to lose the person you love, just like that; having to juggle not only your own emotions, but those of a child, too. It makes me think of the Santa thing and her daughter. It's not something

I can bring up, but I sincerely hope she's aware of what's going on inside that little girl's head.

Anyway, it's none of my business and now I have a mess of pipes to hack about, so I can start again and do the job as it should have been done in the first place. Shoddy workmanship just annoys the heck out of me.

Chapter 6

Luke

Dad For the Day

Picking up Joe is always a bittersweet moment. It's great to know I have some quality time with him and yet the handover is always upsetting. What I wish is that we could have family time together, all three of us. It can't happen, I know, as whatever was good between Anita and me has completely disappeared. Maybe it's just too soon to expect her to be able to put her feelings to one side to join in our fun. But I always try.

'We're going swimming, would you like to come?'

She looks directly at me, raising one eyebrow with disdain.

'Swimming? You know the chlorine isn't good for my hair. I think I'll pass. Besides, I'm meeting up with a friend at the mall to do some shopping. Goodness knows, I don't get much time to myself and I deserve a few hours off.'

I'm such a fool, I didn't mean to upset her, or make her

feel guilty for grabbing a few carefree hours. I just thought ... hoped—

'No, it's fine. I understand. I thought I'd ask, as you know what Joe's like. He loves splashing about in the water and it's great fun.'

The eyebrow doesn't lower and I hold Joe up for a goodbye kiss. She hugs him close, plants a kiss on his forehead and says, 'Mumma loves you. See you later, little guy.'

I know she's pulled between the sadness of letting him go and the desire to grab some precious *me* time. It's different for the guys, isn't it? Most men don't even consider that when a baby arrives it's a truly life-changing event being a mum. It's often something we take for granted. We tend to dip in and out of our kids' lives, a lot of men still being the traditional main provider. And even when both parents are working, I wonder how many men jump out of bed in the middle of the night when the kids start crying? I like to think I did my share, but Anita was always awake before me and out of bed before it registered with me that Joe was even awake. Perhaps it's all down to how we are wired up.

Joe wriggles, clearly eager to be put down and for us to get on our way. He looks up at me expectantly as I grasp his little hand in mine.

'Swimming, Joe?'

He nods. 'Water,' he says in that sing-songy little voice of his. It sounds more like 'vauta', but his words are getting much easier to understand as the weeks go by. Apparently he's a little behind on his speech, considering he's now seventeen months old, but my mum says boys are often like that. Girls, apparently, are much quicker to talk.

'Right, little man. We have one job to do on the way to the pool. Daddy has to drop something off as Granddad forgot, so we're taking the scenic route and going via the forest. Trees, Joe? Wanna see some big trees?'

Joe nods enthusiastically, although I'm not sure he understands. You don't get many big trees in the middle of a busy town, so I hope he's going to love the detour.

He's happy enough in his car seat and as we leave behind the built-up area of town and the landscape changes, he's fascinated by the open fields.

'Look Joe, sheep!'

'Eep.' He repeats, pulling his finger out of his mouth and pushing the wet digit against the car window. 'Eep.' A once-clean window is now covered in smears and it makes me smile. Today I feel like a dad again.

As we pull up outside Bay Tree Cottage, I unclip Joe from the seat and he claps his hands. 'Baa, baa,' he shouts. He thinks we're going to look at the sheep up close.

'No, Joe. But we are going to see a great view.'

I grab the roll of flashing from the boot and walk down to the cottage, both arms full. Then I realise I need to ring the doorbell, but the lead is even heavier than Joe. Just as I'm considering my dilemma the door opens and it's Maya.

'Hi, Maya. I'm just dropping this off and wondered if your mummy was around?'

'Baba,' Joe says, not wanting to be left out.

'Maya's a big girl, Joe. You're the baba.'

Maya laughs. 'He's funny and cute!' She reaches out and he grabs her hand. Elana walks up behind Maya, smiling.

'Ah, what a sweetie. Who is this little chap?'

'His name is Joe.'

'Mum. Can he come in and play, please?'

Elana looks at me and then smiles down at Maya.

'I think that's rather up to Luke.'

She tilts her head in my direction, clearly quite happy to invite us in.

'Well, I didn't mean to interrupt your day. I was just going to ask if I could store this in the hallway. I'll need it on Monday and it's not something I can leave outside. It's just that I don't have the van at weekends.' I turn my gaze in the direction of Joe.

'Oh, sorry. That's heavy and you have your hands full. Step inside, please. I'll put the kettle on.'

Elana disappears and I put Joe down. At first he clings to my leg, but Maya starts talking to him and, before I know it, he's toddling after her as she encourages him inside.

I'm relieved to dump the roll of lead as I'm not sure how much longer I could have carried it. It's only as I turn to enter the cottage that I notice the photo on the windowsill. It's Elana and her husband. I recognise him from her screensaver; he's holding Maya, who is probably only a few weeks old.

'What will Joe drink?'

Elana's voice catches my attention and I quickly check on the kids before I join her in the kitchen.

'Water will be fine. He's not very good with a cup still, but he's okay if I hold it for him.'

She hands me a mug of coffee and carries a tray through into the sitting room.

'Take a seat, Luke. So, do you babysit often?'

Maya is on the floor showing Joe one of the apps on her iPad. There's a small monkey running around collecting bananas and as they both stab their fingers at the screen, he runs faster and faster.

'Sort of, he's my son, actually.'

Elana takes the seat opposite me, a look of mild surprise on her face.

'Oh, I didn't realise you were a family man.' Her face looks a little flushed.

'I'm older than I look,' I retort. Her cheeks are now beginning to glow. 'It's complicated. We split up when Joe was six months old. I have him every Saturday.'

Quiet ensues as we both turn our attention to taking sips of coffee that is way too hot to drink. Maya and Joe are having lots of fun and now they have crayons and a colouring book.

'Just make sure he keeps his crayon on the paper, Maya. He's still learning the rules.' Maya smiles back at me as Joe does a squiggle all over a Christmas tree she drew for him.

'That's sad,' Elana says after a few minutes have elapsed.

'Yeah, well, it wasn't my decision. But you know what it's like, life has to go on.' The moment I finish speaking I realise that she might think I was referring to her situation, too. She probably doesn't realise I know, so now I'm the one feeling embarrassed. I glance across at her and our eyes meet.

'It certainly does,' is all that she says. There's no emotion in her voice, though, and no hint of acknowledgement beyond the obvious. It's a relief, as I have to remember she's a client.

'He's a happy little chappie, so you must be doing something right. It's hard for the kids when things go wrong. It's a constant worry, isn't it?'

'Yep. I don't like to think of him paying the price for our mistakes. But you're right, he is happy most of the time. Sometimes on handover he wails when I have to leave and that breaks my heart.'

'Do you want to try him with his drink?' Elana holds out the plastic cup.

I take it and hold it out to Joe. He immediately toddles over and with his hand on one handle, and mine on the other, he drinks half of it in one go.

'Ta,' he mutters and then heads straight back to Maya and the colouring book.

'Aww … he's a little darling. I can't really remember Maya at that age; I'd have to look back at the photos. I vaguely remember that every time she tried to pick something up off the floor she would topple over. Her head seemed to be heavier than her body for ages, as she was very slim. She constantly walked around with a forehead that looked like she'd been fighting!'

We laugh and for some reason Joe decides to join in, which makes Maya laugh, too.

'Look, I really didn't intend to disrupt your day and we'd better get off. I'm taking Joe swimming and then we're going to visit my parents. Thanks so much for the coffee and I'll be here at seven on Monday. The weather forecast is dry but overcast, so fingers crossed I can get that lead work sorted and then make a start on the repointing.'

'It's been a real pleasure and Maya has enjoyed playing with Joe. Next door are away this weekend and she's missing the company of her friend.'

'It must be nice having a best friend living next door. Lucky too, given this location. I haven't seen many other kids around.'

As I scoop Joe up and he gives Maya a big wave, we head out to the front door.

'It's one of the drawbacks when you have kids, but we thought the benefits outweighed the negatives. It's safe for them to play outside, there isn't much passing traffic, and nature in all its glory is literally on the doorstep.'

I don't think Elana realises she said *we* and I pretend not to notice. I guess it's hard to switch from being one half of a happy couple to being a widow. Even the word itself sounds grim and it doesn't suit her. Grief is a process, I believe, so I'm sure it's not easy going through each stage. I suppose splitting up with someone is quite similar in some respects. I'm grieving for what could have been and still trying to work out what to do next.

As I strap Joe back into his car seat I can't help thinking that this is the sort of life I'd envisioned for my family. I just thought it was a few years away and by then I'd be financially secure. Instead, it's all one big sorry mess. They do say you get the life you deserve and I guess Anita and I aren't being punished, but paying the price for letting life sweep us along. No baby should be a surprise, it should be something that is planned. My aim now is to make sure I keep them both as happy as I can, given the circumstances.

Chapter 7

Elana

Living Life Under a Cloud of Dust

I sit in front of the screen with my email to the publishers open in front of me. There's a massive sense of accomplishment as I press the send button and, at long last, the outline of Aiden's biography is winging its way to their offices. They promised they would get the payment for stage one processed by the end of next week. I'll have to wait to find out what changes they want once they've had a chance to consider my initial thoughts, but that doesn't affect payday.

I told Seth Greenburg, Aiden's business manager, I'd give him a call once it was done. I grab my phone, sitting back and looking at the screen with a measure of satisfaction and relief.

'Seth, it's Elana James. The outline is done and on the way. I doubt I will hear anything now until the New Year, but as soon as I do, I'll let you know what they have to say. I've plenty to be going on with and I'll begin fleshing out some of my notes from the various interviews.'

'Great. I'm sorry Aiden couldn't be available as often as we'd hoped, but it's going to be a case of grabbing time with him when you can. I mentioned the idea of you perhaps accompanying him on tour in March, but he's doing a special gig on New Year's Eve at Eastleigh Court. It's invite only, as it's a private party for Morton Wiseman, but I wondered if it might be an opportunity for you two to meet in person. I think you'll understand a lot more about him when you see him perform live.'

Is Seth worried about what I think of Aiden and concerned I'll focus less on his talent and more on his infamous temper? And why can't I seem to get a clear picture of who this guy is, because even as I try to piece it all together nothing seems to fit.

'Well, um, I'll have to think about that as there would be a few things I'd have to rearrange at this end. Is this *the* Morton Wiseman, you're talking about? The actor?'

'Yep, this year's number-one sexiest man alive, or so the polls say. He's not the best influence on Aiden, I'm afraid, but they've always been good mates. Look, I appreciate you might already have plans, but I think it would help if you meet up before you start getting down to the detail. Research is one thing; what other people tell you is another, but you also need to see the guy beneath all the hype.'

Seth is a really genuine man, very professional and very astute. He knows he can't influence what I write, but I think he can see that I'm going into this with an open mind. I know sensationalism sells books, and the publishers will expect a full account of the years Aiden was using illegal substances, but he has changed. Yes, he still has a short fuse, but from what I've pieced together so far, there is often a lot of provocation before he explodes.

'I understand. Leave it with me and I'll do my best. Can you email me the details?'

"No need. I'll send a car to pick you up late afternoon on the day and it's only just over a two-hour drive. Aiden's performance begins at nine. I'm happy to book a room at a local hotel for you if you can stay over; it's going to be a late one.'

'Thank you, Seth. I'll email to confirm when I've sorted things at this end.'

I put down the phone thinking I rather walked into that one. New Year's Eve has never been special, usually the three of us watching a film together before Maya went to bed. Then, Niall and I always watched one of our favourites – some of them we'd seen over and over, but never tired of the storylines. Should I feel guilty about leaving her with Mum and Dad, just so I can work? And how do I feel about dressing up and being around celebrities? The answer to that is nervous as hell. It's certainly not something I thought about when I took this job on.

'Mum, are you ready to play Monopoly now?'

'Yes, honey. I've just finished.'

'Can we light the fire?'

'No, Maya. Luke is starting work on the chimney tomorrow. Then I have to book the sweep and I'm not sure he's going to be able to come before Christmas. We might have to pile the fire grate up with logs and pretend this year. Do you mind? Maybe I could buy some red lights to put in between them, so it looks like a fire?'

She stands with her head crooked to one side, considering my offer.

'It's not quite the same, Mum. I suppose it's better for Santa, though. I wonder if he's ever burnt his feet? You know, on the hot bits in the bottom.'

I have to concentrate hard not to smile, but keep my expression as serious as hers.

'That's why he wears stout boots. He's been doing it a long time, Maya, and even when there isn't a fireplace he has a master key that fits every front door.'

She jumps up and down on the spot, her eyes wide with excitement.

'I wondered about that! He listens, too, Mum. Doesn't he? I've been talking to him and hoping he was listening.'

My frown is back, the smile no longer hovering. What has she told Santa that she hasn't told me?

'Well, yes, he does listen but he's very busy in the run-up to Christmas so it's probably better to write to him. I can post a letter for you, there's still plenty of time. It's express delivery to the North Pole at this time of year.'

What goes through the mind of a six-and-a-half-year-old child when they are missing their daddy at Christmas? I remember something Luke said, yesterday. 'Life has to go on.' It's the same whether you are a child or an adult.

'Think about it, Maya, I'm sure Santa would be very happy to receive a letter from you.'

'It's Monopoly time!' She shrieks, and I'm not sure whether or not my words have even registered with her. It would help me to know what's important to her this Christmas, aside from having a roaring fire, which doesn't look very promising at the moment.

'Go on in and set it up on the coffee table. I'll pack this away, make a quick coffee and then I'm all yours.'

Her beam is reward enough. I quickly scoop the small pile of papers into a stack, slip them into the box file and then, with the mouse, click to change screens.

Diary Log – day 490. 20 days to Christmas. Pressed send on the Aiden Cruise book outline – now awaiting payment. Time to change my screensaver, I think, something Christmassy to show Maya I'm getting in the mood. Hoping she will write Santa a letter so I can gauge what's going on inside that little head of hers. We're surviving – just.

As I make a cup of coffee, I wonder what I'd write in a letter to Santa. What would I ask for? What do I want? My mind is blank, like a chalkboard that has been cleaned and is ready and waiting for someone to begin writing on it. Except that I have no idea what to ask for, even if Santa was real and could deliver whatever my heart desired. Everything I wanted was wrapped up in Niall. All I want now is a rosy future for my daughter, but should I also want something for myself? I suppose what I'd really like is for someone to wave a magic wand and make Bay Tree Cottage perfect. If we can't have Niall, then maybe we can surround ourselves with a home that still feels like he's here with us. I'm only guessing Maya feels that way, too, but I'm pretty sure it would be very different if we moved somewhere new. The problem is that until she's prepared to tell me in her own time, I'm second-guessing. Okay, Santa, find a way to sort out this cottage once and for all. I don't care if it's a lottery win, although I'll have to remember to buy a ticket – or an unexpected cheque in the post.

I look down at my slipper-socks, covered in white concrete dust, and sigh. Just make it happen soon, Santa.

Chapter 8

Elana

Santa to the Rescue

By seven a.m. Luke is already on the roof clambering around. The intention was for Maya to have an early night after several hours of board games yesterday, but we ended up reading quite a few bedtime stories. She went to sleep a little later than usual for a Sunday night. Her last words were that it had been a lovely day and that actually brought a tear to my eye. The cottage doesn't feel full any more with just the two of us and she obviously feels the same way, but we'd laughed a lot. It had turned into one of those days that you re-live with a smile on your face, as it's a reminder that life can still be good.

I pop out to put some rubbish in the bin and pass Rick on the drive.

'Hey, Elana. How're things?'

'Hey, stranger. Good and I owe you a big thank you. I don't know what I'd do without you and Eve looking out for me. I hear you've been busy.'

He's carrying a large pile of files under one arm and a small suitcase in the other.

'It's not a problem; I'm only sorry it meant more expense for you. I'm off to London again; at this rate it would be easier to rent an apartment up there. The travelling is the worst part, although usually I can work on the train. Today I have to take the car as I'm dropping off files and then heading off to Surrey.'

'Well, just drive safely.'

We exchange glances and Rick nods in agreement; I didn't mean to say that, as immediately we both think of Niall.

'Will do and enjoy your week,' he calls out as I head down to the cottage.

Today I have to phone Mum about New Year's Eve, to see whether they will be able to have Maya. I did think of asking Eve first, as she's having a small family party and it would be great for the two girls to keep each other company. However, I know that it's a night Mum and Dad rarely go out and they love spending time with Maya. Since Niall passed away there are few reasons for her to go and stay over, so I know they'll be delighted.

When I open the post I'm rather surprised to see an envelope with Mum's writing on it. Slitting it open, it's a card with a picture of some hand-tied roses on the front of it. Inside is a cheque, folded in half, and the note on the card says:

This is a Christmas present and you can't refuse something that's given with love at this time of year. Mum and Dad xxx

When I unfold the paper it's for five thousand pounds. My legs wobble a bit and I sink down onto the dining chair.

'What the … I can't take this!' Talking to oneself out loud probably isn't best with a six-year-old around, so I stuff the handful of post into my filing tray on the desk. I shout up to Maya to clean her teeth and come straight down afterwards, or we will be late for school. Amelie is probably already waiting for us as it's my turn to do the ferrying this week.

All the way to school, and back, I can't stop thinking about the cheque. Yes, I need it, but will my conscience allow me to take it? I have a roof over my head and we don't go short of anything – all it lacks is a little cosmetics. Is that really enough justification to begin emptying my parents' little nest egg?

When your thought processes are churning it's almost like having two voices in your head. Good cop, bad cop. Okay, that's not quite right, but it's how it feels.

They're going to be upset if you don't take it.
There goes their dream trip to Australia.
No more concrete dust – a floor you can clean!
Mum will admit that she wasn't looking forward to the long flight anyway.
How selfish are you prepared to be?

It's a temptation to just take it and say thank you, but it doesn't feel right. In the end, when I arrive home I go straight inside and phone Mum. An hour and quite a few tears later, I place the cheque on my desk, ready to take it to the bank this afternoon. Mum is over the moon about having Maya to stay on New Year's Eve, but I'm still feeling as if I've been talked into doing something that will rob them of one of their dreams. I've become a liability and somehow I have to turn that around. The time has come to stop making excuses and start grabbing hold of life again.

I'm going to do such a great job of this biography that lots of new work will come my way and then I'll repay my parents every single penny. As a rush of enthusiasm rolls over me the door bell chimes, interrupting my determined, 'I am woman, hear me roar' moment.

It's Luke.

'Sorry to bother you, Elana. The flashing is done and that's the really noisy bit out of the way, now. I need to use your outside tap to mix up the cement for the chimney, but it appears to have been turned off, so it must have a separate stop valve. Do you mind if I take a look?'

'No problem, help yourself.'

Luke steps inside and I leave him to forage under the stairs. On his way out he shouts out a quick thanks and I hurry to catch him before he shuts the door.

'When you stop for lunch do you think you could pop in? I'd like to talk to you about some of the outstanding work on the cottage. If you haven't prepared anything, I could make us some sandwiches.'

He nods his head. 'Sure. I have a pasty if you could nuke it in the microwave for me.'

I can't help laughing at the thought. 'No problem. See you in a bit, then.'

He's so easy-going that's it's hard to understand what could have gone wrong with his relationship. Yes, he's very young, but he seems mature and level-headed enough. Maybe going through the experience of fatherhood and a break-up has made him that way. I catch sight of myself in the hallway mirror and run a hand through my hair, thinking it's about time I had it cut. I lean in, noticing that the little crow's feet around my eyes seem much deeper these days. And I now have an awfully sharp frown line on my forehead that seems to deepen with each week that passes. That's another awful thing about grief, it ages you.

Diary Log – day 491. 19 days to Christmas. Must remember not to frown quite so much. Yes, bad things have happened – the worst – but I'm lucky in that I still have people around me to love and who love me unreservedly in return. Time to remember to count my blessings – appreciate what I have, as opposed to what I haven't … And Santa, thank you! I didn't realise you could work that fast.

Chapter 9

Elana

Moving Forward Means Accepting Change

Sitting around the kitchen table with Luke, he seems remarkably relaxed and there's no indication that he feels I'm encroaching on his lunch break. The re-heated pasty on the plate in front of him looks anaemic and unappetising, but that doesn't put him off as he tucks into it quite heartily. Alongside his plate I've buttered some thick slices of beetroot-and-apple bread and he's already devoured one slice.

'I'm sorry to be a pain and you must really long to just get on with the original job you're here to do, so you can finish. It's just that—' I stop to find the right words, my eyes sinking to the dusty, grey concrete floor.

'It's just that you are living in a partially finished cottage and while you're pretending everything is fine, it isn't.'

My mouth goes dry as I look up at him in utter surprise.

'Oops. Sorry, that sort of came out sounding a bit, um,

well – blunt. Some things sound harmless enough when you think them, but unexpectedly harsh when you try to put them into words. I hope I haven't offended you, that wasn't my intention.'

He doesn't seem upset, quite prosaic, actually, and it hasn't stopped him munching his way through the last of his pasty. I toy with my neat little sandwich.

'No, not at all. Spot on, really. I try not to let it get to me because up until now there was nothing I could do about it. You see, my husband died last year. Since then virtually nothing has been done on the cottage. It's like living in two different homes at the same time. Upstairs is a reminder of how the whole place should look: the moment we descend the stairs it's rather like camping out. Yes, the new kitchen is in place, and I managed to give the walls a coat of paint to tidy it up, but we never expected to live like this for months on end. The dust permeates everything and it's ruining the sofa, and I worry about how much of it Maya is inhaling—'

Luke hasn't moved, but he has stopped eating. That's not a good sign. I feel rather silly, now, as if I've just emptied my head of a jumble of words that won't really mean anything to a young man like Luke.

'Life isn't very fair at times, is it, Elana? I'm really sorry for what you've been through. I could seal the floor for you, to stop you worrying about Maya—'

'Oh, no, really, I wasn't ... didn't mean. You see, I've been given a present that will allow me to have some of the work done. Obviously I'm going to ask your company to give me a quote. But I need help making a list of the jobs that need doing and their individual costs, so that I can decide what exactly I can afford to have done. I mean, is it wise to have the flooring sorted, or will the walls need re-plastering, first? I'm afraid I don't have a clue about building work in general. Filling, sanding and painting I can do myself, but I have no idea if there's damp, or any other serious problems that are more important than a nice, clean floor covering. Could you help me on that? I'm happy to pay for your time.'

He picks up the last piece of bread and begins chewing.

'I'll tell you what, invite me to dinner this evening and I'll do a thorough inspection. Then we can sit down after Maya's gone to bed to look at potential costs and priorities. Or is that over-stepping the mark?'

'Not at all, it's helpful. Really. Do you like beef casserole?'

'I'll eat anything, if I'm honest. I'm used to microwave meals for one these days, but even before that Anita wasn't a cook. Highlights for me are trips home for some old-fashioned, hearty dinners. Anyway, I have to get back to work now. My client is a rather demanding lady.'

He starts laughing and I join in. I hope I'm not the proverbial home-owner from hell, but then it's not that I keep changing my mind, more that the list of jobs that need doing seems endless.

***

'Mum, here are the words I have to learn for the Christmas play. I'm the wishing star!'

'Wishing star, you say? And you have words?' That's a little puzzling.

'Of course! I grant each of the three wise men a wish. A bit like Santa, I suppose.'

My heart skips a beat. This could be my opportunity.

'Well, I'm sure you'll do a great job. Do you want to write that letter to Santa this evening? Luke is joining us for dinner as he's going to make a big list of all the jobs that need doing in the cottage. I think it's time we began to sort things out, don't you?'

She stares at me without blinking, what did I say?

'You mean, we have money?'

She's six, well, six and a half, and I can't believe my own daughter just said those words. What has she overheard me saying – does she worry about our future, too?

'Yes, darling, we have money, of course we do. We simply have to use it wisely. Mummy has just been so busy that I haven't had time to decide what to do next. Wouldn't it be nice to have a lovely clean floor, one where we could walk about without raising dust clouds?' I force out a laugh, trying to lighten the moment.

'You mean like in Amelie's cottage?'

Was I being very naive thinking that, at that tender age, kids didn't take much notice of their surroundings?

'Well, maybe not quite as stylish as Hillside View, as I don't think cream carpet would be practical for us. But some rather nice wood flooring would make things a lot cosier, don't you think?'

Maya gazes down at the assortment of rugs covering about eighty per cent of the floor.

'I like the colours, I just don't like the dust.'

'Me too, darling. Hopefully Luke will come up with a plan so we can get the work started very soon.'

Maya comes close, putting her arms around my waist and hugging me with great force.

'I'll write that note to Santa, Mum, before it's too late.' She sounds subdued and I can only assume that this has, unwittingly, raked up some old memories of Niall and me working upstairs together. On several occasions Maya, too, wielded a paintbrush, usually preferring to paint in circular sweeps rather than going for coverage. And, more often than not, getting more paint on herself and the floor than the walls. But those were fun times, for the most part. Times I didn't realise she would readily remember.

I head off to check the slow cooker. Luke usually finishes work for the day at about five-thirty, so he could be knocking on the door shortly. As I set the table, it seems strange putting out three place settings again. I purposely set a place for Luke in the chair opposite the one Niall always occupied. I hope it's not going to upset Maya as she's usually quite bouncy. Sadness comes in fleeting moments, until I can distract her. I won't know until we all sit down together how she's going to react.

As the big hand on the clock hits the six, there's a tap on the front door. I wonder why he didn't ring the doorbell.

'Hi, thanks for coming, Luke.'

He looks hesitantly at me and doesn't appear to be making any attempt to take a step forward and come inside.

'I realised afterwards that I kinda invited myself along this evening and that might have been out of order. I can come back another time just to take a look, if it's inconvenient.'

'Hey, you are doing me a huge favour and I would have suggested the same thing if you hadn't. Come in, please.'

'Maya, when will you be finished?' I call out, leaving Luke to wrestle with the laces on his boots. Silence reigns.

'Do you mind if I wash my face and hands? I have a towel, so I'm not going to leave mortar everywhere, promise.' He indicates a backpack slung from one shoulder.

'That's fine, of course. There's a cloakroom leading off the utility room. Help yourself.'

Maya still hasn't answered me.

'Maya, are you on your iPad?'

I'm expecting her to shout down, but she's in her bedroom and from the dull thumping, she probably has her Disney CD playing. When I go up to check, popping my head around the door discreetly, she's at her desk writing. I back out slowly, not wanting to disturb her, and creep back downstairs.

Luke has changed his trousers and shirt, which surprises me, and I look at him with a smile.

'I always carry something a bit tidy in the van, just in case. I've also had the odd occasion when I've worked until late on an empty property and ended up sleeping on the floor. A change of clothes is essential in this business.' As he smiles his eyes twinkle and I hadn't noticed that before. He seems more relaxed this evening, maybe enjoying the fact that the working day is over at last.

'It can't be easy working up so high all the time, in all

weathers. Please, take a seat. What would you like to drink? Hot, cold or something alcoholic? I have wine and beer.'

Instead of pulling out a chair he stands there looking at the table and clears his throat.

'Um, where would you prefer me to sit?'

At that precise moment Maya appears, letter in hand. It's one of those split seconds where everything and nothing happens all at once. No one moves but I glance at Maya, who glances across at Luke, whose eyes nervously seek out my own, before we both return our gaze to Maya.

'You can sit in my chair if you like and I'll sit in Daddy's chair. Mum, I have my letter.'

She walks past us both, placing the hand-written envelope on the table. Then she slides one of the place settings around in front of Niall's seat and hoists herself up onto the chair.

'Is it nearly ready, because I'm starving?' she states, quite casually, unaware of the way Luke and I are watching in amazement.

With that, I give Luke an encouraging nod and he walks across to sit down next to Maya.

'What are you hoping Santa will bring you this year, then, Maya?'

It's not a straightforward question and, with a lot of seriousness, Maya begins to explain that she's between toys; too old for dolls and too young for her own real computer. The look on Luke's face is priceless. I'm sure he was just being polite, but what follows is a critique of the most popular toys and why Maya wouldn't be pleased to find them under the tree on Christmas Day.

Out of Maya's line of sight I hold up a beer in one hand and a bottle of white wine in the other. Luke nods in the direction of the beer and I carry two across to the table, together with an apple juice for Maya.

'It's serious stuff, then,' Luke says in earnest to Maya. 'What if he gets it wrong?'

'Oh, he won't. He brought me my iPad last year and I didn't make up my mind about that until Christmas Eve. I nearly had a bike, but Mummy said it was a bit difficult to have one here because of the hill.'

'Sensible decision. Anyway, what's the final verdict, then, for this year?'

'A piano.'

I look at Maya, stunned. A piano? Where on earth did that come from? She doesn't know how to play the piano and, unless they've been doing it at school, I wasn't aware she'd ever seen one up close. Luke can see I'm speechless and begins to laugh.

'Well, I'm sure whatever Santa brings you will be the right thing. Don't you agree, Elana?'

I nod enthusiastically, wondering how on earth I'm going to talk her out of this idea. Besides, I have other plans for her Christmas present.

It's funny how with children you worry about the things that you perceive are likely to upset them. Then they totally surprise you. Maya chattered away quite easily, as did Luke, and the meal passed very pleasantly. It was actually nice having some company. Usually we only get that when we're away from home, as I still shy away from inviting people here. Who wants to eat surrounded by a hollow room with bare floors and a thin layer of powdery dust covering everything you touch?

Fortunately, Luke takes it all in his stride and he even distracts Maya when I slip Santa's envelope off the table and onto my lap.

Chapter 10

Luke

A Working Arrangement

Kids are funny at times, and I don't mean in a humorous way. Clearly, Elana and Maya don't have many dinner guests and I'm sure there are several reasons for that. But Maya was so relaxed over dinner earlier on, as if it was the most natural thing in the world for me to be here. In truth, I'd spent most of the day on the roof being mad at myself for making such a stupid suggestion. I only said it because it's easier to help Elana out if I do it in my own time – not that Dad would mind, I'm sure, but I'd feel better about it. There didn't seem any point in driving all the way back to the flat, only to return later, but even I was surprised when I casually invited myself for dinner.

I'd been mulling it over all afternoon and ended up thinking that I had made a big mistake. Two, in fact. First of all Elana might think I fancy her, or something, hence the inappropriate suggestion. Secondly, either Maya, or Elana, could have had a meltdown if I was the first male to sit down at the table with them since their loss. Did I need to worry? Not at all.

In fact, Maya has only just gone upstairs, after some coaxing from Elana, to get ready for bed. She's going to have some iPad time instead of reading, which I gather is a treat, while we make a start down here.

I'm waiting for Elana to come back down, as I don't want to go poking around on my own.

It's a credit to her that although it is a work in progress there's still a very comfortable feel to this cottage. She's tried to soften the ugliness by painting it white throughout and the colourful rugs add a fun element. With only the side lights on, the unevenness of the walls and the fact that the windows badly need replacing isn't quite so obvious. You don't even notice the bare patches of concrete in between the splashes of colour. She's a homemaker, that's for sure. A twinge in my chest reminds me that I didn't choose a homemaker to settle down with. Anita feels that things should be done for her, that life owes her something. I tried to explain that the deposit on the apartment took everything I had and after that we could only buy things as we could afford them. I worked a lot of overtime to get the basics, but my absence seemed to annoy her even more. And then, of course, she was disappointed that we could only afford to buy the more reasonably priced stuff. Every penny had to stretch as far as we could make it.

I guess Elana is in much the same position, although her situation is entirely different. Elana asked how soon she could get the chimney swept and start using the fire again. When

I told her it takes about twenty-eight days for the mortar to cure, both of their faces fell. I'm not sure what that was about, but it didn't go down well. It's not as if it's needed for extra heat, so I guess there's a bit more to it.

'Right, sorry about that,' Elana traipses down the stairs, stopping on the last step to put her dusty slipper socks back on.

'Those will be a thing of the past, soon,' I comment and she looks up, smirking.

'If only!'

'Two very powerful words, there. I spend most of my days thinking the same thing.'

Damn it! Why did I say that? I've been sitting here letting everything get to me again and this isn't the time, or the place.

Elana flicks the switch on the kettle. 'Time for coffee, I think. I know what it's like, Luke. Don't feel awkward.'

Our eyes meet and I nod, because we both understand it's all about acceptance.

'Right, I'll grab my clipboard.'

As I walk off into the dining/study area to grab my back pack, Elana explains her dilemma.

'I know I can only afford to get a few things done, but as I'm not sure when I'll get another influx of spare cash, it's going to be tough deciding what can, or should, wait. I have to make the decision with my head and not my heart, if you know what I mean.'

'Do you have the original survey report handy, by any chance?'

'I'll dig it out. Here you go: coffee is on the side table.'

As Elana disappears back upstairs, I move out into the sitting room with clipboard and pencil in hand. On closer inspection most of the walls aren't in a poor condition, exactly, they're just not totally smooth as in a new property. All of the wood seems to be sound, although there's a little wood-worm in one of the overhead beams, but none of it is active. There doesn't appear to be any damp, but the window frames are rotten and they all need replacing. The fireplace isn't original and is in good condition. As I walk around I continue making notes.

By the time I walk back through into the open-plan area, Elana is sitting at the table with the report.

'Great, let's have a look.'

I take the seat next to her and we both lean over the document, scanning the pages for anything that jumps out.

'Ah, the woodworm.' I point to the paragraph and Elana nods.

'Yes, we had the wood treated before we moved in, just in case anything was still live.'

'Good, even if it's old stuff it's always best in a property of this age.'

By the end of the document, I only have two concerns.

'There are some blown areas of plaster under the stairs. I noticed it when I turned the outside tap valve on and it's mentioned in here. It also talks about similar areas across that back wall. Let's take a closer look.'

I drain my coffee mug and then grab the clipboard, heading off to take a look at the under- stairs cupboard.

Crouching down with the door open, there's no smell of

damp. I turn on my small pocket light and train it on the back wall.

'Elana, if you look over there you can see that there's no visible signs of mould, or anything that indicates water ingress. This hollow plaster will need to be hacked away, I'm afraid. But let's check further along the wall.' I stand up and walk her over to the bottom of the staircase.

'If we pull out this unit I think you'll find similar problems along the entire run. I had a look at the ground levels outside this morning and I'd say that in the past the level outside has been lowered to cure a persistent damp problem. The exterior wall was then treated, but over time the moisture left in the wall has affected the bonding of the plaster in a few places.'

Sure enough, as I ease the cabinet forward and begin tapping the wall, I demonstrate the difference in sound between plaster that is firmly attached, and the hollow sound where the moisture has forced the plaster away from it.

Elana gives me a grimace.

'I had no idea there was even a problem. Is it difficult to fix?'

'Don't panic. This is minor stuff and there are people who will ignore the problem until it spreads, cracks, and eventually a chunk of plaster falls off. It's a messy job hacking off the blown areas, but once it's been patched you'd have a sound surface to re-paint.'

The worry line on her forehead deepens.

We move on into the kitchen, which is the easiest room. The newly fitted units are fine. The areas that need tiling above the work tops are sound and the ceilings throughout have been replaced. It then takes about twenty minutes to measure up the downstairs to get the square meterage for the flooring. And then we're done.

'The good news is that there are no really nasty surprises here. And the survey report confirms that. Shall we take a seat and start making that list so you can prioritise the work?'

***

An hour and a half later Elana seems relieved that although she's only going to get a few things done within her five thousand pound budget, she has a good grasp of the outstanding jobs.

'Thank you for explaining things in detail, Luke. It really helps. I didn't know where to start, if I'm being honest.'

'Hey, it's my job. If you are happy to accept that the plaster has to be remedied first, then it will probably take about a week in total, with drying time, before you can paint over it. However, that won't stop me from laying the flooring, assuming you pick something that is a stock item. It's a pity you don't have enough money to replace the downstairs windows, too, as that will be quite a messy job at some point in the future. But it's a costly one.'

'I think I need a strong coffee, will you join me?' She's frowning again, but maybe she has a headache. It's been a lot to take in.

'That would be great, thanks.'

'I'll just pop up to check on Maya – can you carry these

biscuits through to the sitting room? We might as well make ourselves comfortable. Back in a couple of minutes.'

I watch her walk across to the staircase, stooping to take off those dusty socks, and then taking each step carefully to move soundlessly up to check on her daughter.

Even though they are two instead of three, this is still a good life for them both. It's not perfect, but Elana is clearly a survivor.

I head off to the sitting room, put the small tray on the coffee table and then make my way out to the downstairs cloakroom, phone in hand.

'Dad, it's me. I'm at Bay Tree still, so I'll be quick. The lady asked me to price up the outstanding work. She only has a small budget, so she can't afford to have all of it done immediately. Is there anything we can do for her?'

'This is the widow lady, right?'

'Yep.'

'Up to you, my son. There's always flexibility in the price if you're prepared to do it yourself, or I can help out. If it requires Andy or Greg's involvement, then obviously it has to be the going rate. It's the extra petrol, pulling them off other jobs, etc. You know the score.'

'Thanks, Dad. I'll talk to you about it tomorrow.'

When I return to the sitting room Elana is curled up on the sofa, having changed into leggings and an over-sized jumper. I don't make a comment because it's not my place, but she looks very different. Amazing, even.

'She's sound asleep. I needed to get out of my work clothes, too. I hope you don't mind. It's time to relax.'

'It's a long day when you have a kiddie around. That had never crossed my mind before Joe came along.'

I lower myself onto the sofa opposite her, taking the mug of coffee she's holding out to me.

'Here's to an action plan,' she says, raising her own mug in the air and I do the same.

'Look, I'll be straight with you. Most of the work here is stuff I can do without any help. Labour is costly and usually the only way to save money is on the materials. Like you have cheaper flooring, or things are made good rather than being replaced. I think we can help each other out a little here.'

I hope that didn't come across as sounding dodgy. Her reaction is merely a blink, she's still curled up and hugging the coffee mug in her hands as if to warm them.

'Sounds interesting. Tell me more.'

I lean forward, placing my mug back onto the tray and clear my throat.

'I have a lot of free time, except for Saturdays. Being able to earn a little money on the side would be very helpful at this moment in time. You'll get more for your money because I won't have to charge you the firm's usual hourly rate IF you're prepared for me to work outside of normal hours.'

Elana is watching me, her eyes scanning my face.

'But it's a family business you work in, isn't it?'

'Yes, and that presents another problem. We're committed right through until early March. Admittedly, after that we could then have two people working here, but it's still a wait.'

'Ah, and you've just been kind enough to sort my other issues, which have, no doubt, put you behind on the jobs you should have been attending to instead. Luke, I'm really sorry I didn't think this through and I don't want to cause any problems for you with the family business.'

'Hey, I said we could help each other. Dad's more than happy for me to do work on the side, because we actually turn a lot of work away. But I can't do it in the firm's time, as obviously we have wages to pay and overheads. What I do in my own time I can charge you for at a very reasonable hourly rate. We can see how far we can make that budget of yours stretch.'

Elana's eyes are wide open and I can almost hear her thoughts churning away inside her head.

'And this is of mutual benefit? You don't mind spending your relaxation time doing more of the same?'

'I don't exactly have much to do outside of work these days and, if I'm being honest, I need every penny I can get. Are we on?'

'It looks like we have a deal, then.' Once again she raises her mug in a toast and as our eyes meet what I see reflected back at me is a genuine smile. I realise a weight has just been lifted from her shoulders. As our mugs chink, it's good to see the sense of relief reflected in her body language as she begins to relax.

Chapter 11

Luke

The Best-Laid Plans

'Luke, I'll put you on Hillside View's conservatory job in January, alongside Greg. I've scheduled it to start the first day back after the Christmas holidays. You'll be there for two weeks, so at least it will mean no additional travelling if you are still sorting out Bay Tree.'

'Thanks, Dad. It just seemed like the right thing to do and the money will come in handy.'

'I thought you had that software thing to test? Have you gone cold on the idea?'

Dad obviously hears more than I give him credit for; I always thought he switched off whenever I talked about anything IT-related.

'No, it's ongoing. But it can wait.'

'Don't take this the wrong way, my son, but I hope you're going into this with your eyes wide open.'

Before I can respond, Mum walks into the office, which is in the garage conversion next to the kitchen.

'What's this? The job at Bay Tree?'

'I was just offering a bit of advice.' Dad glances at Mum, who narrows her eyes a little, warning him to stop there. He shifts uneasily in his seat and then hoists himself up, to leave the two of us alone together.

'Dad means well, Luke.' Mum walks over to place her hand on my shoulder. 'He's worried that a woman on her own in that situation is going to be understandably lonely. You're an attractive young guy who is helping her out. We just don't want you getting hurt again so soon after ... well, so soon.'

'Look, Ma, I'm all grown up and I know I've made mistakes, but I've also learnt a few things along the way. It'll be fine and it means I can put some money away. It must be hard living with concrete floors when you work from home. And then there's her daughter, Maya.'

I stop short. I've already said more than enough. Way more than enough.

'You're not the sort of person to pass up the chance to help someone out, Luke. We're not trying to interfere, my son. You're your own man, always will be, but sometimes a little advice goes a long way.'

I stand and she hugs me fiercely, wishing more than anything that she could solve my problems.

'I'd better get off. I need to pick up a few materials on the way. Thanks, Mum, I know Dad means well and I won't go falling for the widow lady.'

I give her a cheesy grin and she laughs. 'Well, I'm proud

to have a son who has a heart and is prepared to help someone in need. As long as that's the aim, then you'll end up with a little nest egg and the widow lady will end up with a job well done.'

I look back at her over my shoulder, 'Well, that's the plan.'

***

When I arrive to start work there are no lights on downstairs in Bay Tree cottage, which is a little unusual. Normally I can see Elana moving around inside as I walk past the kitchen window. When it's time for the school run, Eve appears with Amelie in tow.

'Morning, Luke. Another bright day – we're very lucky for this time of the year.'

'No Maya today?'

I stop and lean on the scaffolding, smiling down at them.

'No, she has a sore throat, poor little thing. Catch you later. Oh, thank your dad for confirming that date for the conservatory. We're away for the first ten days in January, so I'll give you a set of keys.'

'Okay. Have a good day at school, Amelie.'

Amelie waves, then scurries off to the car. So Maya is poorly. I thought something was up. My mobile starts vibrating and I yank it out. It's Anita.

'Hi, is everything alright?'

'We're good. I wanted to ask a favour.' She sounds distinctly upbeat and she's never asked for anything before as a favour. Normally it's a demand.

'Fire away.'

'I want to take Joe away for a break at New Year. It's one of those holiday-camp things and if I go with a friend and her daughter, then we can share accommodation so it will be cheaper. It means you'll miss seeing Joe for one Saturday. But I thought maybe we could just change the day, you know, without going back to court?'

'Sure, you deserve a break and it's a great idea. I'm happy to chip in on the cost. Just let me know what alternative day suits you and I'll make sure I'm free.'

'Thank you, Luke. I'm really looking forward to it. I'll be in touch. Have a nice day.'

Have a nice day? Is this the same person who was screaming at me the last time she rang, saying I had no idea what pressure she was under?

Well, it seems a little bit of that nest egg will at least be giving them both a treat. It's nice to be able to offer that without having to worry about where I'll find the money.

The funny thing about hard work is that it keeps you fit, whether that's just your mind, or mind and body, and it usually results in a financial reward. Lack of money can make life incredibly difficult, so when life is tough it makes sense to just keep working. Don't focus on the results, focus on the job in hand and gradually you pull yourself out of that big, black hole of nothingness.

Anita left her parents' house to move into the apartment I bought in our joint names and she didn't have to worry about anything. With a baby on the way that was enough for her to deal with and prior to giving up work she spent most of her salary on clothes for herself and the baby. But she's never really had to struggle or lie in bed at night in a cold sweat worrying about paying the bills. I think that's why she's finding it so hard now, even though, compared to many people, she still has it relatively easy. Maybe one day she'll see that I wasn't neglecting her, just doing what I thought was best for us as a family. And now I'm back to square one, still working hard and still trying to avoid falling into the abyss. When I told Elana it was a mutually beneficial arrangement, I really meant it.

Chapter 12

Luke

I'm Not Being Rude, But Hello and Goodbye

With Maya feeling poorly, Elana and I agreed that I wouldn't start work inside until tomorrow. I've managed to free up most of the day so I can get the worst bit done in one hit. It suits me as all the guys are off on a night out this evening and I initially said I was going to pass. It's not really my thing, but now there's no excuse and I really ought to put in an appearance for an hour or two.

Looking at myself in the mirror, wearing a crisp shirt and my hair styled, I realise it's been quite a while since I tidied myself up. I suppose that was a part of the attraction about working in IT. You don't end up covered in grime each day and it means using your head and not your muscle. It's probably rebellion, because I'd been helping Dad out on jobs since I was a young teen. It was his guidance that led me into roofing and I also completed a City and Guilds construction diploma at college. He wanted me to be an all-rounder and

I wanted to be a good son. When it became clear it wasn't for me, he didn't say anything, but his silence was worse than a falling out. And now, just three years later, here I am – back where it all began.

The doorbell buzzes and it's Greg, from work, as he's giving me a lift. We're the two youngest of Dad's team and he's a good friend.

'Hey, mate, some lucky woman is in for a treat tonight, you clean up well.'

We do our customary man shake – butting knuckles and then the handclasp.

'Mate, you smell like one of those women's sections in a department store. You sure that's a product for guys that you're wearing and you didn't pick up the wrong one?' I tease.

He claps me hard on the back, 'Nice one. You're just jealous. Still, us single guys have to show the married ones how it's done.'

'Well, that might be true for you with your flash car and all, but I'm in for a few drinks and then a taxi back for an early night.'

Greg shakes his head, laughing all the while.

'Okay, Uncle Greg is here to rescue you from yourself. Which do you prefer – a blonde or a brunette? I'll keep my eye out.'

I grab my coat and as we walk out, Greg casts an eye around the tiny bedsit.

'Better not bring anyone back here. Is this bedsit really all you can afford at the moment?'

I nod, pulling the door shut.

'Yep. Supporting an ex and a child doesn't come cheap.

But, hey, company is the last thing I need at the moment, anyway.'

He winks. 'We'll see about that.'

***

The bar stools are uncomfortable, there are too many people packed into too small an area and the music is grating. I must be getting old. Old at twenty-four isn't exactly a confidence-builder. I look across at Greg, who is chatting up a woman with long, dark hair. She's a looker and the eye contact between the two of them shows she's clearly interested. I'm sitting in the middle of a group of older, married guys, who are all trying to act as if they do this every night. I suspect half of them are wishing they were ten years younger and the other half really want to go home and sit in front of the TV.

Suddenly, Greg pushes through the crowd, heading in my direction with a look on his face that makes me quake. Oh no, he hasn't—

'Your luck is in, she has a mate. Long auburn hair, single and works in administration. She's going to love you. Office types always drool over builders.'

'Greg, I'm not in the mood and this is a woman you are talking about, not a stereotype. I've had enough, mate. I'm finishing this and getting out of here.'

'Really? You're going to pass on the opportunity for some scintillating conversation to go home alone?'

I slap him on the back, good-naturedly.

'That's a big word, Greg, I'm impressed. Please pass on my apologies, but I'm off.'

I leave him standing and push my way through to the door, throwing a 'Goodnight gentlemen' over my shoulder. I doubt anyone can hear over the music, anyway.

Outside the air is cool and it's a relief. There's a taxi rank down at the end of the road and I head off in that direction when suddenly, someone calls my name.

'Luke? Are you Luke?'

A young woman is walking towards me, increasing her pace as I turn to face her. Damn it, Greg, you told her my name.

'Hey, I don't mean to intrude but I've had enough, too. Your friend, Greg, said you were getting a taxi home and I wondered if you wouldn't mind sharing. I don't like travelling alone at this time of night.'

It's only nine o'clock, so I'm not sure whether this is just a ploy. If I wasn't such a gentleman I'd say *no* and be on my way. But up close she looks genuine enough.

'Okay. Sorry, I don't know your name.'

'Lisa, hi,' she offers her hand.

'It wasn't anything personal, but I only came out for a couple of drinks tonight.'

She blushes. 'Oh, oh, that's fine. I mean, it's just that my friend was getting on well with Greg and I didn't want to spoil it for them. She recently split up with her boyfriend of five years and it hit her hard. He, um, he is single, isn't he? He said he was.'

She swings her arm as she walks, her hand holding a bright-pink handbag. I bet it's a designer one, it looks expensive. Greg seems to gravitate towards women who are high-maintenance and that's his downfall.

'You don't have to worry about Greg. He's sound, just hasn't found the one.' That seems to reassure her as we walk up to the first taxi in the queue and I open the door.

It turns out she lives two streets away from my flat, so it's no hardship, but she doesn't stop talking the entire time.

'Well, it was lovely to meet you, Luke. If you ever fancy a coffee or something, here's my number.'

I take it because it seems rude not to and wave off the money she offers towards the fare.

'Thanks and I'll handle the fare. My pleasure.'

'Nice to meet a real gentleman for a change, Luke. Hope to hear from you.'

As she slams the door shut I fold the paper in two and put it in my pocket, where it will sit until I pass a bin. No offence, but she just reminds me of Anita way too much. Been there, have the t-shirt and it no longer fits.

Chapter 13

Elana

Getting it Right is Far From Easy

Diary Log – day 493. 17 days to Christmas. What will Santa bring? Maybe a grand piano won't fit in the sleigh. If only I had a magic wand!

'**M**um my head really, really aches.'

'I know, honey. Another hour and you can have some more medicine. Are you comfy? Warm enough?'

Maya is snuggled up on the sofa under her favourite velvety-soft throw.

'I'm warm. It would be nice to light the fire, though.' She stares across at the empty fireplace.

'Oh, darling, I'm sorry. It's going to have to be logs and some fairy lights this year. I'll pick them up this week, ready for when we put up the Christmas decorations.'

'But, Mum, won't that be in Santa's way? Besides, it won't be the same.'

To my horror, tears start plopping down onto her nightdress and she swipes at them impatiently. I sit alongside her, pulling her into me.

'Hey, it's one year, that's all. Next year the chimney will be working and we'll light it every night leading up to Christmas. I promise. And Santa will be fine, he'll understand.'

She looks up at me, her raised temperature giving her face a pink hue.

'You're hot, darling, time to throw off the cover and cool down a little. What's this about you wanting a piano?'

I figure changing the subject might help – if she gets upset her temperature will spike.

'Melissa at school is having one. She's having lessons and says it's fun.'

Oh dear, this sounds very much like it's going to be a whim.

'Well, it is fun, but it's also hard work and you have to practise every single day if you want to learn to play it properly. We could buy you a little keyboard so you can see if it's something you'd enjoy doing. I think that's better than asking for a bigger piano, to begin with. It takes up a lot of room so you have to be very sure it's a present you are going to really love.'

Maya sinks back into the cushions, tiredness overcoming her.

'Maybe. Melissa says it's going to cost a lot of money, but her Daddy told her she can have it anyway.'

Do kids brag to each other? It sounds to me like some bragging has been going on here and I'm not too impressed.

'Santa usually knows exactly what to bring, Maya. Perhaps we should leave it up to him. What do you think?'

Already her eyes are drooping. I adjust the cover, so only her legs and feet are covered and sit quietly until she drifts off to sleep.

The pressure of getting it right is starting to build. I can't do anything about the fire, and I'm gutted about that because to Maya it's clearly meaningful. Somehow I have to make this year magical, but I can't replicate last year because we have moved on. I don't think just *us* time, on its own, will do it now she's a year older. But how do I make it all that little bit special? I'm hoping that if Luke can perform a miracle, then by Christmas Eve, between us, we can make the cottage feel more like home. Will that be the little bit of magic that Maya is looking for this year? The comfort of knowing that I'm committed to the dream her daddy and I began? If it doesn't work, then this year could be a total disaster and I will have let her down.

Chapter 14

Elana

It's a While Since I Looked in the Mirror

This morning Maya is, thankfully, much better. Her temperature is back to normal and she's eating well. I'm keeping her home from school, but she should be well enough to go in tomorrow. It's only one day, then she'll have the weekend off anyway, so I think it's the right decision. Friday week school breaks up and we're going to do the tree the following day. Santa usually decorates the rest of the cottage after his visit, but we have a ritual which involves back-to-back Christmas music, hot chocolate and careful placement of a gazillion tree decorations. At least, it feels like that many.

Luke arrived early and warned us that when we return it's going to look pretty grim because hacking off the loose plaster will expose bare brickwork. As instructed, I've covered everything up and put away anything breakable. At the moment he's hanging large dust sheets to block off the stairs and the sitting room, so that the dust will be contained in the open-plan area. It's been agreed that we will pop into next door's for the day and that I'll come back to help with the clearing up when he's done. Everything has to be looking the best it can by Christmas Eve; the hopes of a six-year-old are riding on it.

'Maya, pop on your fleece and your jogging bottoms. I'm just going to grab a few things from my wardrobe to show Eve.'

'Are we dressing up?' Maya looks hopeful.

'Not really. Mummy needs Aunty Eve's opinion as I have to work on New Year's Eve. Remember? You're going to stay with Grandma and Pop overnight.'

'Ooh, yes. Grandma said I can have popcorn and we can watch my favourite film.'

'Did she, now. Well, that's a nice little treat to look forward to. Makes me wish I didn't have to go out.'

Maya smiles at me, shaking her head from side to side.

'It won't be the same if you're there, Mum. Grandma says it's our little secret, so I'm not supposed to tell you.'

It's funny how their minds work at that age. Innocence and lies are so poles apart that it doesn't occur to Maya that she's leaking Grandma's little secrets. I find myself chuckling, thinking how lucky I am that my daughter has such a special relationship with my parents. Niall's parents do contact us from time to time, but they find it hard, still. Whether that will ever change, I have no idea. I hope it does, but at this moment in time I just can't see how. Grief is a process that is different for every single person going through it.

A trawl through my wardrobe doesn't inspire me at all

and I can only find three dresses that would be even remotely suitable for a posh 'do'. All were expensive, but my style tends to be understated and even to my eyes they look a little drab.

'Right, we're off, Luke. When it's time for cleaning up to commence just knock on Eve's door. Good luck.'

He winks, 'Enjoy the dressing-up party.'

I laugh, but it's more of a groan as he has no idea how big a deal this event will be for me.

With my arms full, Eve ushers us inside. We settle Maya in front of the TV and she's happy enough to lie back with a drink and biscuits to hand.

'Don't forget it's back to school tomorrow young lady. Think of today as a treat.'

She smiles up at me, knowing full well I probably should have sent her to school today, but more than happy to enjoy a day off.

'Right,' Eve mutters, grabbing one of the garment bags. 'Let's get started.'

The full-length mirror in Eve's master bedroom doesn't do anything for the first dress. I look like a corporate employee in a little black dress that just doesn't scream anything at all.

'What do you think?' I ask her, hesitantly.

'One word comes to mind. Boring. It doesn't do you any favours, if you want my honest opinion.'

I slip it off and move on to the next one.

'Are all three dresses black?' Eve asks, looking me up and down with much the same expression as she had for the first one.

'Yes, but this one fits better, don't you think? The other one has a lacy panel.'

'Well, number one is a definite no, this is a maybe. Try on number three.'

My confidence is waning. What on earth am I going to do? I can't justify spending a small fortune on a new dress that I'll probably only wear once. Slipping on the last dress, when I turn and look in the mirror I don't feel quite so disheartened.

'It's better,' Eve sounds rather more enthusiastic, at last. 'But even with the lace panel it still lacks impact. You need a splash of colour, my dear. Hmm, let me think.'

She begins rifling through drawers, pulling out a few colourful scarves and throwing them down on the bed. Finally she turns, holding up a plain, but vivid, fuchsia-red silk scarf.

'Red? Really?'

She drapes it around my neck and over my left shoulder. Taking it loosely across the front of the dress, she holds the other end up to my right shoulder.

'If we pin it to each shoulder then it's like a silk cowl, so it won't keep slipping off. Just stand back and look at the overall effect. This dress fits you like a glove and the pop of colour turns that little black dress into a statement.'

I have to admit she's right. Red just isn't me under normal circumstances, but this isn't an everyday event.

'A touch of red lipstick, matching nails and clutch bag, and you're going to look like a model!'

A little head pops around the side of the bedroom door and Maya shrieks.

'Mum, you look like a film star!'

Eve and I both start laughing. Eve digs into a wardrobe and comes back with a matching clutch bag and I have to admit that even though I'm not wearing any make-up and sporting a pair of very un-glam socks, I feel good about myself.

Eve takes Maya down to put on a DVD as I change and slip the dresses back into the garment bags. Downstairs in the kitchen there's a pot of tea brewing on the table.

'You really think I won't look out of place?'

'You look amazing in that outfit. Slip into a pair of five-inch heels and you'll measure up against the best of them,' Eve replies with gusto.

'Well, I'm not sure about that. I just don't want to look totally out of place. You know, a drab, hideaway mum who never gets to see the light of day because she's like a hermit.'

'You, drab? I think if you ran that past Luke, you might be shocked by the answer.'

My head whips upwards as I scan her face.

'Luke? What do you mean?'

She pauses to pour the tea, leaving me hanging. When she does, eventually, break the silence she sounds very casual indeed.

'Oh, nothing in particular, I suppose.'

'You can't say that without explaining yourself. Luke's a hard worker, very polite and in need of some cash. Our arrangement works well on both sides. He's very young, though. I could almost be his mother.'

Eve begins laughing. 'For goodness' sake, don't go saying that to him, Elana. You'd shatter his illusions.'

'Do you think there's something going on between us? If

105

that's the case, you couldn't be more wrong. I spend all my time worrying about my finances rather than thinking about making small talk. And poor Luke seems to be struggling to handle his own personal life.'

'Really?'

'What do you mean, *really*?'

'You have no idea how attractive you are! It's such a shame, because if you just made an effort to open your eyes ... a little fun could bring you back into the land of the living.'

'It's almost obscene. I'm thirty-four and he's probably half my age. I'm shocked at you, Eve. Okay, I realise that's an exaggeration, but those are the years in which life teaches all of us a lot of lessons. I've been there and done it and he hasn't – yet.'

'Luke asked a few questions about you, not wanting to say the wrong thing about Niall. Now that shows sensitivity. And he's such a genuine type. Besides, you're exaggerating. I don't know how old he is exactly, but you most certainly aren't twice his age. I never thought of you as someone with prejudices and I think you're being a little unfair in your assumptions, there. He comes across as having a very mature outlook on life.'

Now I feel like I've been backed into a corner.

'Of course that's not the case. It wasn't what I meant, at all. Why a good-looking young guy like Luke would even think about someone like me, well, you have a vivid imagination there, Eve.'

We stare at each other across the table and her face breaks into a grin.

'So there's no little undercurrent of physical attraction bubbling away beneath the surface? If you say not, then I suppose I have to believe you. Just be careful there.'

I'm horrified. What does she mean?

'Why? Is there something I should know? Am I in danger?'

'Not at all. I think the only danger likely to arise here is a little misunderstanding.'

I grimace. Oh no.

'He's a really good guy, Elana. His heart has been broken and he's in a very difficult situation. Why wouldn't he develop a little crush on the beautiful widow who deserves a little happiness back in her life?'

I gulp down a lump in my throat that feels the size of a golf ball.

'Niall was my soul mate. It's still hard to think of starting over again with someone else.'

Eve sighs, reaching out across the table to touch my hand.

'None of us are saints, Elana, and it's always a mistake to impose that on anyone – whether they are here, or not.'

I'm so shocked by her words, that even though I don't know if I agree with that statement, I let it go. I take a long, deep breath to calm myself down before replying.

'If I've given Luke the wrong impression that's something I'm going to have to sort out. It hadn't even crossed my mind, to be honest with you.'

'He might be younger than us, but he's been through more than a lot of guys we know, Elana. Wisdom comes through experience, so don't go dismissing him as some inexperienced young guy who falls for every pretty face he sees. I might be reading this all wrong, but I thought that as your friend it was best to mention it. He might not even realise he finds you interesting.'

I really can't see why Eve is going on and on about this. I wonder if Luke has said anything else to her about me? I would hate to have made him feel uncomfortable.

'I sincerely hope that's not the case, because I might be about to lose my builder, then.'

It's a sobering thought, but there's no way I'm going to risk Luke thinking I'm in any way interested in him. It wouldn't be fair, even if it sours our arrangement.

Diary Log – day 494. 16 days to Christmas. It feels more like a ticking time bomb than a ticking clock. How am I going to get everything done in time? And now I have to consider whether having a young guy around the house so often is going to unsettle Maya.

Chapter 15

Elana

Can it Get Any Worse?

After every high, there has to be a low. Six hours later and I'm wearing a dust mask, have a woolly scarf wrapped around my hair and am dressed in a disposable boiler suit. I'm brushing up rubble while Luke shovels it into bags and if I was worried about dust beforehand, this is something else.

'Is it worse than you thought it would be?' He asks, his voice slightly muffled by the face mask.

'Yes. I just hoped it wouldn't be quite as bad as I feared. Some of these patches are really big.'

'You don't know what's going to work loose until you start hacking at it. We'll leave the hanging dust sheets up until tomorrow to stop it travelling into the sitting room and upstairs. Overnight it will settle and in the morning it will need to be mopped with water and all the surfaces wiped down with a wet cloth. Don't try to dry dust it, as that will just send it back up into the air. Trust me when I say that by the middle of next week you'll have a perfect wall, as I'll skim over the rest to even it up. It will simply be a case of letting the plaster dry out. Then it can be repainted.'

'You're the expert.'

He gives me a grin and immediately I feel myself colouring up. This couldn't be misconstrued as flirting in any way, could it? He is the expert, as I know nothing about building work and this isn't about trying to flatter his ego.

Eve pops in to check on progress and immediately offers to have Maya overnight and do the school run in the morning.

'Don't worry about anything,' she assures me. 'You have enough to cope with here. Just pack her school things and drop them over. The girls are putting everything away, ready for bed. If Maya needs you for anything I'll give you a call to pop round. Is this really going to be tidy by Christmas?'

Eve and I survey the mess.

'Yep, you can count on it.' Luke isn't fazed and I shoot Eve a warning glance not to make any unsuitable comments.

'I'll leave you two to get on with clearing up, then. Good luck.' And with that she's gone.

'How late can I work tonight, Elana? I mean, there won't be any noise but I'd like to get some render on so that I can top-coat with plaster as soon as it's dry. I don't want to put you out, though, if you've had enough for one evening.'

I glance at the clock. It's nearly seven. I did say I would cook tonight.

'I just want it done, so it's entirely up to you. I'll pop something in the oven for about an hour's time. When this is cleared I have to jump back on the computer for a bit, anyway. So you won't be disturbing me.'

'Great. And thanks, I'm starving. Don't feel you have to cater for me, though. I'm going to be around quite a bit and I'm used to fending for myself.'

There, Eve is wrong. He's giving me a get-out if I want one. He's never overstepped the mark and he doesn't intend to, so I can relax.

I don't know what's up with Eve these days. It's as if she feels she has to look out for me all the time. I might not be in a happy place, exactly, but I'm surviving. Maya seems perfectly relaxed whenever Luke is here, so I really can't see a problem.

***

After I pop round to give Maya a goodnight kiss, Luke and I stop briefly to eat, plates on our laps, in the sitting room.

Luke insists on bringing in a clean dust sheet to throw over the sofa and we sit, side by side, eating in silence. In fact, it's so quiet that I grab the remote and turn on the TV. The news is on and the weather forecast is predicting some heavy snow later this month.

'Great,' Luke says between mouthfuls of pasta and meatballs. He sounds dispirited. 'Ironically, this year we have a lot of outside jobs on and we're going to have some disappointed customers once the temperature starts dropping.'

'It can't be helped. I can't even begin to think about the garden here at the moment. Wouldn't it be nice to only have one project to cope with?'

He nods, mouth too full to speak for a moment.

'Great food, by the way – appreciated. You mentioned you were away New Year's Eve? If I can't get everything done by Christmas, I can pop in then to finish up.'

'Great, if you can. But please don't feel you have to be here at every opportunity. Besides, you have Joe to consider.'

'No – change of plan. Anita is taking him away for a few days with a friend. I said I'd swap days and I'm just waiting to find out what suits her.'

That sounds like a rather one-sided arrangement to me. He shrugs and I say nothing.

'If you can decide on the flooring and we can get it delivered soon, I'm thinking it might be possible to start on the floor in between waiting for the walls to dry.'

'Wow. I wasn't expecting that! Just the thought that this could look tidy and clean for Christmas is a boost. I've not been feeling very festive and this year seems a lot harder, for some reason.'

Luke's face reflects pity and I mentally berate myself. He's not a friend, he's here doing some work and listening to me droning on isn't exactly what he signed up for.

'Sorry, that just slipped out.'

'Worried about the piano?'

We both start laughing at the same time. As we exchange glances his eyes do that twinkly thing again and I realise he's teasing me.

'Well, we might need to consider getting an extension built first to make room for it. I'm hoping Santa brings a desktop version this year to give us a little time.'

'Ha, nice one! I've bought Joe some of those large building blocks. Thought I'd start him off young in the hope that one day he'll join the family business. Geez – did I really just say that? I must be turning into my dad.'

I smiled and shook my head.

'Anyway, like I said, don't feel you have to feed me – I can always grab fish and chips on the way home if you're busy. But that was great and I appreciate it.'

'Hey, I have to eat, too. It's the least I can do and it's no bother at all.'

Eve is so wrong about Luke. He's not a guy who is looking for a little romance, or a distraction. Like me, there's too much going on inside his head to cope with already.

Have I turned Niall into a saint? We all have our flaws, but he was a good man. Eve was wrong in what she said; I don't choose to be alone because no one will ever match up to him. I'm not ready yet, and I'm not about to jump into a casual relationship for the sake of easing my loneliness. That wouldn't be fair on anyone.

Chapter 16

Luke

Home From Home

I keep forgetting Elana is a customer and relaxing my guard. When she does that too, it's tempting to slip into a zone that implies some sort of purposeful friendship. What isn't helping is that we both seem to be in a similar situation in our lives. At a sticking point where it's hard to see what's going to happen next. Usually, when you sit down and eat with someone who is little more than a stranger to you, it's a date. So I'm having trouble finding the right level of conversation.

Still, by the time next door's conservatory is finished, come mid-January, everything should be wrapped up at Bay Tree Cottage. It sounds like it will be a while before Elana can afford to think about replacing the windows, or looking at the outside work that needs doing. By then she could be in a whole different place with her life and, no doubt, I'll have moved on a little, too.

The mobile starts to vibrate in my back pocket and I yank it out, leaning against the wall. Today I'm clearing up all of the rubble outside Hillside View, which was left over from when the foundations for the conservatory were laid.

'Greg, my man, what's up?'

'I was about to ask you the same question. Where've you been lately?'

'Oh, I'm doing some work on the side that will take me through into January. I need the cash, so it's evenings and weekends.'

'Ah, I was hoping to catch up with you at the office for a chat. Do you remember Lisa?'

'Lisa?'

'She said she gave you her telephone number but you still haven't given her a call.'

Oh, that Lisa.

'Been too busy working, mate. Have you seen her, or something?'

I feel guilty about having thrown away her number, but it wasn't as if I'd asked her for it, or promised to call.

'I'm seeing her friend still, and she mentioned it. Seems Lisa was hoping you'd be in touch. Surely you can afford to take one night off?'

I roll my eyes and let out a groan.

'You shouldn't have told her my name, Greg. I threw her number away because there's no point in meeting up. She isn't my type. Look, I'm in the middle of something, so I'll have to catch you later.'

'Shame, she's seems pretty keen to see you again.'

'Again? We shared a taxi. I think it's best you break the news.

I have to go, but glad to hear it's working out for you. Thanks for the call and sorry if she had the wrong impression.'

Damn it! Greg means well but I'm just not interested.

'Girlfriend trouble?'

Eve appears with a mug of coffee and the sound of her voice makes me jump.

'Me? No. Just a mate who is trying to fix me up and it isn't happening.'

Why is it that women always want to know what's going on?

'Life is short, Luke. You only have to look at Elana's situation to appreciate that. But it's also easy to make a mistake and sometimes you end up having to live with that.'

Eve walks away, leaving me to ponder over her words. Yeah, she's right, but I don't think she was talking about just me. Eve's one lucky lady, so what would she have to regret?

Maybe I bring out the mothering instinct in women and she's just trying to be helpful. What I don't need is another Anita situation. Actually, what I don't need is another woman in my life full stop, whether or not they are simply trying to be helpful.

I look at the pile of debris I still have to clear and start shovelling.

***

When I finish for the day and go round to Elana's, Maya answers the door and the sounds of Slade in full-on Christmas mode filters through into the porch.

'Ah, we have the oldies on again. How are you today, Maya?'

I walk in and slip off my boots.

'Good, thanks. Mum says if the music is too loud and it bothers you, I have to turn it down. I think she has her ear plugs in, as she's working.'

I smile at Maya's earnest look and shake my head.

'No, it's fine. I like a bit of Christmas music. You go ahead, it doesn't bother me.'

'Thank you, Luke.' She turns and shouts out, 'Mum, Luke said the music is fine.'

Elana appears, iPod around her neck and ear pieces hanging.

'Sorry, Luke. Are you sure it's okay? I'm editing and it will be about an hour before we eat, if you'd like to join us. Had a good day?'

'Just clearing up the rubble from next door's garden. Hopefully the skip can go in the next day or two, so it will be easier for parking.'

'Oh, don't worry about that. If you need me for anything, just shout. Well, you might have to wave your hands as I'm using whale music to counteract Maya's noise. Editing requires concentration. I've washed through and the dust is much better. I've moved the computer into the kitchen, so it's all yours. I'll just make some coffee and then get back to work.'

Obviously Elana needs to concentrate, so I nod and make my way through to the dining room, carrying a bucket of plaster. Shortly after I spread out the dust sheets on the floor, she reappears with a mug, but her ear pieces are back in and I give her a thumbs-up, by way of a thank you. She smiles at me before turning to walk away.

Maya appears from behind the hanging sheet I put up in front of the sitting-room door.

'Luke, if the chimney isn't dry yet, should we put up a sign for Santa to let him know?'

Her forehead is scrunched up in earnest as she awaits my reply. It takes me a moment or two to think of something.

'Well, Santa is a chimney expert. In fact, he was the one who let us know something was wrong and he will be pleased to see it looking like new. But it should be fine by the time Christmas Eve comes around, anyway, so I don't think you have anything to worry about.'

She gazes up at me, putting a finger up to her lips and then glances behind her at Elana, whose back is towards us. Then she leans in to me to whisper.

'He'll get the letters I'm leaving for him, then? I don't want Mummy to see them, as it's a surprise.'

I stoop to her level, plunging the trowel into the plaster to lift a large scoop out onto the hawk.

'What's that?' She continues to keep her voice low.

'It's a tray for the plaster so I can hold it up close like this and then spread it on to make the wall good. I promised Mummy it would be perfect for Christmas.'

'That's one of the things on my list,' she whispers, her voice now barely audible. She swings her head back around to check on Elana, who is typing away.

'Well, I'm working on it, so you can put a tick against that one.'

'Thank you, Luke. I wasn't sure whether Santa would have time. How do you spell your name?'

119

'L-U-K-E.'

'Got it, thanks.'

With that she disappears behind the sheet, leaving me more than a little intrigued. Shouldn't kids be making lists about the toys they hope Santa will bring them? Why on earth is Maya making a list of jobs around the house?

As I trowel on the plaster and the new surface begins to take shape, I try to imagine Joe at Maya's age. What will be in his letter to Santa? I hope it's just the usual kids' stuff and even though our situation isn't the best, it will be a normality that we will have made acceptable to him. I guess in the case of a death, there is no way to make it normal. Now that *is* a tragedy.

Chapter 17

Luke

Opening Up

After dinner both Elana and Maya disappear upstairs as I continue layering on the plaster. I'm conscious that I have Joe tomorrow and need to finish this tonight. But I can't get Maya's words out of my head and curiosity gets the better of me. I head across to take down the dust sheet in front of the sitting room door and fold it roughly, ready to take outside to shake it out. My gaze trails over to the fireplace. It's none of my business, but still I can't drag my eyes away. Kneeling down in front of the grate I bend my head to look upwards into the void. Sure enough, there is a small pile of white paper neatly folded and sitting on the ledge to the right-hand side. I sit back to listen for a moment and clearly they are both upstairs in the bathroom as the shower is running. I lean in and before I can stop myself I gather up the papers in my hand and sit back on my heels, staring down at them.

Maya's writing is very neat and well controlled, although

I'm no expert on the abilities of a six-year-old. I'm just surprised it's so legible.

There are four folded pieces of paper in total and on the front of each she's written, 'To Santa'. On the first one, beneath the handwriting, is a little drawing of a star. The others feature a bauble, a Christmas tree and the final one has a heart. Immediately I see the heart, I gather up the slips of paper to put them back on the ledge. Even a six-year-old has the right to a little privacy and, besides, it's not my name on those letters. Maybe Elana is aware of them and has the situation in hand; either way, it's none of my business.

By the time Maya is in bed and Elana comes back downstairs I'm ready to head off home.

'What a difference in just a couple of hours. I have a solid wall again, no more exposed brickwork. Thanks for taking down the dust sheets. And you were right, yesterday was the worst day.'

'It was best to get that mess out of the way. It's pretty even, not perfect, but much better than it was and it's sound. Gradually the patches will dry out and when it goes a pale-pink colour I'll seal the wall with a coat of primer. Do you want me to do the top coats? It will need two to cover it properly.'

Elana is standing next to me and a waft of her perfume, warm and mellow, suddenly reminds me of summer. She turns her head to look at me with grateful eyes.

'You're a saviour, Luke. I'm happy to do the painting and I'm conscious Christmas is getting closer with every hour that passes. I can wield a paintbrush, but I can't lay flooring.'

I nod; fair play to her that she's prepared to roll up her sleeves and get hands-on.

'Niall was good with his hands and there was quite a bit he could do, not professional stuff, though. I was always the painter. I guess the only skill you need for that is attention to detail and patience.'

Her face changes suddenly and she looks embarrassed.

'You must really miss him.' Darn it, why did I say that?

'Don't mind me, it's just that sometimes the memories come flooding back when you least expect them. It's survivor's guilt. I want to move on but—

She's inches away and before I can stop myself my arms are around her. I half expect Elana to recoil in horror and to push me away, but instead her head falls against my shoulder and she sinks into me. I don't feel I have a right to hug her, so I stand there with my arms loosely draped around her, almost holding her upright. The seconds stretch into minutes and then I gently withdraw my arms and stand back. I glance at her to double-check I don't need to make a very quick exit before she begins shouting at me.

She swallows, hard. 'Thanks, Luke. I needed a hug. It's lonely at times, you know? I wonder if Maya understands that. Or will she be hurt to think I'm letting her daddy go if I decide it's time to move on?'

My heart begins to pound inside my chest. 'I'll put the kettle on,' I mutter and turn to walk into the kitchen.

Her body language wasn't warning me off, that's for sure, but I still can't believe I just did that. I keep looking back at her as I grab two mugs and shovel stuff into them while waiting for the kettle to boil. It looks as if she's taking a moment to compose herself and then she walks towards me, lowering herself into one of the seats around the table.

'I really am sorry for putting you on the spot, there, Luke. Along with survivor's guilt comes the awkwardness other people around you feel when they sense your inner turmoil. People are naturally uncomfortable and they don't know what to say, or do. Thanks for not making me feel ... foolish.' What can you say to something like that? For some crazy reason it's important to me that she knows I'm not simply feeling sorry for her. I hugged her because at that moment I wanted to be the person who was there for her. What that means, exactly, I can't be sure. But I do know that it's not in my nature to go around hugging women for the sake of it.

'It's okay, I understand. There are times when I get this sense of anger building up inside of me and I work it out in the gym. It's the frustration of knowing I can't change anything that's happened and it's hard to accept. I'm not comparing my situation to yours, please don't think that, but I understand the feeling of being overwhelmed at times.'

Elana takes the coffee mug from me as I sit down opposite her. The frown on her forehead is back and there's a look in her eyes that isn't anything to do with sadness.

'I can't bring him back, Luke. He's never going to be sitting at this table with me again. I can't change that and it isn't my fault. And yet it's hard to accept it's over, which sounds ridiculous. I mean, death is the very definition of no going back. I don't want to be alone forever and that hug kinda reminded me of that.' Now she looks uncomfortable as the colour rises in her cheeks.

I'm conscious that no matter how attractive I find her, she's a customer and I definitely crossed the line. All I can do is try to redeem myself so she doesn't think I took a liberty.

'You're doing the only thing you can, and that's to focus on Maya and rebuild your life one day at a time. My mum is the one I turn to when I'm feeling desperate and she keeps saying the same thing over and over again. We have to learn to accept the things we can't change and move on. It sounds harsh, doesn't it? But I've come to realise that the danger of ignoring those words of wisdom is that the pain never lessens. It's a way of keeping it raw, of punishing ourselves because when things go badly wrong it has to be because of something we've done, isn't that right? But now I know different. I made the choices I made based on what I knew at the time and there's no way I could see what was going to happen. As you said, there's nothing you could have done to change what happened, Elana, it wasn't within your control. That's what you have to accept and I know that's very easy for me to say, but it's not a platitude. If you learn to embrace the concept, you can change your future but you can only take it one day at a time.'

I've just poured out everything I've been thinking since I met Elana and now I'm feeling her pain. Elana's head is bowed over her coffee mug.

'I'm listening,' she says, so quietly I have to strain my ears. 'There's no way to compare levels of pain and I appreciate that you know what it's like. It's the constant pressure to be strong when other people are around, in order to avoid the pity factor. I see it in the eyes of my family and friends all the time. Then there are days I could scream and I just want life to be normal again. But the old normal, so it doesn't involve me stepping outside of my comfort zone. I find myself resenting Niall for putting us through this. How can I do that to him? It wasn't his fault, either. And then I feel guilty. Again.'

What I hear is someone who is holding back her emotions and I reach out to grab her hand.

'No, it wasn't his fault, but it's also true that you didn't deserve for this to happen. Your life has been torn apart, literally, and no one is ever prepared to cope with that. Learn to cut yourself some slack, Elana, and don't feel you have to be this superwoman figure who can roll with the punches. Life hurts at times, and this is one of those times. It's not weakness to admit that, it's simply the truth.' I squeeze her hand and then pull back, immediately grabbing my coffee mug to make the action seem more natural. Holding her hand was unnerving me, the feel of her skin against mine seemed too natural and left me wanting more.

'My counsellor would be impressed, Luke. Maybe you missed your calling.'

'That was a bit heavy; I hope I wasn't crossing a line. It just touched a nerve with me. There's something about this time of the year that makes it even harder trying to act as if everything is fine when it isn't. I mean, I'm back with my parents this Christmas, just the three of us. How sad is that?'

Elana looks directly at me and smiles, the corners of her

mouth lifting just enough to soften her face and dispel that haunted look.

'But knowing they are there for you, no matter what, shows how much you are loved. That's something I remind myself of all the time. I'll get through this and so will you. That doesn't make it easy, or take away the pain, but you are right. There is no going back and that's the thing I still struggle with. I keep asking myself why? Why me, why Niall; why does an accident have to happen? But accidents do happen and the harsh truth is that it will never make any sense. Ahh ... I bet you wish you had some simple little job to do, rather than working in the home of an emotionally unstable woman.'

She begins laughing as she raises the mug of coffee to her mouth.

'Every day that passes takes you another step towards becoming stronger. Maya is one lucky little girl.'

A sudden flush of guilt washes over me as I remember Maya's handwritten letters sitting on the ledge up the chimney. Now obviously isn't the time to raise it with Elana, she has enough to worry about.

'If you ever need a listening ear, I'm only a phone call away.'

When Elana closes the door behind me and I walk up to the van, the quiet darkness all around feels alien to me. The emotion and warmth I've left behind leaves me feeling exposed in some way and the chilly breeze is akin to being attacked with knives. I'm going home to an empty flat, cold and drab. Time to take your own advice, Luke. Tomorrow is another day and there's no point in looking back. But you also can't fool yourself that you are becoming a part of someone else's life just because you recognise another soul who is suffering in much the same way. Elana needed a hug and you were the only one around. Don't fool yourself into thinking it meant something.

Chapter 18

Luke

Why is Life so Complicated?

'Greg, it's Luke. Sorry I didn't get to return your call yesterday but it was a late one. I'm just heading over to pick up Joe, so I'll drop by yours on the way for a quick coffee.'

Greg answers the door, looking unusually smart considering it's early Saturday morning.

'How're things? Still seeing the same lady?'

'Cheryl, yes. She's pretty special and it's going really well. I'm in a bit of a spot, though. Seems she promised Lisa she'd talk me into dragging you along for a foursome. Believe me, mate, it wasn't my idea but she won't give up on it. I know what you said, but could you do this as a favour? An hour, max, and then you walk away and everyone is happy. You know what women are like, they won't give up until it's obvious you aren't interested. Cheryl thinks that you would like Lisa if you just gave her a chance.'

129

He rolls his eyes upwards and gives a shrug. I let out a loud sigh, knowing this is the worst idea ever.

'Okay, as a favour. But it isn't going anywhere and I'm not going to pretend I'm even mildly interested in her just to get you in the good books of your latest love interest. Text me where and when. And this is a huge favour because it means I'll be pulled away from this job I'm doing. I hope you feel guilty.'

'How is the widow lady?'

The label seems to have stuck and for some reason I suddenly take offence at it.

'Her name is Elana and I'll be working there for a couple of weeks. I told you, I need the money and Anita and Joe are going away at New Year to a holiday camp with a friend and her daughter. I said I'd chip in on the cost of that.'

Greg claps me on the back, a big grin on his face.

'You've saved my life, mate. Pity Anita didn't ask you along instead of her friend. Seems a bit unfair.'

Greg has no idea and, in fairness, I can't expect him to understand.

'It wouldn't work, trust me. I just need to earn what I can at the moment to cover everything. I won't stop; I have a few things to pick up before I collect Joe.'

He shrugs, probably thinking I'm a mug because he has no idea what a huge responsibility it is to have a family to support. To him I'm a single guy, so should be as free as he is to spend my money how I want. And now he's roped me into something that I know isn't right, because it will imply an interest that just isn't there. I suppose the sooner we get it over, the better.

***

I end up at Anita's on the dot, but instead of simply handing over a bag and encouraging Joe out of the door, she invites me inside.

'Joe's watching TV; I'll just grab his bag.'

I stand inside, pushing the door shut behind me and just a little surprised that Anita seems so relaxed. She reappears, handing me a full back pack with Joe's things.

'I was wondering if you'd like to have Joe overnight sometime, you know, as we'll be away the last Saturday in December. I know it's only the Lakeside Park Resort, and you could collect him and take him out for the day, but it would be easier if he stayed with me. What do you think?'

'As I said, it's not a problem and I'd love to have Joe overnight, if you're sure.' I mean, this is a big step forward for us. Maybe it's time, at last, to put the old hurt behind us and forget personal hang-ups, so we can concentrate on what's best for Joe.

I can't wait to call in to see Mum and Dad, and when I break the news Mum lifts Joe up in her arms and hugs him close, spinning him around in her excitement.

'Are you and Daddy going to come for a sleepover?'

Joe, bless, nods his head. 'Leep. Dada.' He continues nodding, enthusiastically. Maybe he does understand a bit of what's going on, because he seems excited.

'That's such good news, my son.' Dad chips in, beaming from ear to ear.

It's only one night, but all they get to see Joe since the split is an hour or two if they are lucky, once a week. In the summer we'll be able to go out on a few trips together, but in winter it's harder to find things to do. So I usually take Joe swimming, or to one of the play centres. He loves slides and the bouncy castle, but it requires a lot of energy to keep an eye on him and help when he gets stuck or tries to be too adventurous.

'It looks like we're finally reaching that point where it's no longer about us, but all about Joe. It's a relief, I'll be honest.'

Mum manoeuvres Joe down onto her hip and comes across, placing a hand on my shoulder.

'It's about time, Luke. Maybe now you can relax a little and start living again. You're too young for life to be solely about money worries, responsibility and work. It's time to bring a little fun back into it, because if you're happy then Joe is going to notice that. Kids can sense anxiety.' When a mum has her mothering head on, all you can do is agree. In my heart I know she's right, but it's not a road I'm in a hurry to go down again. Then I remember Greg.

'Actually, I'm making up a foursome with Greg very soon.'

It's an offering and at least it will put a temporary halt to all her worrying. She'll take it that I'm making an effort for myself, as long as I don't enlighten her about the truth of the matter.

'Good for you! But don't go using Greg as a role model, his track record shows he has an aversion to commitment. Obviously you won't go jumping into anything serious without a lot of thought, but having a long succession of women passing through your life is equally as problematic.

It's all about balance, my son. We just need to get some back into yours.'

'Yes, Ma. I am listening.'

She gives me one of her 'through the eyes of a mother' looks. She thinks I'm a catch and that I deserve the love of a good woman. She doesn't see the screw-up I am, so I'm hoping that I can turn that around before reality dawns. Whatever I get myself into in future, I will at least be going into it with my eyes wide open.

Mentally I begin making a list of the perfect woman for me:

Ability to love someone with their heart and soul.
An understanding that kids come first, always.
Willing to work as a couple and not sit back and take things for granted.
A confident and competent person in their own right.
Honest, open and in touch with their emotions.

Mum would laugh if she could hear my thoughts. If that's my tick list for the perfect woman, then it strikes me I probably sound more like a middle-aged man than a young go-getter.

Chapter 19

Elana

Time to Shop!

The envelope with confirmation of funds being transferred into my account arrives in the post and it's almost as though Christmas has finally arrived. I hold it in my hands and pull it to my chest. My Amazon wish list is all set up and ready to go.

'Christmas is happening,' I whisper, under my breath. We have one week until Maya breaks up from school for the holidays and there's so much to sort out. The flooring and underlay were delivered late yesterday and that used up a third of the money Mum and Dad gave me for the work on the house. Now I can happily hand over the first chunk of cash to Luke for his labour costs to date, which will be a huge relief. I had to hold back in case there was a problem with the money being transferred, as I'm at the top of my overdraft facility.

At least it looks likely I'll have enough to keep us going

until the next payment in April, the big one for the biography, combined with the other smaller jobs I've also completed. Assuming, of course, that I get all the information and co-operation I need so I can deliver the full manuscript. Working hard and focusing is something that comes naturally to me, so letting anyone down just isn't an option.

Niall, I've done it and there's still time to pull it together for Maya. As I send out that thought I cast my eyes around; can he hear me?

'Mum, can we finish the bead strings for the tree?' Maya's voice filters down the stairs.

'Yes, we can. I don't need to work today and I think we should pop out and do some Christmas shopping; what do you think?'

A little head appears, poking over the top of banister rail.

'Oh, Mum! Could we? I want to buy you something very special.'

My heart squishes up inside of me. Shouldn't she be excited about touring the toy shops, her mind full of what Santa might bring her?

'Grab your coat. We'll make a day of it.'

***

Diary Log – day 495. 15 days to Christmas and finally it's all going to happen! As young as she is, Maya can tell when I'm under pressure and suddenly it's been lifted. A lot can happen in 15 days!

Money doesn't make for happiness. However, having to wait for funds to arrive so you know you can pay the bills for the next four months and afford to put food on the table is another matter. Unless you've been in that situation and have a child depending upon you, then you have no idea how the pressure builds.

We had a really fun day, with burgers, chips and ice cream. Stopping on the way home to buy freshly made biscuits, with the largest chunks of chocolate I have ever seen. We didn't spend much in the end because that wasn't what it was about; it was about the feeling that if anything did take our fancy I could say 'let's get it'. Maya made me turn my back while she looked for her *special* gift for me and then I stood there patiently while she counted out two handfuls of change from her money box.

The lady serving her was lovely and she even gift-wrapped it for Maya, who wouldn't put it in my bag and insisted on carrying it herself. I'd overheard her whispering to the lady as she wrapped it up, 'It's perfect. Simply perfect!'

'You have a very lovely daughter,' the woman remarked as Maya gave her a wave goodbye.

'Thank you, I've been blessed.'

If only she knew the full story, she'd probably be in tears. I was fighting to keep my eyes from misting over, that's for sure.

As we shopped for Mum and Dad's presents, Maya showed as much interest as if it was something for her. Niall's parents' present I'll order in the morning, as we always bought them a hamper from Harrods. They are a couple who have everything they want and it's one of the few gifts that probably wouldn't end up in the charity shop in January. Sad, but true, and even Niall knew that.

For Eve and Rick we chose a diamond-shaped lead crystal paperweight. It was a little more expensive than some of the others, but they've been so supportive I wanted to give them something special. They have a display cabinet for their collection of paperweights and each has a story behind it. I think that's rather romantic, as quite a few celebrate wedding anniversaries and birthdays. Now they have one from us to thank them for being such special friends.

For Amelie, Maya chose a Collectibles unicorn named Fantasy.

'Mum, that's perfect. Amelie has most of them but she doesn't have that one.'

The little figurine seemed to stand out on the shelf. It was lovely to see Maya so excited to find something she regarded as the perfect thing for her best friend.

We bought a present for her teacher and one for her favourite teaching assistant. I then picked up some chocolates for the postman and my list was complete. After Maya goes to bed tonight I'll jump on the PC and then Christmas will be delivered in a series of boxes over the coming week.

One large, online food shop and even if the snow they forecast does arrive, we'll be all set up. Someone up there is surely looking over us. However, while Amazon can deliver most of Maya's presents, there's one special one I still have to organise. What I want this Christmas is to hear a happy, happy, shriek of unfettered joy and disbelief!

Chapter 20

Elana

The Empty Space at the Table

Sunday morning is always a leisurely wake-up as Maya comes into bed to snuggle and we talk about everything and anything. Today Amelie is spending the day here, so Eve and Rick can visit the mall. The girls are going to finish the bead chains for the tree, which is an important part of our ritual. This year Maya is assembling them in a rainbow of colours; last year it was single colours for each strand.

As we await Amelie's arrival I busy myself in the kitchen, preparing pancake batter and slicing brioche ready to toast. As I'm washing the raspberries Luke arrives and I hear Maya in the porch, chattering away to him.

'Sounds like a great shopping trip,' he muses as Maya dances around him. Looking down at his feet I notice he has the holey sock on his right foot again. He catches my stare and grins back at me.

'Behind on the washing again. For some reason I keep

139

losing socks. They go into the machine in pairs, I swear, but I end up with a collection of singles so the holey ones never get thrown in the bin.'

'It's the sock fairy,' Maya informs him in all seriousness. 'Mummy says she likes to take one now and again to decorate her house.'

Luke and I burst out laughing; be careful what tales you spin to young children as they will quote them back at you.

Once she's out of earshot, I indicate for Luke to take a seat at the table and pour him a coffee.

'Breakfast won't be long; we're just waiting for Amelie.'

'How are you doing today? Glad to hear you had a good one yesterday. Maya is in high spirits.'

'Be prepared, this is just the start. Once school finishes it's going to be like someone's been force-feeding her doughnuts. Oh, maybe Joe's too young for you to have seen the sugar-rush effect. Well, Christmas is like a double dose.'

I make a face as I warn him and then break into a grin. Maya's festive cheer is infectious and I can't believe how low my spirits have been lately.

'Actually, I'll cook you a couple of pancakes now and I can feed the girls in a bit. I'll try to limit them to Maya's bedroom and the sitting room. I've moved my PC into the sitting room, too, so I won't be in the way. What's on the agenda today?'

Luke sips his coffee while leaning back in the chair with one arm hooked around the ladder back. He looks relaxed and I'm almost tempted to ask how it went yesterday with Joe, but I decide it's best to leave it to him if he wants to begin that conversation.

'Hey, you're spoiling me, but who doesn't love pancakes? Well, today it's going to be a bit noisy to start with as I'll be ripping off the skirting boards. I will move that stack of flooring first, though. Is it okay if I pile it up in the porch so I don't have to keep moving it around as I work? I want to get the underlay done in the dining room and make a start laying the laminate. I'll do the cutting outside, so although it will involve a bit of hammering inside, there shouldn't be much mess.' Luke talks me through his plan as I place a breakfast plate of brioche, jam and pancakes in front of him.

'Maple syrup is in the jug. I've been told that keeping your builder well fed is a wise move. It keeps him coming back for more.' I wink at him and he puts his head back and laughs out loud.

'Pretty see-through, am I? To be honest, after a day out with Joe and a lot of crawling around on the floor playing with cars, I'm starving this morning.'

He eats like a man who hasn't been fed for a while and although I'm pretending to wipe down the work tops, I watch surreptitiously out of the corner of my eye. There are some appreciative noises as he eats and he makes quick work of the pancakes and raspberries.

'Now that's good. I think I should be paying you for my meals if you insist on catering for me like this.' He looks up at me quite seriously.

'And that reminds me! I drew out some cash for you; it's in an envelope on top of the stack of flooring. As soon as you have a moment let me know exactly how much I owe you and I'll draw out the rest. Are you happy for me to pay you week by week?'

He frowns, then shovels the last piece of brioche into his mouth as he rises from the table. He nods several times until his mouth is empty.

'Thanks, appreciated. I'm keeping a record of the hours I work and giving you a forty-per-cent reduction on the firm's going rate. Least I can do,' he smiles. I watch as he brushes a few crumbs from the corner of his mouth. Then he grins at me in that boyish way of his. It's easy to forget he's not some brash twenty-four-year-old who hasn't a clue about real life, when he gives me that trademark look of his.

I suppose it won't be too long before his broken heart begins to heal and he'll fall under the spell of some other young woman. I hope, for his sake, that next time it's someone who won't disappoint him.

I realise he hasn't moved; he's standing with his hand on the back of the chair looking directly at me.

'That's quite an intense look you've got going on there. Problems?'

I shake my head and turn back to the sink to swill off the cloth in my hand.

'Just a stray thought, you know how it is. If the girls get in the way at any time, just shout. I'm going to be doing some work tucked up in the corner of the sitting room.'

'Will do,' he calls over his shoulder as he walks away from the table.

What would it be like to live here with another man? To cook him breakfast and hold hands over a table at which I can still see Niall sitting across from me? I can't even contemplate being in a place where I want to invite anyone into our home, or our lives. Doing the dating thing in a restaurant and then moving on to the next step and bringing someone home makes my stomach churn at the thought.

'You're a lost cause, Elana, and you know it', my doubting alter ego seems to whisper in my ear. Only the chimes from the doorbell springing into life interrupt my thoughts.

'Maya, Amelie is here.'

Chapter 21

Elana

Is a Little Sparkle a Dangerous Thing?

With Maya and Amelie playing quite happily, and Luke working like a man on a mission, I sit down at the PC. Who is Aiden Cruise? How does he manage to get himself out of every scrape and still keep the public on his side? I genuinely believe that's the question the publishers are expecting me to answer. I guess this guy must either be very lucky indeed or have a guardian angel watching over him.

Then it hits me, like a light bulb being switched on in a darkened room. My contact with Aiden has been patchy and unpredictable. One moment he's supposed to be available, then he's not. Then I get a call and he's there, so no matter how inconvenient it's been I've had to drop everything. I get him to answer as many questions as I can fire at him before he says he has to be somewhere else. The only constant throughout the entire process so far has been Seth Greenburg. He's an old-school gentleman, very professional and although he doesn't make excuses for Aiden, he's constantly smoothing the way. He makes Aiden look a lot less erratic than he actually is and he does that with great skill.

I dive into the growing box of information, interview sheets and photos I've pulled together over the last three months. Some of this stuff is pretty damning and I realise there's hardly anything about Seth. Okay, let's see what the Internet has to throw up. As I type in his name and press return, I'm rather shocked to discover that Seth hasn't always been a manager, but his background is in stage and theatre. He was a producer for many years and it looks as though he worked with some of the top names. His career extends back quite a way. I'm intrigued as to why he decided to step into the role of the infamous Aiden Cruise's manager. There's an article here announcing his appointment, shortly after Aiden had been arrested following yet another late-night bar brawl. The charges were dropped within twenty-four hours of Seth's appointment. Coincidence?

I pull up my timeline chart on the screen, mapping some of the high and low points of Aiden's career. From the number-one hits to the clashes with photographers, and several fracas that made the headlines but never resulted in charges. But a pattern is emerging that since Seth appeared on the scene suddenly there is a lot more positive press and a lot less of the negative. It's unlikely that Aiden has been increasingly lucky dodging the repercussions of his actions, as he's still known at times for his cavalier attitude. Clearly that has also, in the past, made him a target. But it's beginning to look as if he's calming down, becoming much more conscious of his public image. Or is it simply due to the fact that he has someone looking after him who is very skilled at making bad news go away?

Seth has personally handled all of the arrangements for my New Year's Eve trip to meet Aiden. He has ensured that everything is taken care of from the moment the car picks me up until the moment it drops me back home in the early hours of New Year's Day. Like a magician, he smoothed away my concerns, even though I hesitated because I didn't want to leave Maya. But at no point has he left me feeling that I've been put out simply to accommodate Aiden. Am I, too, being managed, manipulated to ensure that what's included in the book is controlled? All I have is hearsay and the hard facts are the ones Aiden and Seth choose to present to me.

My head starts to ache as I realise that I'm going to have to be on my guard from here on in. The publishers are paying for my services and my brief is to get to the heart of what makes Aiden Cruise the bad boy everyone is prepared to forgive. He's being paid an enormous amount of money for his side of the story. I'm the person who has to marry the two halves – what other people have to say about him and what the man himself chooses to tell me.

Maya's face appears in view and I yank out the ear pieces of my iPod.

'It's lunchtime, Mum. Can we have a picnic in my bedroom?'

Maya and Amelie are both staring intently at me. I turn the PC into sleep mode and urge them back upstairs. 'Of course. Give me five minutes and I'll bring it up. You haven't been getting in Luke's way, now, have you?'

'No, Mum. Have you seen the new floor? It's amazing.'

Maya is clearly impressed, but then we've been living with concrete for such a very long time. Maybe she doubted it would ever be finished. As I walk through my heart actually rises in my chest as, aside from the ugly gaps along the bottom of the walls from the missing skirting boards, there's an expanse of walnut laminate.

'You seem surprised,' Luke looks up, surveying my reaction.

'Yes, this is real progress.'

'Well, don't be too impressed. This is the easy part and it goes down quite quickly. It's all the cutting around the door-ways that is labour-intensive and takes the most time. The finish is what you wanted?'

'It's perfect. I mean, already the room sounds less hollow. Maya's given you the thumbs up.'

'I know, she told me.'

'The girls are having a picnic up in Maya's room, so I thought I'd do sandwiches for lunch. How late are you working, because I'll prepare something hot for dinner, later?'

'I'll keep going until early evening, but I want to stop soon and do some of the cutting. I don't think it's fair on your neighbours if I'm outside using the circular saw past late afternoon.'

'Sandwiches are on the way, then.'

As I work on lunch I reflect on the fact that I love it when there are other people here with us. Luke mumbles to himself as he works and I wonder whether it's a tune that's playing in his head and he's being respectful by holding back. If we weren't here would he turn out to be a closet singer? I love watching him work, the way his body moves and how absorbed he becomes with the job in hand. He's an artist with his hands and I admire his skill. Luke is just so easy to be around and he's really good company. I wonder if we'd met at a party whether we'd have been attracted to each other and started talking? I smile to myself; daydreaming is a luxury I can't afford and I reluctantly drag my eyes away from his muscular arms to focus on what I'm doing.

Maya and Amelie are giggling away upstairs; goodness knows what they're talking about. But it gives the cottage a buzz that's been missing for a while.

When I take up the girls' tray I see they've made a den, using Maya's throw, and the floor is covered with felt-tip pens, magazines and notebooks.

'Looks like you've been having fun, girls.'

'We're making scrapbooks, Mum.'

'That's a great idea. Just don't forget to stop and eat.'

Even before I reach the door it's as if I'm not there, as two heads are busy ripping pages out of magazines. 'I want Justin Bieber,' Amelie exclaims and I shake my head as I make my way out of the room.

Walking into the kitchen Luke follows me on his way back from the downstairs cloakroom.

'Just in time. Take a seat.'

'Thanks. Could I trouble you for a large glass of water? It's hot work.' He begins rolling up the sleeves on his plaid shirt. Obviously he must be feeling comfortable, as he launches straight into the pile of sandwiches on his plate.

I take my seat, trying hard not to look at Niall's empty place at the table.

'You're rather quiet today. There's nothing wrong, is there?' He talks between bites, chewing way too fast for it to be good for his digestion. But I could sit and watch him eat as a pastime. He devours his food with the same level of energy he tackles his work.

'The main job I'm working on at the moment is a biography. I'm at that stage where I don't quite have all of the information I need to see the whole picture, but what I do have has to be written up. It's rather like putting a jigsaw puzzle together.'

'Sounds fascinating,' he pauses to wipe his mouth with the paper napkin. Instead of taking another bite of his sandwich, he sits back ready to listen. I hadn't intended saying anything further but his eyes remain very firmly focused on me.

'I think I might have a bit of a dilemma brewing, if I'm honest.'

'Time for some detective work, maybe.' He begins eating again but doesn't take his eyes off me.

'That's why I'm away New Year's Eve. I'll be meeting my subject face to face for the first time. The problem is that I think I'm being fed information by him and his manager, whereas the arrangement is that I should be given unrestricted access. That hasn't been the case so far.'

'Is that what they call being a ghost writer? Wouldn't it be easier to write your own stuff, instead?'

I shake my head, swallowing a mouthful of food and realising I was hungrier than I thought.

'I trained as a journalist and fiction isn't my thing. I mostly edit children's books, the occasional young-adult novel and text books. I've worked for a couple of the newspapers over the years, but editing is easier as it means I don't have to traipse around in search of a story.'

'Bet there was a buzz, though. It is kind of isolated here and you don't seem to get out much.'

Suddenly the look passing between us feels a little uneasy. It was merely an observation, of course, but is it a polite way of saying my life looks rather boring?

'It's hard to pick back up again as everywhere I go family and friends are thinking of me as one half of a couple. It's a constant reminder to them of what's happened. Niall was as much a part of their lives as I am, but now everything is different. If they aren't worrying about unwittingly saying the wrong thing, they feel they should be encouraging me to look to the future. As the months passed I accepted the invites to dinners and meals out, but people tend to like round numbers and so you find yourself seated next to people you don't know. They think it's helpful drafting in their single friends in the hope that one of them will prove interesting. To be frank with you, it's all rather ghastly. For the moment I'm happy enough to concentrate on work and Maya.'

Luke sits back, his plate empty. His eyes flick over me, as if he's weighing me up.

'Maybe it's time to think a little less and have a bit of fun, instead.'

Is he flirting with me? I can feel my cheeks growing hot. I immediately run my hands through my hair, conscious that this morning it's even more wayward than usual. I must look a mess in my tracksuit bottoms and baggy sweater.

'Is this me we're talking about, or you?' I counter in an attempt to divert his attention.

His jaw drops a little and the sparkle is back in those eyes of his.

'Fair play, I'm just repeating some advice I was given this week. I wanted to see your reaction, out of interest. I sure as hell have no idea how to shake everything off and have a little fun. I'm not even sure I know what it means now. I seem to spend all my time stressing over Joe and how he's handling the situation. Any time left I'm caught up with worrying about money, or lack of it.'

The eye contact grows and neither of us blinks until Maya and Amelie come running downstairs with empty plates, filling the room with their boisterous antics and asking if they can have some ice cream.

Chapter 22

Luke

Life Can Be Scary For a Whole Host of Reasons

Greg's text is the last thing I wanted to wake up to on a Monday morning.

Hey, mate. It's all arranged. The four of us will get together on the twenty-eighth. Cheryl has tickets for a buffet at The Rage Machine, so come prepared to party as there will be a DJ and some great music. It's only one night and I'll owe you. G

Owe me? He'll be in my debt for the rest of his life. It's the in-place for singles and it's noisy. I've never been into knocking back shots and trying to dance in a place so packed with bodies that you can't help getting up close and personal with complete strangers. If that's the sort of place Cheryl and Lisa frequent, then we're not going to have anything in common. Besides, I come with baggage, not least because I no longer feel like the carefree, single guy I think they will be expecting and doubt I ever will again.

When I pull up at the office Dad says we have to head off to do an emergency repair on a broken window in the town centre. Seems there was a stag do last night that ended up way out of control. When we arrive it looks like someone went on a rampage. Even though the metal grill protecting the glass is still in place, something sharp has been pushed through at force. It's mindless vandalism for no reason at all, as there's no way anyone could get their hands through to grab any of the goods inside the store.

I hate days like this and, to make it worse, it starts to rain. Repairing unnecessary damage is rather soul-destroying and I find myself getting wound up over Greg's text.

'Is everything okay my son? This rain is a pain we could do without today. I said we'd board it up and the glass should arrive tomorrow. If you need to get back to Hillside View, I could get one of the other guys to help me.'

'No, it's fine. Another half a day and the skip will be full and I'll have it collected. I'm done then and you can put me on something else.'

Dad slides the boarding into place and I begin hammering.

'How's Bay Tree going? If you have your hands full I could write you out of the schedule through to Christmas.'

He's trying to be helpful, but I know it's always a juggling act at this time of year. Three of us are multi-skilled, including plumbing, and I know he's turning a lot of work away. Emergency call-outs command a premium rate.

'I'm on target, no worries there.'

'We're really looking forward to the weekend and having you and Joe stay over. He's a grand little chap.'

'Thanks, Dad. I also appreciate it as I'm a bit nervous, if I'm honest. What if he gets upset when Anita isn't there at bedtime? I mean, he's still a baby really.'

'Well, it's probably going to be easier with Mum around to help out. I'm not sure I could have coped on my own when you were young, either. I'm happy to sit down and have a play, but the minute they get grumpy I don't have a clue.'

Sadly, I feel exactly the same way. Do I know my son well enough to judge what he wants when he's tired and his routine is broken? What if he ends up screaming and inconsolable, wanting his mum? What if I end up having to bundle him into the car and admit defeat? Anita is bound to see that as yet another failure on my part.

***

'Four more days, Luke, and there's no more school.'

Maya is sitting on the floor next to me, watching as I mark up a piece of laminate ready to cut.

'I thought you liked school?'

'I do, but I like the Christmas holidays more. And I'm going to be staying at Grandma's house at New Year. We always have fun. Mummy says they spoil me, but I like it.'

I wonder if Joe will ever get the chance to have alone time with his grandparents. I can see by Maya's reaction that it's a real treat.

'What are you having for Christmas, Luke?'

Maya tilts her head to one side, studying my face as I sit back on my heels to consider my answer.

Before I can think of something suitable to say, Elana appears and answers for me.

'Lots of new socks and some peace and quiet. Maya, Luke is trying to work, darling. He's had a long day and, besides, it's time you popped into bed.'

Maya turns her back to Elana and gives me a conspiratorial look.

'Who wants socks for Christmas?' She asks, under her breath but loud enough for me to hear. I can't help myself laughing.

'Night, Maya. Sleep well.'

As they climb the stairs and I get back to work, it occurs to me that there's usually a good reason why mums bear the brunt of the work when it comes to rearing kids. Every question Maya asks makes me stop and think, whereas Elana has an instant answer and it's always the right one. It's the same with Anita; she just knows what to do without having to think about it. Mums have that natural ability, whereas maybe dads have to learn it. Over time I hope that I can become the sort of dad who Joe will not only look up to, but with whom he'll feel safe. Safe to share his secrets, as well as safe in the knowledge that I'll always be there for him when he needs me.

Chapter 23

Luke

Reluctant or Unwilling?

When Elana reappears she looks tired.

'I'm having a glass of wine, would you like one, or maybe a beer?'

'A beer would hit the spot. Give me half an hour and I'll join you for a chat.'

She glances up at me from underneath her eyelashes, enquiringly. Usually I down tools and we sit, talk for a while and then I get back to work. Tonight I want to ask her opinion about something because she's about the only one I can ask who won't have a biased view.

'Great, shout when you're ready.'

As usual, the last piece of the day is the one that just won't fit properly, but I'm conscious that Maya is probably snuggling down to sleep and you can't hammer boards together without making some noise.

I tidy up and head into the sitting room to see if Elana's busy. It can wait if she's on the PC and I'll go home instead and just make it an early night. As I hover in the doorway, she's stooped over in the fire grate picking something up.

'This just fell down the chimney.' She straightens, holding up one of Maya's little letters in her hand and with a puzzled look on her face.

'It was actually on the ledge. There are a few of them. I sort of thought you knew she'd been writing to Santa.'

Elana indicates for me to sit down, handing me a beer and a bottle opener.

'Maya gave me a letter to post, which I did, but I took a peek first. It was a short list and everything is on order, except the piano, which has been replaced by a small keyboard.'

She's smiling, so it hasn't upset her that I knew what was going on.

'How did you find out about them?' She asks and I guess I'm not completely off the hook.

'The fireplace seems to be a big deal to Maya for some reason. She wanted to know whether it was safe now and that Santa wasn't in any danger come Christmas Eve. For a kid, she's great at applying logic. You have to be careful what you say, because she considers every word.'

'I know. She's one bright little girl. It's a dilemma, though, isn't it? What do I do? Read what she's written so I know what's going on inside her head, or accept that everyone has the right to have secret thoughts?'

Elana looks down at the little letter lying unopened on the coffee table. It's folded into four and on the upside it says

'Santa'. It's the one with the heart drawn underneath Maya's handwriting.

'I keep a daily diary; it's one of the self-help techniques you learn when you go for bereavement counselling. Well, I say daily, but now I just add to it once in a while. I guess that means I'm making progress. It's not something I'd ever share with anyone and I'd be horrified if someone else read it.'

We lapse into silence. We all have things we might not be too happy to share with the world.

'Anyway, I'll have to mull it over. So what's new with you?' As usual she's giving me the chance to talk without any pressure. I take a swig of beer, trying to collect my thoughts and not really knowing how to approach this.

'I'm having Joe overnight this weekend, first time ever. Okay, we'll be sleeping over at my parents' house. I will admit I'm a little anxious about it, but it's a huge step forward and shows that Anita thinks I'm up to it. It's all about the kids, isn't it?'

There's a little furrow lurking on Elana's brow.

'Yes, it is and they always come first. But is this only about Joe, or is it about Anita, too?'

Her eyes narrow slightly as she takes in my sharp intake of breath. 'Be honest with yourself, Luke.'

I cast around for the right words, my head processing so many thoughts coming at me from all angles.

'Not, it's not. But I'm not sure anyone else around me can understand what it's like to have their world fall apart, except you. I suppose it's only natural that I should still feel some sort of residual guilt because we failed Joe. A part of me wonders if she's reaching out to me for another reason and I don't know how to handle that. Any wise words of advice?'

'If you were sitting there telling me that you loved her, really loved her, then I'd say get in your car now and go tell her how you feel. Don't let another second slip away without letting her know that, just in case there's a chance you can still make it work. I don't know Anita at all, but what I do know is that a woman wants to be loved for who she is, not just because she's given birth to a child. She'll always be in your life, as you will be in hers, because of Joe. But if you don't truly love each other what possible hope could there be for your long-term relationship as a couple?'

'I'm trying to hold on because I can't seem to let go. What did I do that was so wrong?'

I put down the beer bottle and lean forward, cradling my head in my hands.

'Luke, it takes two people to make a relationship and it takes two to break it. Nothing you've said indicates that Anita is asking you to give it another try, am I right?'

I nod, knowing full well she's right. 'It's time to face facts, isn't it? It's really over.'

'It's only natural to want to cling on, Luke. I know that only too well. Letting go is a process, a painful one. Added to that, you have to learn to cultivate a very different kind of relationship with Anita as you move forward. Working on that benefits you all, including Joe.'

I rub my eyes, tiredness suddenly hitting me like a slap in the face. Or maybe it's the onslaught of thoughts, fragments of angry outbursts and rows I don't really want to remember.

'I'd better go. That was helpful, thanks. No point in trying to kid myself. If there was anything left to salvage we wouldn't be a year down the road and still apart.'

'Can I ask what really triggered this?' Elana's voice is full of sympathy.

'I let Greg talk me into making up a foursome.'

She smiles, the sides of her mouth hitching up slightly. Her eyes reflect a sudden warmth, indicating that she understands.

'You are drawing a line and stepping over it. Time to be brave, Luke. Maybe you need to begin following your own advice – what was it you said to me about it being time to have a little fun, for a change? You're still very young and this is just a little stumble on life's path. You need to start trusting your intuition and developing a little self-belief.'

'Thanks. Helpful.'

As Elana follows me out to the front door we walk in silence and I realise that giving advice is easy; learning to take it and act upon it is the hard part.

'With age comes wisdom,' Elana adds, as I turn to say a final goodnight.

'Perhaps. But I think some people are born with a lot more common sense than others. I just don't want to be that sad person who keeps making the same mistake.'

Elana shakes her head.

'Then stop looking back and start looking forward. That's going to be my New Year's resolution and I think it's one that applies to most of us, don't you?'

We exchange wry smiles and I walk out into the chilly night air, feeling alone and miserable. Life seems to be rubbing my nose in my misery by bringing me close to a woman as special as Elana. If it wasn't for the job, our paths would never have crossed and I'm well aware of that. Outside of our respective situations we have little in common, but it's just so easy to be around her. And it has been from the start. Perhaps that's partly why she's so relaxed when I'm around, because she knows there could never be anything serious between us. I'm just not in her league.

Chapter 24

Luke

Here I Go Again

The more I get to know Elana, the more I realise that she's just the type of woman I need in my life. Someone who has a genuinely good heart and a lot of common sense. We've become friends almost without realising it. I guess that's because we're both vulnerable at the moment and it's easy to connect on that level. I admire her strength whenever she's around Maya, but ironically it's her weaknesses that draw me to her. They make her more human and more approachable, somehow. Those moments at the end of the day when we're grateful to sit down and unwind, feeling relaxed in each other's company. It's easier to talk frankly with someone who isn't a part of your life because you don't have to hide anything. Was I a little too honest last night, though? I asked for her advice and then wondered if a part of me had an ulterior motive. What was I hoping? That Elana would throw her arms around me, hold me close in the hope of rescuing me from myself?

It's clear she thinks the age gap between us means we're worlds apart, but when we share our feelings and worst fears we're closer than I've ever been with anyone else. It's like walking along the edge of a cliff with a sheer drop on one side and the safety of land on the other. Something is drawing me to her and away from the safety zone. I know that if I told her she's the most exciting woman I've ever met, she'd never open her door to me again.

Or maybe I'm tired of living in limbo and trying to grab on to something, anything, which will make me feel like I count for something. Anita represents the life I know, one that might work still if she was prepared to meet me in the middle and make an effort. Elana is never going to be interested in me because I have nothing to offer a woman like her. But she made me look at my motives and in my heart I know that Anita doesn't love me. The truth of the matter is that I don't think she ever did. Did she purposely go out to trap me, by getting pregnant? If that's the case, then it trapped us both, but I wouldn't change that for a second because Joe's arrival is the best thing that has ever happened to me. What Elana made me stop to consider last night was that I'm in danger of making a huge mistake for all the wrong reasons. She's right and even if Anita is beginning to see me in a different light, I'm no longer the person she once knew. I want more out of life. I want to be with someone who makes me feel alive. Why is it that what I want always seems to be outside of my grasp? I guess I have to learn to make the most of the opportunities that come my way, instead of trying to reach for the unobtainable.

***

'I'm hungry, how about you?' Greg and I are ankle-deep in mud, sorting out a collapsed drain. It's overcast and grey, with intermittent rain and one of those days when the job has no appeal whatsoever. We're in all-weather gear, but still it's miserable work as the rain seems to find a way through to the layers beneath. We head off to the van, throw our boots and waterproofs into a tarpaulin in the back, and go in search of a pub with an open fire and some good, home-cooked food.

When it arrives it doesn't take long to clear our plates, then we sit back contentedly with stomachs full, appreciating one of life's simple pleasures. It won't take long to work this off when we get back, but it serves to raise our spirits.

'How's the job for the widow lady going?'

I roll my eyes. 'I wish everyone would stop calling her that. She has a name.' I realise that was a bit abrupt, but I'm finding that reference increasingly irritating. 'It's Mrs James to you.'

Greg laughs, but it comes out as more of a snort.

'But you're on first-name terms, I assume.'

'Her name is Elana. We chat, but that's it.'

'I'm glad of that because Lisa's really looking forward to our night out.'

'And Cheryl is no doubt very grateful for your organisational skills.'

Greg downs half a pint of orange squash and wipes his mouth with the back of his hand.

'Among other things. Hey, she thinks I'm great, what can

I say? She's one smart lady. Did I tell you that I'm going to meet her parents this weekend?'

'Well, that's a first for you. Should I be thinking about reserving a date in the not-too-distant future?'

That makes him chuckle.

'We're a long way from that, mate. After seeing what you've been through I'm in no hurry whatsoever to start thinking about domesticity. And anyway, I believe in long engagements. If the woman you're with is going to turn into a monster it's best to find that out before you walk down the aisle.'

'Is that what you really think? Or are you exaggerating?'

Greg leans forward, lowering his voice a little.

'Mate, you wouldn't listen, remember? It was doomed before it began.'

It's too depressing to get into this and, besides, there's no point.

'Lesson learnt, so tell me about Lisa. What do you know about her?'

'She's twenty-one, works in a bank and split up with her childhood sweetheart about six months ago. There's no bad blood between them because, according to Cheryl, it just sort of fizzled out. She's been on a few dates but is still looking.'

'That's it?'

Greg gives me a stare.

'She loves going to the gym and reading romance novels. Heck, what do I know about her? I'm just giving you what Cheryl told me to pass on if you asked the question.'

I thought as much.

'Nice rack,' he adds and I wince.

'Can't say I noticed and besides, it was dark when we walked to the taxi. What does she know about me?'

Greg casts his gaze around the room, before looking me in the eye.

I suddenly know what he's thinking. 'You haven't told Cheryl about Joe, have you?'

'Look mate, take a bit of advice from someone who is a little more clued-up about women in general. You don't drop that on them at the start, it's something to talk about after you get to know her a little.'

'It doesn't feel right, Greg. You need to fill Cheryl in so she can pass that on to Lisa.'

'So you're prepared to meet up with her, with an open mind, then? I thought you were doing this just as a favour to me?'

He smirks.

'Let's just say that splitting up with Anita hasn't been easy. It's only natural I'm being cautious, who wouldn't be? It's not a case of having an open mind, more a case of I'm not really ready to let anyone back in, yet.'

Greg sits back sharply in his seat, throwing his hands up in the air.

'Well, at least you aren't cutting yourself off from the outside world completely. You're no fun these days, Luke, and it's sad to see. The old you is still in there, somewhere, I know it. Just relax a bit and we'll have a great night out. It's just a date, mate, and what a way to start a new year, having a good-looking woman on your arm. Besides, you might surprise yourself and relax a little, for a change.'

Maybe I'm being rather uptight about this and it probably

reflects how serious everything seems to be in my life at the moment. This Lisa lady might be in a similar position and being pressured by Cheryl to go out with me. Friends often mean well and sometimes, no matter how bad an idea is, it's just easier to give in.

Chapter 25

Elana

What Lies Beneath the Surface

If I'm going to spend next Friday painting the walls, then I have to get as much work out of the way as I can. With school finishing in just three days, and the tree to sort on Saturday, it's going to be a busy few days.

I've made quite a bit of progress on the manuscript, feeling I've done justice to introducing Aiden and painting an accurate picture of his childhood. The over-protective mother, the absent father and his formative years surrounded by a group of friends who stuck together through good and bad. The problem was that a lot of it was negative energy and there was a distinct lack of a positive influence at a very developmental time in his life. No wonder he hit his teens feeling life owed him something better. When he was plucked from a very mundane life, at such a young age, and virtually overnight became someone idolised by a growing band of adolescent girls, it was overload. Not only that, but he fell prey to an inner circle of employees whom, it seems, had no problem ignoring his excesses.

All it took was one audition for lead singer in a new group being formed by one of the most powerful producers in the industry. His edgy good looks and that sense of craziness hovering around him made him irresistibly dangerous to a generation of young girls. Then came the years when day after day he was in the tabloids and he became the hunted. There were so many photos that certainly wouldn't have made his mother proud. Out of control, he had several trips to an exclusive rehab clinic, but he never stayed the course. After each visit, within days he was back to his old habits and he went through a long period of hiring and firing managers. A few simply chose to walk away, but then along came Seth. Something definitely changed after that, although from the interviews I've conducted no one else noticed any remarkable change in Aiden, or his habits. However, I wonder if there was a new level of awareness and a closed-door policy when dealing with publicity. Eventually the press found a new target. Did he just become old news, or could it really have been something engineered by Seth?

My admiration for the guy who, it seems, was able to turn things around when it was clear that Aiden was living on the edge, continues to grow. Suddenly, the doorbell breaks my concentration.

'Hi Eve, come in.'

'Sorry to pull you away from writing about a life of glitz and glamour. I just wanted to ask if you could do the school run this afternoon for me. I have to drop Rick at the station, he's off to London for a few days.'

There's a hint of exasperation in her voice and she seems a little tense.

'Is everything alright? Sorry, come inside and I'll put the kettle on.'

'Well, I really didn't mean to interrupt, but thanks.'

As soon as she turns to step into the open-plan area she stops. 'Wow! You have half a floor!'

'I know, it's wonderful, isn't it? He's amazing; I mean ... it's amazing.'

'No, I think you had that right first time. Luke is amazing. Hard-working, easy on the eye—'

'Eve!'

She follows me down to the kitchen end of the room and hovers as I make coffee.

'What? It's the truth. And you have lovely smooth walls, although the colour is a bit random.'

I laugh, although it's beginning to even out as the plaster patches dry and take on a much paler hue.

'That's my job this weekend. Luke is hoping to finish the flooring before Christmas, although that seems rather ambitious to me. He's confident, though, and it would be amazing to be able to clean through and know the concrete dust will be gone for good. Then I'll just about be out of money until I have a completed draft to hand over to the publishers.'

'It's quite a weight on your shoulders, isn't it, managing your finances? Has any other work come in?'

We sit at the table, facing each other.

'A little. I have the last in that series of three children's books to edit, which I told you about a couple of weeks ago – the fantasy ones that Maya is enjoying. I've also been commissioned to write a few product reviews for some kitchen equipment. I'll be testing out a juicer first and they are going to send over a number of recipes for me to try out. So enjoy your coffee, because the next time you come it might be carrot, ginger and apple juice I'm putting in front of you.'

Eve makes a face.

'I much prefer breaking the seal on a box of juice I've grabbed off a shelf. This isn't inspired by some faddy health kick or something?'

'No. Just the need to take any work that comes my way. Luke's inspection confirmed that all the window and door frames are rotten and beyond repair. So that's a big chunk of money to find. Then there's the extension the other side of the utility room, which needs to be turned into a guest bedroom and study at some point. And, of course, the outside needs re-rendering and then there's the garden to tackle.'

'Now would be a very convenient time to find a love interest who happened to be handy with his hands, wouldn't it?'

I sit back, eyes wide with disbelief that Eve said that.

'I'm paying for his time and it's a reciprocal arrangement. He's happy to work for cash to help out with his situation and I'm grateful to get the work done whenever he has a few hours free.'

'And I rather suspect he's good company over dinner,' she muses.

I give up.

'He's easy to talk to, granted, and we usually end up sharing our problems. It's a bit like attending a broken hearts club, actually.'

'Maybe I should come along, then.'

At first I think she's joking and I laugh, good-naturedly. Then I see that she's serious.

'Are you having problems? You and Rick?'

Eve finishes her coffee and places the mug down on the table, twisting it between her hands.

'You've never heard us rowing? I assumed the sound of raised voices travels when the windows are open, because of the valley. You seem surprised.'

'Shocked is probably more accurate. What have I missed?'

Eve sighs. 'Rick is so focused on his work that even when he's home it's like his mind is constantly elsewhere. Did you know he wants us to move? He has his eye on a bigger house because he feels it's a status symbol. He says he's earning the money and it's time to reap the rewards.'

A cold feeling settles in the pit of my stomach. Maya will lose her best friend and I'll lose the support of two people who are like family to me. But that's selfish. Rick obviously wants his family to have the best life he can provide for them, but clearly Eve doesn't see it that way.

'I will admit I am surprised, and the thought of you moving away is a bit overwhelming. I mean, all that work on the cottage and it's beautiful now. Maybe it was only ever an investment to Rick and I suppose that's partly down to the business he's in.'

'It's all about money, to be honest, Eve. If only he'd been more like Niall—'

Her hand shoots across the table. 'Sorry. I am sorry, I shouldn't have said that, I was just thinking out loud. Ignore me, I ought to be grateful for what I have, we're very lucky.'

Tears fill her eyes and I'm at a loss for words. I thought they were about as close as any couple could get and I don't understand what's going on.

She pulls a tissue from her pocket to mop her eyes and it's painful to watch as she pulls herself together.

'Ignore me. I'm just upset because he's off to London yet again. Amelie's going to be disappointed as we were going to put the Christmas trimmings up tonight. You know what a big deal it all is at this age.'

I nod. 'Yes, we're doing the tree on Saturday. It's funny, but this year Santa seems to be a fixation for Maya. She's been writing him letters and putting them up the chimney. There's quite a little pile of them, even though we've already posted off the one to the North Pole.'

Eve gives me a watery smile.

'Amelie's was a long list and I'm still talking her out of a few things.'

We both laugh. 'Same here. The request for a piano needs toning down a little as Santa is actually going to deliver a small keyboard.'

'Oh, you were let off quite lightly, then. Amelie asked for a pony.'

I raise my eyebrows.

'The worst part is that Rick says if we move to a house with a few acres of land he'll buy her one.'

'But you don't want to leave Hillside, no matter how exciting a move could be?'

She shakes her head, shrugs off my question and stands, thanking me for the coffee and agreeing to do the school run.

I'm sure whatever is going on between them is just a rough patch and hopefully they'll work through it. I can't pretend that the thought of losing them as neighbours isn't unsettling, but that's something I might have to learn to deal with.

Chapter 26

The In-Laws

When I put the phone down I find myself anxiously chewing my lip, an old habit I slip into whenever I'm stressed.

'Maya, can you come down for a moment?'

You would think a herd of elephants was descending the stairs, but it's only one little girl who appears moments later.

'That was Grandma and Granddad James on the phone. They're coming to dinner and they'll be here in about an hour.'

'Are they bringing my present?'

I look at Maya, feeling rather shocked and more than a little disappointed. It's been quite a while since we've had any contact with Niall's parents and this must mean they're finally ready to reach out to us.

'Maya! That's not very nice. Christmas isn't just about presents; it's about spending time with family and friends.'

Maya's face puckers up a little and a pink flush spreads across her cheeks.

'Sorry, Mum. It's just that we haven't seen them in ages.'

'Well, I don't think they're popping in just to deliver presents; they want to spend a little time with us. Daddy would like that and it's our job to make it a happy visit.'

She mulls over my words and then says, 'Okay, Mum,' before heading back upstairs.

You can't tell a six-year-old what not to say, it wouldn't be fair, but since Niall's death each visit with his parents has been a painful experience. Without him there's no bridge between us, although it's clear that they don't want to lose touch. But they are coming to see Maya, whereas I'm just a reminder that their son is no longer here. There's nothing I can do about that and I understand that for them it's very hard to know what to say. The only thing we now have in common is Maya and they have no idea what is happening in our day-to-day lives. It's a barrier that isn't intentional, but is still very real.

The doorbell kicks into life and a glance at the clock confirms that it's probably Luke.

'Hi, had a good day?'

Luke shrugs as he kicks off his boots.

'If you call getting cold and damp while digging out a drain a good day, then I suppose it was.' He laughs and when I don't join in he looks straight up at me.

'What's wrong?'

'Day from hell for me, too. I have the in-laws coming over in an hour for dinner. An ad-hoc visit. You can tell it's

Christmas.' Ouch. That was a bit heavy and even Luke does a double-take.

'Awkward. Is it best I head off home and leave you to it?'

It would probably be easier, but my hopes are pinned on getting this cottage into shape before Christmas and I shake my head.

'No. It's fine. This is our reality at the moment and there's no point in putting on an act. I expect they'll leave shortly after we've eaten, so it's just a meal and a chance for them to catch up with their granddaughter. It might help having another person around the table.'

'You aren't close?'

'I think it's more that the person who linked us is no longer here. I'm not their flesh and blood, but Maya – well, that's a different matter.'

'Sorry, that can't be easy for them, or for you. I'm not the best conversationalist, to be honest.'

He looks as if he'd rather turn around and head out the door.

'If I get stuck you could talk about the work you're doing here. Who knows, they might know someone who needs a builder.'

'If that's supposed to be an incentive, you're wide of the mark. However, I am hungry so I guess if that's the price I have to pay, consider it done.'

'You are a saviour! Now if we can just be ready to jump in if Maya starts talking about anything ... um ... you know, sensitive, then I think that's everything covered. I'm away to cook.'

Chapter 27

Elana

Building Bridges

When Philip and Carol arrive we hug rather awkwardly and I usher them into the sitting room. Luke is on his knees easing a piece of board into the corner with the help of a rubber mallet.

'This is Luke. Luke, Philip and Carol. Maya, Grandma and Granddad are here – we're in the sitting room,' I call out to her as we walk past the staircase.

As usual, movement in Maya's bedroom sounds as if half of her class is running around.

'Good to see the work is progressing,' Philip nods at Luke as we walk past him.

'We'll soon be dust-free. Ah, here she is!'

Maya appears carrying an envelope and stands in the doorway, looking at each of us in turn.

'How you've grown. Come and give Grandma a hug.' Carol holds out her arms, but Maya doesn't move. In fairness to her it's been quite a while since she's seen her and no doubt she's picking up on the fact that I don't feel comfortable, either.

'What's that in your hand, Maya?' I give her a smile, hoping to coax her into action, while indicating for our guests to take a seat.

'It's a Christmas card I made.'

She begins to look a little tearful, her gaze flickering back and forth between us all.

'I think Grandma would love to take a look. Why don't you show her?'

Finally she moves forward slowly, until she's standing in front of Carol with her hand extended.

Carol is amazing, making a big deal of opening the envelope and showing genuine delight as she shares the card with Philip.

'And such a beautifully drawn Christmas tree – we have an artist in the family!'

Maya glows under her praise, eventually happy to sit between them both. As soon as she looks settled I excuse myself to check on dinner.

Luke looks up as I walk out of the room, pulling the door behind me. 'How's it going? Maya was a bit agitated, I had to encourage her in,' he confirms. I'd suspected as much.

'Oh, I did wonder – for a brief moment I thought she was going to turn and run. Thank you! I'll set the table and then start dishing up.'

'I'll go and wash my hands. Are you sure you want me at the table, I mean, I won't be offended and I could make myself scare for a bit.'

'Are you bailing on me? Some friend you've turned out to be!'

He smirks. 'Okay, you win. Let me just sweep up some of these offcuts first.'

I take a deep breath and get busy. It's only pasta with chicken, but that's all I had that would stretch to feed five people. Actually, it's a bit daunting as it's a long time since I cooked for anyone, other than Luke, and he seems to eat anything.

When I pop my head around the sitting-room door, Maya is reading one of her favourite stories out aloud. She's showing off a little, as she usually runs her finger along underneath the words so she doesn't lose her place. Of course, it's all new to Niall's parents and they are looking at her in awe.

'Sorry to interrupt, but dinner's served.'

'It's pasta, my favourite,' says Maya. She clasps Carol's hand, who beams as they make their way into the dining area. Philip stands and indicates for me to go ahead of him. He's such a gentleman and a little stab of pain makes my heart constrict. I feel guilty because I'm not totally at ease with them and they aren't totally at ease with me. It's no one's fault as we've never fallen out, but there are so many things that have been left unsaid.

'Thank you, Philip. I'm so glad you are able to stay for dinner.'

'Not at all, thank you for the kind invitation. I'll be honest with you,' he hangs back a little and I follow his lead, 'we weren't sure whether it was the right thing to come over, or not. We don't want you to feel we're intruding, or causing any upset, but we've missed you both.'

His words touch my heart and a sense of regret washes over me.

'Ah, Philip, you are welcome any time. Please don't wait for an invitation. These days it's just work, school runs and trying to keep up with everything. I feel awful so much time has passed and it wasn't intentional, just life getting in the way.'

'Glad to hear it, just wanted to check. If it's hard for us, it's even harder for you.' The look on his face is one of stoic acceptance. I reach out to place my hand on his arm, unable to trust myself to speak.

Maya and Luke are in deep discussion with Carol, telling the story about the chimney.

'Luke says it's perfectly safe, but we can't light the fire yet.'

'Well, that's a relief,' Carol replies, in all seriousness. 'We can't take any risks when it comes to Christmas Eve.'

As Philip and I take our seats, Maya says, 'Grandma, did you know I'm getting a piano?'

Luke has to hide a smile, as I jump straight in and explain that it might not be a big piano this year, as Santa thinks Maya needs to practise on a keyboard first.

Surprisingly, the conversation flows well as everyone chips in with their own favourite childhood anecdote. Then Philip compliments Luke on the great job he's doing with the flooring. That sparks a conversation about how difficult it is to find a reliable builder and Luke seems genuinely pleased when Philip asks for a card.

Maya more or less chatters non-stop to Carol and it makes my heart sing to see them bonding again so easily after such an awkward start.

When it's time for them to leave, Maya is more than happy to accept their hugs and then I walk them out to the car. Carol takes my arm as I guide her up the incline, which has a few pot holes here and there.

'Thank you, Elana. It wouldn't have been as enjoyable if we'd popped in briefly. It's a lesson learnt and in future we won't leave it so long between visits. Maya is growing so quickly and you are doing an amazing job of raising her.'

'Ah, that means a lot. I'm so glad you stayed for dinner too, it's been fun and Maya needed to spend a little time with you.'

'Well, we've had a lovely evening, my dear. And Luke is a nice man; it's good to know you aren't alone.'

'Oh, but—' Before I can explain the situation, Philip has taken over and is steering Carol into the passenger seat.

As he slams the door shut, she gives me a small wave. Philip turns to face me.

'I think tonight was important for all of us and thank you for making us feel that we're still a part of your life. If ever Maya wants to come and stay for a night, we promise we'd spoil her without reservation.' He smiles broadly and gives me one last hug. I stand, waving them off and trying very hard to stop my bottom lip from trembling as my eyes fill with tears.

Diary Log – day 497. 13 days to Christmas. At last the distance that was opening up between Maya and me, and Niall's parents is beginning to come full circle. Today we made progress and in my heart I never doubted that would happen. I just didn't know how to begin the healing. It's a relief, because we need them to be a part of our lives. I know I have to move on, for Maya's sake, but I was worried it would distance them further from us. Now I don't have any more excuses, do I?

Chapter 28

Luke

Kids Are Harder to Read Than Adults

I had a great evening at Elana's last night, but I didn't get much work done. That was okay, because I could see how nervous she was, but the visit from her in-laws went well. What I didn't mention to Elana was what Maya told me while her mum was outside seeing them to their car.

'Daddy is very happy tonight and he loved my card.'

We continued clearing the plates from the table and I decided it was probably best I didn't overreact to what she'd just said.

'That's nice, Maya. It was a lovely dinner, wasn't it?' It was probably just a kid thing and maybe she was simply saying what she was thinking he might say, but didn't know how to express it.

'He gave me a message for Mummy last night, but I've forgotten it. I was very sleepy.'

I looked down at her face and she smiled up at me without any sign of concern whatsoever.

'We all have dreams and sometimes it's hard to remember what happens. It's nothing to worry about.'

'But this was important. Daddy has never given me a message before and I forgot to ask him to remind me what it was when he came to see Grandma.'

She seemed very cross with herself, as if this wasn't simply her imagination taking over. I was there the whole time and if anything weird had happened, I'm sure someone would have said something.

'It's nice to have memories, isn't it?' I'd told her, not wanting to make her feel awkward. But I also hadn't wanted to encourage her to confuse thoughts and dreams with reality. That can't be healthy, can it? Or do kids' imaginations run riot at that age anyway, and it's inevitable that at times fact and fantasy become mixed up?

'Not when you can't remember and it's important, Luke.' Maya stared at me as if I was missing the point. Was I being reprimanded?

'Of course, sorry. I'm sure you'll remember it. Maybe when you wake up in the morning it will pop into your head. You can tell Mummy, then.'

She had tilted her head to one side, those big blue eyes of hers partly obscured by that mop of curls.

'Did you know that you can't give someone a present when they are in heaven, Luke?'

Elana had walked back through the door at that moment and immediately whisked Maya away to help her get ready for bed. In a way I was rather relieved, because words had completely failed me.

***

After a morning running around to pick up some new skirting board and caulk, I headed back to Bay Tree. Dad didn't need me for anything in particular and I wanted to make up for the time lost last night. Working evenings is fine, but if I can have a whole afternoon outside on the circular saw that should allow me to get most of the remaining boards cut, ready to fit. I'd really like to get the open-plan area totally finished by Thursday lunchtime, then get the base coat on the walls so that Elana can paint on Friday. My weekend is going to be all about Joe.

'I wasn't expecting to see you this early,' Elana looks at me with surprise when she answers the door.

'I'll be working out here most of the time as I have a lot of boards to cut. Will the noise distract you?'

'No, I'll have my iPod going so I won't hear a thing. If you need anything just let me know.'

'Thanks.' I hesitate, wondering if I should talk to her about Maya, then change my mind. It's her working day, too, and I know how annoying it can be if you are trying to do something and keep getting interrupted. It crossed my mind that Maya may have remembered her dream and mentioned it to Elana, anyway. I'm sure she would have known exactly what to say, to put Maya at ease.

My phone buzzes and, yanking it out, I see it's a text, but

the sender is unknown. When I tap on the screen and it opens, it's from Lisa. Damn it, Greg. You should have asked before handing over my number.

Hear you lost my number – shame on you! Looking forward to meeting up.

She finishes with a smiley face.

Life is so easy when you only have yourself to think about. It would be wrong of me to judge her simply because she hasn't yet reached that point in her life. Maybe that's commendable and it demonstrates that she's the type of person who knows what she wants.

Have I been reckless with my life so far? As I work away, tuning out from the task in hand, a whole range of thoughts flash through my head. Was there a point with Anita when I should have realised what was going to happen? I think back to the person she was when we first met – bubbly, happy and fun to be with. Now she's often moody and resentful; not of Joe, exactly, but of me for putting her in this situation. How is any woman ever going to be able to step into the mess that is my life? What I admire most in other people is that ability to learn, change and grow. I'm not sure it's something I'm capable of doing.

As I stop to type a quick response, Elana appears with a mug of tea. I press send.

'Sorry, meant to bring this out a while ago, but I was tied up. This weather is freakily mild, guess the warnings about snow on the way is a bit embarrassing for some forecaster wondering what's going on. It's hard to believe it's only twelve days to Christmas.'

'Mild is good, as long as the rain keeps off. There's a lot to be done still. It's sleepover weekend.'

I didn't think it was at all cold today, but Elana pulls the sleeves of her jumper down over her hands, hugging her arms close to her body. I forget that I'm used to working outside, so the temperature rarely bothers me.

'Kids have good imaginations, don't they?' As I speak Elana looks at me, our eyes lock for a few seconds and I watch as a little smile creeps over her face.

'Tell me about it! I can't keep up with Maya sometimes.'

'Did you ever read those letters Maya wrote to Santa?'

Elana shakes her head. 'It didn't feel like it was the right thing to do. I just put them back. The first time we light the fire they will go up in smoke, as she intended. There's still plenty of wintry nights ahead to have a few cosy times toasting our toes and reading. I've missed having that, too.'

The phone in my pocket pings and I ignore it. Then it pings again. And seconds later, once more. Elana raises her eyebrows.

'You're popular today.'

'My blind date. Well, that's not quite true as I shared a taxi with her a while ago.'

'Oh, I'll leave you to it, then.' Her smile is genuine as she turns to go back inside. I guess she thinks I took her advice seriously, and I suppose letting Greg talk me into this means I am making some sort of effort. However, I'm not the sort of man who spends his day texting back and forth for the fun of it, so I ignore the texts and get back to work. I don't want to give Lisa the wrong impression about me and there's no point in pretending I'm something I'm not. Or that I'm in the market for a meaningful relationship. A drink and a friendly chat I can do, but any more than that and I'm out the door.

Chapter 29

Luke

Feeling in the Way

When Eve drops Maya back after the school run, she rushes into the cottage in an excited mood.

'Hi Luke. Mum, can Amelie come in to play? Please. Please.'

Elana encourages Maya out of the kitchen, as I move the table back up into the dining room, which is now finished. After a bit of back-and-forth conversation, they disappear and when they return both Eve and Amelie are with them.

'I'll re-assemble your desk and get it in situ, if you like, Elana. Is everything in the utility room?'

'Yes, and thanks, Luke. The screws are on the windowsill. The PC is in the sitting room and it's safe to turn it off. I didn't leave anything open.'

Eve says 'hi' as we pass and by the time I begin carrying the parts through, the girls are upstairs and Elana and Eve are alone in the sitting room. The door is open and it's not so much that I'm listening, but their voices carry out into the dining room.

'Are things any better?' Elana's voice reflects concern.

'Not really. When Rick's away we talk several times a day on the phone, but it's not the same. We put the trimmings up last night and it was just the two of us. He doesn't seem to be interested in being a part of family life any more. And all he talks about is work, or moving house, and I'm beginning to wonder if we have any emotional connection left between us.'

I usually try to keep the noise down. This is one occasion when I'm trying my best to generate something, anything, so that I can't hear what is, quite clearly, a private conversation. However, once the desk is in place I have to knock on the door and disturb them anyway, to disconnect the PC.

'Sorry to interrupt. The desk is done and I'll have this up and running shortly.' I begin pulling out the leads and gathering up the pieces of kit.

Elana and Eve sit in silence and I try to work as quickly as I can.

'There, I'll leave you in peace now.'

Elana smiles appreciatively, but Eve sits there looking down at her lap, miserably, as I make my exit. I guess we all have our own set of problems. It's pretty depressing, though, to think that even a couple like Eve and Rick, who seem to have pretty much everything they need, have ended up being unhappy. How can things go so badly wrong? No one sets out to cause problems for themselves, even if they end up causing other people problems because of their idiocy.

Rick's a solid guy; he works hard and is ambitious. But I hardly know them and even I could see that Eve wasn't happy when I was working in Hillside View, so surely it's in his interests to fix that before it's too late?

Guess when you're in the middle of it, it's hard to stand back and see what's going on. I shake my head, as I start sorting out the leads to get the PC up and running again. It occurs to me that life is a form of agony, interspersed with what can often feel like only a handful of happy moments. It isn't about money, having things, or success – it's about taking pleasure from the small things in life. The big things will happen, anyway, to a greater or lesser degree, and all you can do is work hard and keep pushing forward. But moments like taking time to be a family and enjoying the simple pleasures like trimming a tree, for instance, are important. Rick's one lucky guy, but it looks as if he might be about to blow it if he isn't careful.

Maya appears and runs through to the kitchen to fill up two bright-pink plastic drinking beakers sprouting glittery straws. As I fold the dust sheet, a sprinkling of sawdust I didn't realise was there shoots up into the air and settles on the dining table. She smiles.

'Uh oh, you'll be in trouble.'

I stoop under the sink unit to get out the dustpan and brush, but when I turn I see Maya writing in the dust.

'*I'm sorry*? What's that about?' What a strange thing for Maya to write.

'I remembered the message from Daddy. He said he was sorry.' Maya picks the beakers back up and hurries away, leaving me puzzled as I quickly sweep away the evidence of my carelessness. That little girl certainly has one huge imagination and I'm surprised she even remembers sharing her dream with me.

Chapter 30

Luke

Making an Effort

Hey, Lisa, I was working and couldn't get back to you.
Busy day. How was yours?

I press send and leave my phone on the worktop as I push a
load of washing into the machine. I'm trying to get everything
sorted ready to pack a small bag to take to Mum's for the
weekend. I left Elana's early, passing on dinner as there are
chores I need to do here and I made good progress today at
Bay Tree. Ping.

Hey, Luke. Assumed that was the case. Okay day for me.
Didn't mean to pull you away, but wanted to make contact
just to check out that you're happy to meet up.

Fair enough, I'd probably be thinking the same thing if I'd
given her my number and never received a call. I begin typing

and then think, what the heck, texting is too restricted. As I press the call button my throat goes dry and I swallow hard as she picks up.

'Luke?'

'Yep. Thought it was easier to chat than type.'

'Lovely! It's nice to speak to you. I was a bit worried Cheryl might have made Greg talk you into this. They certainly seem to be getting on very well.' She sounds genuinely pleased that I called. I thought it was easier to get the tricky stuff said and see how she takes it.

'So it seems. I'm a bit rusty when it comes to the dating thing, to be honest. It's been a while.'

'Same here. Awful, isn't it? I've pretty much dated the same guy off and on since school. Then one day he made it clear it wasn't going anywhere. It's just easier to keep doing the same thing, without giving it too much thought, isn't it? So here I am, six months on, and still trying to let go of the past.'

I like the fact that she's prepared to be up front. That's why I made the call.

'Has Greg mentioned my situation?'

'No, he just said you were a great guy,' she laughs.

'That was helpful, then.'

'Well, he was hardly going to admit that he probably had to call in a big favour to please Cheryl, who is determined to get us together.'

Straight to the point, I like that.

'My situation isn't straightforward. I have an eighteen-month-old son and an ex-partner who are still very much a part of my life.'

'Oh, I see. That makes sense now. I was a little hurt when you didn't call me, to be honest. I mean, I'm not that bad and it was only a coffee I was proposing.'

Now it's my turn to laugh. She has a sense of humour.

'I just don't know if I'm good company at the moment. Even a year after the break-up it's tricky still. I have to put them first, of course, but with having to work extra to make the maintenance payments, it doesn't give me much time, or money, for things like socialising. I wanted you to be aware of my situation because I don't think it's fair to try to hide it.'

'I wouldn't have guessed. How old are you?'

'Twenty-four, and Greg told me you're twenty-one. Is that right?'

'Yes.'

'I'm not looking to get into anything long-term, if I'm honest, but I'm up for a drink and a chat.' There's a split-second pause before she replies.

'This is quite a brave step for you, by the sound of it. That means I should be flattered.'

It probably would have been easier if she'd cancelled the date and put the phone down on me. However, I feel a bit mean-spirited. Having knocked her confidence once by 'losing' her number, now it would be a bit awkward to refuse going for a friendly drink.

'Obviously a lady who likes to take risks.'

'Some risks are worthwhile, others – well, you live and learn. Let's wait and see what happens. Nice talking to you, Luke.'

***

It's a very disturbed night and I find myself constantly drifting in and out of sleep. My pillow feels like lead beneath my head and I keep turning it over, pummelling it with my fists. Then I realise that all I'm doing is winding myself up and the way to relax is to get up and do something.

It feels like weeks since I sat down at the computer. One glance at my inbox confirms it's full of the same old junk mail, so I haven't missed anything much. There's only one email that's of any interest and it's from Paul, a programmer I met online, and we bounce problems off each other. He's been checking a little software program I wrote and he thinks he's found the bug.

As I trawl down the other emails, highlighting them, ready to press delete, there are a few Facebook notifications. Most of them aren't of interest, but one informs me that Anita Price has changed her status. I hesitate for a second, then click through and her page opens up on the screen in front of me. The header is a photo of Anita with Joe in her arms, and it's an old one. But on the top left-hand side, under her personal information, there's a one-line entry that says she's 'In a relationship' with someone named Chris Johnson.

I can feel the colour draining from my face. I sit staring at the screen. This is the last thing I expected to happen and clearly I must be naive to think she wasn't going to find someone else. Heck, I'm meeting up with Lisa for a date, so why am I so shocked? But this is a real statement for the world to see; it isn't just a date, but something that has probably been going on for a while. There's no hint of jealousy in my mind, just anger that another guy is in her life and around my son, and yet she didn't have the decency to tell me. Suddenly what I thought was that a bad enough night has turned into a nightmare. How am I supposed to handle this? Is this guy seeing more of my son than I am? Then realisation dawns. Anita is handing over Joe to me this weekend so they can go away together. This could actually work in my favour and that's something I didn't see coming.

***

'Dad, if you don't need me again today I thought I'd head over to Bay Tree. I want to finish laying the flooring and start putting the skirting boards back on. If I can get there for a few hours tomorrow, then I'll offer to help out with the painting. Elana said she'd handle that herself, but it's going to be a lot for her to do on her own.'

'I won't need you until Monday. I have a three-day job for you next week, pairing up with Greg. Replacement ceiling and some plastering after a massive water leak. It's an insurance job. You sound tired, my son. Is everything okay?'

"Fine. Just had one of those nights, you know – mind wouldn't shut off and I couldn't sleep. Guess it's the excitement about having Joe this weekend.'

I feel guilty not being straight with him, but he wouldn't know how to handle it, or what to say. I don't want to upset Mum or tarnish the thought of the weekend, so the less said the better.

'Well, try to finish up early today. I'm sure Mrs James will understand.'

'Will do. Give Ma my love.'

Chapter 31

Elana

Peeling Back the Layers

Diary Log – day 499. 11 days to Christmas. It's hard being a single parent. Heck, it's hard being on your own. I'm scared of facing the future without someone by my side – is it selfish of me to admit that? At the moment work is keeping me sane and focused, how sad is that? Maya is growing up fast and I have to set a good example. Change needs to be embraced, and actions speak louder than words.

When I arrive back from the school run Luke is sitting in the van on the drive. He jumps out, grabbing an armful of tools from the back.

'Hello, I didn't think you were going to be here again during the day. I feel bad now, because I stopped off to do some shopping on the way home.'

'Change of plan. I'll finish off today and if you want some

help tomorrow with the painting, then I'm available. Think about it and let me know.'

He doesn't sound his usual self and his face looks a little drawn. When we get inside he starts work immediately and it's obvious he doesn't want to talk. I pack away the shopping, leave a mug of coffee on the side for him and make myself scarce.

I don't know where to start today. I know I said I'd paint through tomorrow, but I have a few urgent things still to sort, including an awkward phone call I don't really want to make. I have presents to wrap, as it's only a matter of time before Maya stumbles across one of my hiding places. It feels like every cupboard has something hidden inside it. Then I have to buy the tree ready for Saturday. It's no use panicking and if Luke is good enough to offer his time tomorrow, then that's not an offer I'm going to refuse.

But first things first. I need to do some digging to find out more about Seth Greenberg and the influence he seems to have over Aiden.

I re-read the interviews I did with each of the other band members, refreshing my memory and trying to assess who seemed closest to Aiden. I need to talk to the person who would be most likely to understand why Seth succeeded where his predecessors failed. I decide that Stevie Harrison is probably the most likely candidate. I was rather surprised to have discovered an underlying sense of mistrust between some of the group members when I talked to them individually. I suppose it's probably understandable, given the circumstances. Aiden grabs the limelight all the time and over the years the other members have become the group behind the star. When the band was originally formed there was, I'm sure, equal status. Certainly each of them is undoubtedly an icon, recognised by their peers as being among the best in their field. But Aiden stands out and while Firehead is news, Aiden is always bigger news.

'Stevie, it's Elana James. I wonder if I could ask you a couple of quick questions?'

'Hey, Elana. No problem. Something you forgot?'

He was one of the easier ones to interview, although there were times when I knew there was a lot more he could have shared. There were incidents that two of the other band members were more than happy to shed light on, feeling no need whatsoever to cover Aiden's back. But as this is a safer topic, I figure I might get the answers I need.

'Not really. I've come to appreciate that Seth has been an enormous influence on Aiden. The two seemed to hit if off from the beginning, am I right?'

'Yeah. Seth doesn't try to lay down the law; he realised that confrontation doesn't work with Aiden.'

'Did Aiden know Seth before he took up his appointment?'

Stevie takes a second before responding.

'I'm not sure where you are heading with this, but as far as I know they didn't have history, if that's what you mean.'

'I'm just trying to understand why they work so well together, when Aiden himself admits he rarely listened to the advice his previous managers gave. What made him trust Seth?'

'Don't know the answer to that one. Maybe Aiden was tired

of fighting at that point. Seth arrived at a time when Aiden was at his lowest and even his mum had given up trying to make him see sense.'

I scribble that down. 'She wasn't speaking to him at that time?'

'Look, I think you have to ask Aiden about this. I wasn't exactly in a good place myself at the time and maybe I'm not remembering it right. Have you interviewed his mum?'

He's clearly not happy to go any further, but there's something he's not telling me.

'Briefly, but Seth sat in on the interview as she wasn't prepared to see me on her own.'

'Well, maybe I don't remember it right. Like I said, you know the amount of drugs we were doing at that time and we were touring virtually non-stop. Life was a bit hazy and it's a wonder nothing really bad happened. Look, I have to go.'

He's being honest, but for some reason I've made him uncomfortable by asking a simple enough question. What does he know that he won't tell?

'Well, thanks for your time.'

'Aiden said you're coming to the New Year's Eve party? So you get to meet the guy face to face at last.'

That's strange. Why would Stevie know that? He wouldn't be aware that every time I was supposed to meet up with Aiden, he'd had to cancel the appointment. So Aiden must have actually told him that. Was I right all along and Aiden has been deliberately avoiding me?

'Yes. Seth suggested it.'

This time the pause is long enough for me to wonder if we've been cut off.

'He can run, but he can't hide.' He laughs and I'm left wondering what exactly that means.

Chapter 32

Elana

Why Do I Feel So Old?

Luke was quiet all day yesterday and left early, saying he had a headache. That didn't stop him working non-stop, though, and when he left the skirting boards were on and undercoated, and he'd applied the base coat to the newly plastered walls. When I said perhaps he shouldn't come back today after all and tried to reassure him I could cope, he wouldn't listen. I hate to admit it, but it's great having him around and I will be sorry to see him go. I know he'll be here off and on through until mid-January, but at some point the money will run out. It's just nice having a man around and, as Eve so kindly pointed out, he's easy on the eyes. Too easy. And smart. And kind-hearted. And about ten years too young.

Ding-dong.

And here he is; I wonder if he'll want to talk about whatever was bothering him yesterday? I can't ask, of course, but there isn't much we haven't talked about. So something really unexpected must have happened.

'Morning. The kettle is on.' As usual, he bends to undo his boot laces and when he stands back up his trademark smile stares back at me. He takes in my old t-shirt and paint-splattered jeans, without comment.

We both peer down at his feet and it's holey-sock day.

'Behind on the washing again,' he smirks.

'Why don't you just throw it away?'

He looks at me as if I've said something really dumb.

'And risk having a day when I can only find one sock to wear?' We both start laughing.

'There are other options,' I reply, but he shakes his head.

'I need a woman to organise me,' he admits.

'I don't buy that. Are you telling me men can't do it for themselves?'

He gives a throaty chuckle.

'This man needs a little help and I'm not ashamed to admit that. But I am good at painting walls.'

'Touché! I'm good at organising, so maybe we should do a deal.' Now I'm really laughing and it's a bit of a relief to hear he's more like his usual self.

'If you sorted through my wardrobe you'd probably throw most of it out. I have a problem letting anything go. If it's old, it's going to be comfortable ... and well-loved.' He throws me a wink.

'Did you just wink at me?'

He pretends to take offence. 'Don't tell me men don't wink at you all the time, because I won't believe it.'

'Well, maybe occasionally, but they're usually much older.'

He groans, then, much to my amazement, walks over to put on the kettle.

'See,' he throws over his shoulder, 'men can do it for themselves. Tea, or coffee?'

***

I have no idea why we are both so relaxed today. Maybe it's because this is a landmark day. Working side by side I realise that there is no way I could have done this all by myself. You can't paint one wall, the whole room has to be done. Luke says we need to give the newly re-plastered wall two good coats and then one coat on the rest so that there is no colour variation.

By lunchtime my arms are aching so much I feel like a wimp. Luke is not only faster than me, but he's fussy and he keeps pointing out that I'm not applying the paint evenly enough.

'Maya is going to be so surprised when Eve drops her back from school. It will add to the excitement of the tree-decorating tomorrow. Your hard work is finally making this feel like a home rather than a building site. I can't express how appreciative we are because this was already going to be a tough Christmas, harder in some ways than last year. Things have moved on and Maya is another year older, so this is exactly what we both needed to make this festive season special. When we look back it won't simply be the second Christmas without Niall, it will be the Christmas we began to feel at home.'

He stops mid-brushstroke, his expression giving little away. Then he clears his throat and it's obvious that my words mean something to him.

'Some jobs are just a little more special than others. You've made me very welcome, been very accommodating and you never moan about anything, Elana. Maya is the same. You have no idea how refreshing that is, believe me.'

He hangs his head, it's obvious there's been a development and whatever has happened is dragging up some old memories. We work in silence for a while, as the hands of the clock slowly tick by and the day begins to run away from us.

After a couple of hours I stop because, once more, my arms are aching but I'm also curious to see if a chat over coffee will encourage Luke to open up.

'You're flagging,' he grins at me across the table.

'I know. My arm muscles are screaming at me with every lift of the roller. I envy your strength and stamina. Next time around I'm coming back as a man.'

'I don't think that would suit you. You're a nurturer and that's a part of who you are. I'm not sure swapping that for physical strength would be fulfilling.'

It was a joke, but he missed the point and I feel badly that he's feeling so sombre.

'However,' he continues, much to my surprise, 'not all women are made the same way. I found out that Anita is letting me have Joe this weekend because she's in a relationship.'

I hesitate for a moment. They've lived apart for a whole year, so surely this can't have come as a total shock.

'And you're upset to think you're losing her to someone else?'

He shakes his head, moulding his hands around his coffee cup and leaning forward to peer inside. He's avoiding eye contact.

'Yes. No. Yes and no. It rams home the stark reality that we'll never be the family unit Joe deserves. But really this is about the fact that she didn't tell me. Is this guy I know absolutely nothing about spending time with my son? I mean, in theory he could be virtually living there, having the quality time that I'm not allowed to have. She announced it on Facebook, of all places. Everyone seems to have known about this before I did and that makes me feel not just like a fool, but like a bad dad. But none of that matters, compared to the fact that Joe is my son and I have to fight for a few measly hours with him each week.'

'Oh, Luke. That's wrong, of course it is, but if she's a good mum then perhaps Joe needs her more than he needs you at this very young stage in his life. If you all lived together you'd still be working every day and only seeing him briefly before bed and at weekends. The time you have with Joe on Saturdays is one hundred per cent quality and bonding time. No one will ever replace you as his dad, believe me, because you love him more than anything in the world. You are prepared to make sacrifices for your son and that is the sign of a real dad.'

He places his mug back on the table and looks up at me.

'It's nice to hear someone say that, Elana. But I hate the fact that I feel jealous of another man coming into my son's life.'

Instinctively I reach out my hand across the table, and suddenly, Luke's hand is there, too.

'Maya and I owe you so much. I know you have the sleepover at your parents' house, but why don't you come and spend the afternoon with us? We have our little tradition of decorating the tree, when I pretend not to notice Maya eating as many chocolate treats as she's actually hanging from the branches. We play silly Christmas songs and games, and make gingerbread men. Maya would love some company, we both would.'

Elana, what are you doing?

'I think Joe would love that. If you're sure, that is.'

'You'd be doing us a favour. I don't want to let go of old traditions, but somehow we have to embrace the fact that it will inevitably be different. Joe is at an age where everything is exciting and they take things in their stride. It might be good for you to see that in action and Maya will be delighted. It's at times like this I really wish she had a sibling.'

'Okay, but we won't come empty-handed, I'll bring a little party food. And Santa Racers.'

Did he just say Santa Racers?

'All will be revealed,' he adds, with a level of mock-seriousness.

'I can't wait!'

Diary Log – day 500. 10 days to Christmas. The numbers stare back at me coldly. There's a stirring in my heart and yet I've never felt more alone. I feel jaded and emotionally tired, which doesn't exactly make me a hot dating prospect. Too much baggage, perhaps. Life, eh?

Chapter 33

Elana

Fun and Games

The trip out to collect the tree is the first item on our list today. Maya can't sit still in her seat and I have to keep asking her not to bob around as she's obscuring the wing mirror.

'Can we have a blue spruce, please Mum?'

'Of course. It's ready and waiting for us.'

'How big is it?'

'Well, I asked for one that would fit in the boot, but I have a stretchy lead to tie the boot shut because I suspect it will overhang a little.'

When we arrive at the garden centre the tree they have set aside is in a net but it's clearly going to be much too long to fit into the car, even with the stretchy lead.

'What are we going to do, Mum?'

The young man who has been trying to fit it in for the last five minutes eventually accepts defeat.

'Can you deliver?'

He shakes his head. 'Not until Monday at the earliest as today and tomorrow are fully booked.'

'Is there anything smaller?'

'Not if you want a blue spruce. They're quite wide trees so they have to be a certain height before they're cut or you would only have one or two layers of branches.'

Maya's bottom lip quivers.

'Let me make a call.' I walk away and dial Luke.

'Luke, we have an emergency. The tree won't fit in the car and they can't deliver until Monday. Do you have the van today, or your own vehicle?'

'The pick-up, but I'm sure it will accommodate up to a six-foot-long tree. I'll swing by on our way over. I'm just about to pick up Joe.'

'Oh, thank you! It's Arcade Nurseries and it will be netted and waiting. See you later.'

I turn back to the guy.

'A friend will come and collect it in an hour or two. Maya, do you think we should go for something a bit bigger? Luke says he can fit in up to a six-foot tree.'

Maya's eyes widen and the guy immediately goes off in search of something to show us. Just the difference of another foot turns what was a dumpy-looking tree into something much more majestic.

'Mum, it's perfect!!' Maya hops from one foot to another, her face a picture.

'Sold! We'd better pick up a few more decorations on our way home to make sure we have enough.' Maya claps her hands, happiness oozing out of her.

'Candy canes, Mum! Dad always loved those and we didn't have them last year.'

She's right, we didn't because we had a smaller tree. It's the little, seemingly unnoticed, things that children hang on to and yet it's so easy to forget that they see the world from a different perspective.

'Candy canes it is, then – and lots of them!'

***

By the time Luke, an excited Joe, and the tree arrive we have a batch of gingerbread men and ladies cooling, ready to be iced. Maya and Amelie had already made a lot of beaded strings and with the chocolate snowmen and candy canes, plus our original box of decorations. It's quite a pile.

'Maya, go and fetch one of your little aprons for Joe. We can roll up his sleeves and hopefully that should be enough protection. Do you like gingerbread, Joe?'

Joe nods, suddenly going into shy mode and clinging on to Luke's leg. However, when Maya returns with an apron with a duck on it, he's more than happy for her to manoeuvre it over his head. Luke stoops to pull up Joe's sleeves and he toddles out to the kitchen, holding tightly onto Maya's hand.

'This is really very good of you, Elana. I was going to take him to soft play, but we do that all the time. Good choice in trees, by the way. If you need me in the kitchen, shout, but I'll just take the netting off and assemble that tree holder. Where do you want it to stand?'

'Thanks, Luke. In the corner of the sitting room, I think – opposite the TV. Maya, you can kneel on the chair and Joe can stand on the one next to it in front of the worktop. I'm coming now and I'll hold him so he doesn't fall.'

Luke gives me a grateful smile and we head off in different directions.

'Shall we let Joe pick a colour first?' I ask Maya, as she spreads the tubes of icing sugar out on the counter top.

'Hey, Joe. Do you like red, or green, or white?'

As I busy myself wiping his hands and pulling out wipes for Maya, Joe takes the green tube from Maya.

'Eetie.'

Maya calls out to Luke. 'What does eetie mean, Luke?'

'Ah, he thinks it's a sweet.' Luke calls out.

'Yes, sweetie, Joe, but we aren't going to eat it just yet,' Maya explains, with all the seriousness a six-year-old can muster.

I can't help but smile. It would be so lovely for Maya to have a sibling, but that's something totally unimaginable. It's funny, though, how looking after someone else, no matter what age you are, is good for the soul.

I literally stand there only to make sure Joe doesn't wobble sideways, while together they pipe icing and stick on chocolate buttons. A few get eaten and the odd finger covered in icing is licked, but the end result is some beautifully decorated gingerbread folk. Luke walks into the kitchen to check out our progress.

'Wow, those are some happy-looking gingerbread cookies. Great job, Maya and Joe.'

'Eetie,' Joe says, nodding his head.

Maya passes him a chocolate button. 'We can eat them after lunch, Joe. Which one would you like?'

After much deliberation they each pick their favourite and we put them to one side for later.

'The tree is all ready,' Luke confirms

'Time to decorate the tree!!' Maya squeals.

As I busy myself carrying the boxes into the sitting room, I leave Luke wiping hands to remove the last vestiges of sticky, sugary goo. First things first, and that's to put on one of Maya's Christmas CDs. The first track is 'Walking in the Air' by Aled Jones. She comes running in, Joe following closely behind her and Luke bringing up the rear.

'We have a tree, we have a tree!' As Maya begins bouncing around, Joe decides he's going to copy her. However, he's a little young to know how to skip, so he does a sort of bunny hop that's very funny to watch. Luke stands back watching him with that proud-dad look on his face. Maya claps her hands and Joe follows suit, clearly delighted that he's able to emulate her.

Luke places the star at the very top of the tree and as we hand him the bead chains and the tinsel garlands he begins working down from the top. I snake the lights through from the bottom and despite a few scratches from the needles, they are soon threaded up through the tree. Once that's done the kids hang the glitter balls, stars, candy canes and chocolate decorations. One or two get eaten, but that's part of the fun and I even catch Luke sharing one with Maya.

'It's a reward, Mum. Luke did the hard part at the top,' she explains.

When we stand back and the lights are finally switched on, it's a delight. Maya and Joe stand side by side, staring at the tree.

'Tree.' Joe says the word so clearly, his voice full of awe.

'Team-working at its best,' Luke adds.

'Is this the best tree we've ever had? I think it might be, Mum.'

I nod, thinking the same, but my heart is torn as I don't want to compare and bring back memories that will suck all the joy out of today.

'I think you're right, the best.' Actually, that's true, but I refuse to let tears come and I swallow hard, maintaining an encouraging smile.

Luke must sense my turmoil, because he places his hand on my arm, giving it a little squeeze. As our eyes meet I know he understands my dilemma.

***

We laugh, we play and we eat. Luke brought a carrier bag full of party nibbles to add to the sandwiches Maya and I had made. With the gingerbread probably taking the sugar intake for the day a little over the top, we add to that with a fresh-fruit platter, but at least it's something a little healthier.

Joe was able to join in with all of the games and loved Twister, although he couldn't reach all the spots. It's a game I found years ago in a charity shop and it's really silly, but you end up laughing a lot as you have to put your hand on one colour spot and your foot on another. Then Luke revealed

Santa Racers. Everyone has a Santa in a different-coloured sleigh with wheels underneath. You roll it backwards first and when you let go it races off and the one that goes the furthest is the winner. The new flooring was the perfect surface and the sleighs headed off at quite a speed. We had such fun and it's such a simple game that after a while we left Maya and Joe to play it on their own, while we grabbed a quiet coffee.

'I can't believe how much Joe has been able to join in. I was nervous about having him for the best part of two whole days, but it's easier to keep him occupied than I thought. I mean, I'm used to six hours, but by the time we visit his grandparents, go swimming, or head off to the soft play centre for lunch, the time flies.'

'Well, judging by how successful the Santa sleighs are you should buy him a set of Hot Wheels. Hours of fun guaranteed.'

'I think you're right. I assumed he was a bit young for it, but he seems to have the knack, doesn't he?'

'Well, he's a bright little thing and when he's pre-school age he's going to love being with a mixed-aged range, by the looks of it. Maya adores him!'

'Anita takes him to a toddlers' group but maybe I could look at doing something like that on Saturdays.'

'Libraries often run little story-time and activity sessions. It might be worth seeing whether there's anything going on locally. Just Google kid's activities and a postcode, you'll be surprised what comes up. If you ever want to bring him over here for a couple of hours, just phone to check we're here first. Maya would be more than happy to play with him. Even after the work is finished, that's a standing offer.'

Luke seems a little taken aback.

'Really?'

'We like having you here, Luke. Both of you.'

Eeek! What am I doing? Am I flirting with him? Of course not. We exchange awkward glances and then I burst out laughing.

'You know what I mean,' I add, just to make myself clear. He gives me a wink and I find myself chuckling. It's lovely to see him so relaxed and happy, especially after how unsettled he's been. Guess this December is a turning point for us both as we move forward on our separate paths.

'See you Monday morning. I'll pop in with the door strips and it will only take half an hour to get them in situ.'

'Have a lovely time with Joe.' I close the door after waving them off. Suddenly the cottage feels strangely quiet, despite the strains of 'I'm Dreaming of a White Christmas,' playing hauntingly in the background.

Diary Log – day 501. 9 days to Christmas. Since we hit 500 the number looks so big. Maybe I should stop counting the days as it's pretty depressing. In fact, I think I'm going to stop the log on Christmas Day. When I had the final session with my therapist, Catherine, she said I would know when the time was right. We had the best day I can remember for a long time, today, Niall. So good, that now I'm feeling guilty. I'd forgotten what it was like to have a day with so few negative thoughts. Then it hit me. This is what moving on is going to feel like and I can't resent that because I know you want us to grab whatever happiness we can. If I had been the one leaving you and Maya alone, I would have wanted you to reclaim a normal life. Not just for her sake, but also for yours. I now understand that you would want the same for me. It feels like goodbye, only it isn't because you will always be in our hearts, no matter what happens. But there's someone who has reminded me what it feels like to be alive again and it's like a breath of fresh air. He's too young for me, of course. He deserves to have someone by his side who can breeze through life, seeing nothing but the joy in it. With age comes wisdom and that isn't always a good thing. Probably what I need is a calming influence, someone with enough life experience to challenge me when I'm in my negative mode.

Chapter 34

Luke

Mixed Signals

Was Elana flirting with me, or is that merely wishful thinking? I look in the rear-view mirror and ask Joe the question. He looks up from his car seat, his index finger in his mouth covered in dribble.

'San-ta.' He states.

'Yes, she could be Mrs Santa, Joe. Pretty perfect, really.' I'm talking to myself, of course, as Joe stabs his finger at the window, leaving little snail trails of dribble.

And then there's Lisa. When I received her text last night I didn't know what to do. She's suggested we meet up before the dreaded foursome and that we don't tell Greg, or Cheryl. I tend to agree that it seemed like a sensible suggestion as the pressure is beginning to mount. Who wants to feel under scrutiny as you answer those inevitable introductory questions. But she's suggesting tomorrow night and I can't think of a reason why not, but I'm hesitating over committing. If I leave it much longer to reply then it will make it awkward. She knows I don't tend to text when I'm working, so I hope she'll just assume I'll get back to her later today.

'Mumma,' Joe says and my head jerks up. We're driving past a woman who looks nothing like Anita, except for her hair colouring.

'We'll see Mumma later, Joe.' The last thing I want is for Joe to become upset because he's missing his mum. 'We're going to Grandma's house next.'

'Gan-ma. Gan-ma.' He chatters away in his own little language, but the first two words are very clear. 'Dada.'

'Yes, Joe. I'm Dada.' And no one else is going to take on the role of a second dad. You might have another male influence in your life, but you can only ever have one real dad. It makes me think about kids whose dads walk away early on in their lives. Why would a man do that to their child? I'm beginning to learn how painful a split family life can be, but I'd never walk away. The thought of some guy taking my place if he moves in with Anita and Joe hurts like hell. It's going to be hard to swallow a sense of bitterness. But that won't help Joe, and every Saturday I'll be there to make sure he never forgets that I love him and he's my boy.

'We're here, Joe. Time for lots of cuddles with Grandma and Granddad.'

After several hours of playing on the floor and watching a nursery rhyme DVD, Joe ends up falling asleep next to me on the bed. We decide not to move him into the junior cot just yet. I'm happy enough to spend the evening next to him doing a little work on the iPad. I respond to Lisa and agree to meet her in a pizza place in town about an hour after I drop Joe off. I'll pop home and change, but I won't be dressing up. Just casual, but with a little more attention to detail, I suppose. It's holey-sock day yet again, by the feel of it, and I wiggle my toes to confirm. I'm unlikely to be bringing her back here, so I think I'm safe. I really must go shopping one of these days because Elana is right, it's just that I don't feel comfortable buying stuff like that, or clothes in general. Too much choice and it's ages since I bought anything new. Anita used to buy all my clothes as she was fussy about appearance. Hers and mine. Me, I guess I'm a bit of a slob by nature. I like stuff to be clean, but comfort comes first. But, most of all, what I need now in my life is a good woman and that's not something I dreamt I'd be thinking about for a long time to come. I guess Anita moving on is doing me a favour; it's certainly been a wake-up call.

***

Anita isn't in the mood to talk and clearly she's alone in the house. Handing Joe back is harder than I thought. Much harder than after our usual Saturday visit. Just being able to be with him at bedtime and when he woke up this morning reminded me of what I'm missing out on. I know there is no going back now, but Mum pointed out something yesterday that hadn't occurred to me. If Anita decides to settle down with this new guy in her life, maybe she will be looking to have more one-on-one quality time with him and be prepared to let me have Joe more often. Starting a new relationship with someone else's child as a part of the bargain isn't the easiest of situations. Maybe the thought of Joe being around all the time will be something he has to get used to. Mum said I shouldn't fall into the trap of making assumptions and basically repeated what Elana had said. It was actually a little depressing, as it made me wonder if I brought out Elana's mothering instinct. She's attractive and I'm attracted to her, despite trying my hardest not to be. I'm getting confusing signals as her body language is saying one thing, but I think her head is telling her something else.

I'm fooling myself if I think I have what it takes to attract a woman like Elana. She's used to a man who had his life and career sorted; someone she could look up to. But my feelings aren't just physical and if I don't watch out I'm going to get hurt. Besides, there are widows who never remarry, although she's so young and vibrant that would be such a waste. Not just for her, but also for Maya, as it was obvious that Joe and me being there yesterday really lifted their spirits.

Anyway, as Mum said, I shouldn't make assumptions and that applies to thinking about Elana, also. Would she even look at a builder, someone whose hands are rarely smooth and unblemished; usually sporting traces of paint or filler that can take a while to wear off. No doubt her husband was more intellectual: Mr Nine-to-Five with a big salary. Okay, one day Dad will retire and I'll run the business, but it's never going to make a fortune. Hopefully it will be enough to allow me to afford a mortgage on a decent house and continue to provide for Joe and Anita.

There's no point in dwelling over things I can't have and I'm an idiot to keep dreaming about Elana. I guess life is all about grabbing whatever opportunities come your way and making the most of them. If something doesn't work out then that's life, getting angry or frustrated about it doesn't help anyone. And I'm going to have to empty my head of all this stuff, as when Lisa arrives I need to pay attention. I haven't even given Lisa a real chance and yet, in theory, everything checks out. She's attractive, mature enough to handle Joe being in my life, sensitive and age-wise she's only a couple of years' younger. Elana isn't even an option for me, so why can't I let go of that thought?

I glance over the menu, glad we decided to come here because at least talking over a meal makes it a little less awkward.

'Hope there's something veggie on there.'

I look up to see Lisa staring down at me and she hovers, clearly expecting me to stand to greet her. Should I shake her hand? Before I can consider it, she leans in to give me a hug. I manage to respond in a similar fashion so it appears, I hope, that it was my intention, also.

'Have you been waiting long?'

'Ten minutes. The traffic was lighter than I thought. Maybe everyone is all shopped-out and Sunday evening in front of the TV beckons.'

'Well, lucky us, then. Meeting someone interesting always beats watching a re-run or the latest reality TV show.'

I try not to make a snap judgement. She's probably nervous. I know I am.

'You still haven't told Cheryl we were meeting up? Greg doesn't know yet either'

'I think that's for the best. Actually I prefer speed-dating, if I'm honest. It's a great idea. Anyway, tonight we might decide we really get on and want to go ahead with our double date.'

Speed-dating? Does that mean we fire questions at each other and only get five minutes to make a decision? She's beginning to make me feel very old, or maybe I mean old-fashioned.

'So, what's it like having a son? You must tell me all about him. I still can't believe you're a dad.'

By the end of the evening I realise just how nervous Lisa was at the start, and once she relaxed it wasn't some quick test but a genuine 'tell me more about yourself'. The result was that she didn't make me want to run away screaming, but it was too early to say whether there was a real connection between us. You know what I mean, that little quiver of excitement that keeps on building, if you are lucky. Or it goes away and you realise the spark was just that initial little surge of hope that this person could become someone special.

She was genuinely interested in Joe, very sensitive about avoiding questions regarding Anita, and quite open about her own situation. She left me with a question that I couldn't answer, so I said I'd think about it and let her know.

'Most guys I meet are rather boring, or into football – which I hate, or are looking for a one-night stand. What are your top three turn-offs in a woman?'

At that point I said I needed to give it some thought and for some reason that seemed to impress her. If only I could get Elana out of my head, then maybe I could give Lisa the chance she deserves.

Chapter 35

Luke

What You See is What You Get

After sleeping on it, I think I might have been too hasty jumping to conclusions about Lisa. Although why I have this need to find something wrong with her doesn't even make sense. I mean, on paper she's a good candidate. Well, in the flesh she's great as well, but I'm trying not to do the 'being ruled by your trousers' thing. She's very pretty, petite, with long auburn hair and an athletic build. Something about her implies energy, vibrancy. I decided on my top three turn-offs.

1. *A person who doesn't understand that kids come first – always.*
2. *Being mothered – I have a perfectly capable mother of my own.*
3. *Being pitied. We all have baggage and for those who haven't, well, it's coming.*

The problem is that while Lisa has passed number two with flying colours, it's too early to tell if she really understands the impact of having little Joe in my life. And then there's number three. If I'm honest, she doesn't seem to be the sort who dispenses pity; but then even her break-up doesn't seem to have been much of a test. Is she the sort of person who sits back and lets life happen to her? Is that a good thing, if that's the case?

In the end it comes down to one simple question. Is there any reason why I should cancel this double-date thing? On the drive to Bay Tree Cottage my thoughts keep going around in circles. I find myself comparing Lisa to Elana, which is stupid. For starters, a relationship with Elana isn't even an option and, besides, it's unfair as Lisa doesn't have anywhere near as much life experience. But I feel so much older than Lisa, as if I have to make allowances for her lack of years. So the fault lies with me – I've turned into this boring guy who is so scared of making another mistake, I'd rather stop living my life. Why would Lisa even be interested in me? Unless she's doing this for Cheryl's sake, the same as I'm doing this because Greg's on my case. I'm a fool. Lisa is just waiting for a reason to get out of it and last night she was offering me the chance to back out. Doh! What an idiot I am! It feels like a pressure has suddenly been taken away. I take a deep breath and relax a little, pushing my shoulders back to release the tension building in my neck. All I have to do is text her and let her down easy.

The front door of Bay Tree Cottage opens to reveal a smiling Elana gesturing me inside.

'Morning. You look serious today. Was everything okay when you dropped Joe back?'

'He was fine, a bit clingy, but Anita handled it well. I didn't ask any questions about her weekend and she wasn't in a talkative mood. She was on her own, though.'

'Ah, I did wonder—'

Elana's face is empathetic and I know she feels for what I'm going through. Her eyes don't move from my face.

'What?'

'I just thought there was something else. You look troubled. Coffee?' She calls over her shoulder as she walks off into the kitchen area.

'Hi, Luke. Are you staying?' Maya appears wearing a onesie, with a pen and notebook in her hands. She looks up at me with a big smile on her face.

'No, just a quick visit to lay these,' I manoeuvre the thin strips around the dining table and lay them flat on the floor.

'Mum, can I have a gingerbread man for breakfast?'

'No, darling. Cereal or toast, but you can have gingerbread for your morning snack.'

'Aww, Mum. Can I have toast and juice in bed, then?' Maya can tell from Elana's face there's no point in arguing and comes back with a counter-offer. Elana nods and Maya disappears back upstairs.

'She was very upset last night,' Elana whispers. I walk closer, leaning back against the worktop counter next to her.

'When you and Joe left it was a little flat, if I'm honest.

We sat down for a few hours to read together, which was nice, but it reminded us both of last year. It was too soon then for either of us to be more than numb, but this year it's all different. It hadn't occurred to me that it was going to get worse before it could get any better.' She lets out a huge sigh and as our eyes meet. For the first time ever she looks defeated.

'Hey,' I step forward and, before I know it, she's in my arms. We both seem frozen, unable to pull away and the seconds pass. The warmth of her body against mine is like an electric shock. It's been a while since I've held a woman this close, but this isn't any woman, it's Elana. She reluctantly pulls back and I release her, but everything is in slow motion. I don't want to let her go and she doesn't really want to draw away.

'Sorry, but I needed that. Thanks. You're a good friend, Luke.'

Her words remind me not to read anything into this; she's just hitting one of those lows. It comes out of nowhere; in my case it's usually in the early hours of the morning.

'Glad I could be of service.' I give her one of my trademark grins, just to reassure her that I haven't misread the signals. 'Maybe you two need a break. Disney has a new film out and it's on at the local cinema.'

She pushes back those wayward blonde curls with the back of her right hand as she pours boiling water into the coffee mugs.

'Great idea! To be honest, we have nothing much planned this week and Christmas still seems a long way away.'

'Well, cinema today, then bowling tomorrow. Hey, how about the Christmas market? If you pop into the mall I think there's a children's cookie-decorating competition on, as well. You don't have to work, do you?'

'A little, but it's mostly Maya quality time. Once you've laid the strips, I suppose I won't see you again until you're back in January for Eve's conservatory?'

My throat constricts and then I realise Elana's just trying to plan her week and checking I won't need to call back in again.

'Well, the next three days I'm working with Greg on an insurance job. After that, yep, I'll be back this side of the valley in January.'

'Well, if you find you have time on your hands and you're passing by, just pop in for a coffee. You know we'd love to see Joe, too.'

There's genuine warmth in her voice and it occurs to me that she understands that I, too, am alone. Yes, I need the money, but Anita hasn't offered to let me have Joe over Christmas, so we'll be opening presents when I have him on Saturday. Then, I'll be at my parents' house for a few days, pretending to be celebrating the festive season.

'Thanks, I might take you up on that.'

'Seriously, any time. We'll be at my parents' house for two days, but aside from that we're here. We'd enjoy the company, so even if you're just at a loose end and feel up to a game of Monopoly, or something, feel free to join us.'

It would be so easy for me to take this the wrong way. She's mothering me, and while it's one of my top three turn-offs, I can't take offence. The fact that Elana is taking time out from her own troubles to think of my situation makes me feel special. Now I'm being really stupid, but the truth is I love being here. It's a place where there's lots of sadness, but there's also a lot of love – more than enough to go around and encompass anyone in need. Well, I'm certainly needy.

Chapter 36

Luke

It's Never Going to be Simple Ever Again, is it?

The insurance job means three days working alongside Greg and a part of me wishes Dad had put me on something else. I know he's going to grill me about my life and I wouldn't be surprised if he's also annoyed I haven't been answering my phone much at the moment. I know I've missed a few of his calls and he's stopped leaving messages.

'Hey, stranger.' Yep, he's annoyed with me.

'I've been busy, what can I say?'

'Too busy to answer your phone? Or have you been *busy* with the widow lady.' He cocks an eyebrow.

'Greg, seriously, man, you must stop calling her that. She's a great person going through a traumatic time with dignity.' As soon as the words are out I could slap myself on the forehead. That sounded like something my dad would say.

'Mate, you have it real bad. I suppose you're cancelling the Lisa meet-up, then?'

I see red, choosing to take a sudden flash of anger out on some splintered wood. After a few hefty bashes the whole thing comes out in one piece. Greg gets the message and goes quiet.

'No, I'm not cancelling. And I've already met up with Lisa.'

Greg stands back, a look of disbelief on his face.

'Really? You did? A couple of us have a bet on and that's not something we saw coming.'

Now I laugh. I should have guessed.

'Oh, so what are the odds?'

'Three to one you go back to Anita. No one thinks you'll go out with Lisa. This is going to upset the pot.'

'That's borderline cruel, you know that, betting on someone else's misery. Going back to Anita isn't an option because she has a new man in her life. Not that I've met him.'

'Mate, you're joking!' He seems shocked, so that means no one's talking about it and the word hasn't circulated yet. That, at least, is one pressure less.

'And Lisa's okay, so I'm not pulling out. You can continue to receive Cheryl's undying gratitude without guilt.'

He stops work, leaning back against a pillar to look at me quite intensely.

'Well, I wouldn't be pushing it if I didn't think I was doing you a favour. Lisa slays it, man. I mean she's one neat little package.'

I roll my eyes. 'Greg, when are you ever going to grow up? Does Cheryl really like your immature style, or is she just humouring you?'

He pretends to wince. 'Hey, she finds me irresistible, what

can I say? Some of us have it and others, well, they know how to put a downer on a situation. I bet you've talked about Joe, then.'

'We did. It's not a deal-breaker, but she was surprised.'

'Can't see why. These days you're twenty-four going on forty. You need a night out and a few shots to remind you that life isn't supposed to be a grind. And I'm not joking here. You're back working for your dad to keep him and your mum happy. You are also working all hours to keep Anita happy. What about what you want out of life?'

'Greg, you're missing the whole point. When you have a kid your life changes forever. Any woman coming into my life now has to accept that Joe is my number-one priority and that Anita isn't going to disappear. In a way she still calls the shots and that's the price I have to pay as a dad with a failed relationship.'

We head off to the van to grab the first sheet of plaster-board.

'You know, Luke, you've just put me off having kids for life. Not sure Cheryl is going to approve of you once she hears you talking. I get the distinct impression she's looking for the whole package – marriage and kids. Hearing you speak I'm not sure that's something I'm ready to sign up for yet.'

I start chuckling and he actually looks a little embarrassed.

'Hey, this is going somewhere, isn't it? Mr 'I Like To Party' is beginning to cave in. Mate, it happens to the best of us.' I slap him on the back as he begins easing the board towards the rear door of the van.

'Between you and me, I'm scared stiff. You won't mention

it to anyone, will you? I mean, it's not like I've asked the question or anything.' His anxiety is real and all I can think is 'you have no idea what you are getting yourself into'.

***

A quick pub lunch gives me time to text Lisa.

Got my top three turn-offs. It took a while!

She responds instantly.

Thought you'd gone cold on me.

I find myself smiling as I text.

It was a tough question. I'm a slow thinker.

She sends back a smiley face.

We need to meet up to discuss this. I don't want to start off on the wrong foot. I'm not used to going out with a man who is a thinker.

Oh, interesting.

I hate to disillusion you, but I think you'll be disappointed. Maybe I should just have said 'slow' and left off the 'thinker'.

Back comes a smiley face lying on its back with tears of laughter spraying out like a fountain.

I think you are being modest. Besides, I like what I see. So are we on for tonight?

Greg raises his head, trying to glance at the phone in my hand, but I wave him off.

'Just arranging to meet up with Lisa again tonight. Don't you dare say a word!'

Chapter 37

Elana

Is There Such a Thing as Just a Kiss?

The presents are wrapped, although I had to do it surreptitiously in the bedroom while Maya and Amelie watched *Frozen* for the umpteenth time. I swear I could sing that song from memory and get all the actions right without even thinking about it. In fact, this time last year it was another of the crutches that saw us through the festive season.

'Time to take Amelie back home, now, Maya. Eve will be waiting.' I call up to them and hear two instant groans.

'But Muuuuum—' Two pairs of feet clatter down the stairs, noisily.

'Maya, it's time. Pop your coats on, girls, it's a cold wind out there.'

Sure enough, as we head down the steps to Hillside View, the wind blasts us with an icy chill. But as I look in front of me I can see that the front door to Eve's cottage is ajar. Puzzled, I turn to look at the girls, who have run off and are chasing

Maya's scarf, which has been blown into the hedge. As they disentangle it, I walk down the last few steps while I'm waiting for them, to investigate.

As I push the door open a little wider there's no one in sight, but I can hear loud voices and as I step inside the door I realise there's an argument in progress. Hesitating, I look back at the girls, but they're now trying to launch Maya's scarf into the air, chasing each other around in circles. I'm about to retrace my steps when what I hear freezes me to the spot.

'You keep trying to make this all about me, but I still remember that day I walked in on you and Niall. And don't think I haven't noticed you watching that builder guy. Are you that desperate for attention?' Rick's tone is furious as I try to comprehend the sickening words he's throwing at Eve. I want to move, to make an exit, but my feet won't move.

'Leave Niall out of this. And Luke? Well, maybe if you were here more often I wouldn't feel so isolated. It's all about the money to you, isn't it?'

Niall? Luke? I remember when Eve was talking about Luke and asked whether I had any feelings for him. It was an odd thing to ask and now I wonder if there was something a little more to it. But this is Eve. I know her, or at least, I thought I did.

Niall's name echoes around inside my head. What did Rick mean about walking in on him and Eve?

The sound of the girls chasing each other up the path to the front door makes me spin around and I step back outside. Plastering a smile on my shocked face, suddenly Rick's behind me and he pushes past, muttering an apology.

Eve appears in the doorway, looking distraught. One look at my face and she knows that I must have overheard the last bit of their conversation.

The squeal of tyres on the drive signals Rick's escape and we exchange glances.

'Elana, I think you'd better come in. Amelie, it's time to get ready for your dance class. Perhaps Maya can pop upstairs and help you choose which leotard to wear tonight.'

'Thanks, Mum.' Amelie throws her arms around Eve's waist and then heads off with Maya in tow.

I'm standing here bewildered.

'I wasn't eavesdropping, Eve. But when I heard Rick mention Niall's name I froze.'

She turns and I follow her inside, expecting her to ask me to take a seat. Instead we stand facing each other and I can tell by her body language she doesn't know what to say.

'What did Rick mean when he said he remembered walking in on you and Niall? What were you doing?'

'He thinks he saw Niall kissing me, but it was a long time ago. And it wasn't—'

'Mum, I can't find my blue one, is it in the ironing basket?'

Eve shakes her head in exasperation, as I will myself to remain calm.

'I'll get it for you now, Amelie. Sorry, Elana, can you just hold on one moment? This is impossible—'

Instead I call out to Maya.

'Time to go, darling. Or Amelie will be late.'

'Sorry,' Eve whispers and her apologetic look seems sincere as I turn on my heels and leave the cottage.

You don't *think* you saw two people kissing; they either were or they weren't. Eve didn't laugh it off, in fact, to me the look on her face was one of pure guilt. Is it true what they say, that we only see the things we want to see? What did I choose not to see?

***

I hear the sound of a car pulling up on the drive and I crane my neck out of the porch window. As I begin to pull back, Eve walks across on her way to my front door. She's dropped Amelie off at her class and come back to talk to me. I stand there, staring at the door and not wanting to open it. She rings twice, but I just can't bring myself to reach for the handle.

'Elana, please open the door.'

Her voice is just loud enough to hear and it's clear she's crying.

'I can't.'

Silence.

'Please. Please don't leave it like this; I need to explain.'

Reluctantly, almost like a robot, I watch as my hand reaches out in front of me. An eternity seems to pass as my hand turns the mechanism and slowly the door inches open. I'm appalled by what I see. Eve's face is almost unrecognisable, puffy and red from constant crying. She keeps wiping her face with her sleeve, trying to stem the flow, but it doesn't stop.

I turn without speaking and walk inside. She follows me through into the utility and beyond, into the extension, which is about the furthest away from the sitting room we can get. It's a bare room we've never used and has always felt chilly and uninhabited. It's home only to a few boxes of things we seldom use. I don't want Eve in my home and I don't want to know about her troubles. That sounds harsh after the support she's given me, but this feels like a stab in the back and any friendship we had is over.

'Say what you think you need to say and go. I don't want Maya overhearing one word of this.'

I stare at her coldly; the tears that keep filling her eyes and brimming over leave me unmoved. I don't know what she's told Rick, but it's all lies.

'It was nothing, nothing at all. It's all my fault, it's all my fault.'

I turn my back on her and look out of the window, peering out onto the garden and realise it's snowing. Tiny little pieces of white floating in the air, as if someone has torn up a sheet of paper and sprinkled the pieces from above. All I can think about is how excited Maya is going to be when she sees it. Behind me, Eve has composed herself and begins speaking.

'I can't talk to Rick about it because ... because he won't understand and Niall was so kind to me.'

I spin around, anger beginning to replace the feeling of numbness.

'My husband was so kind to you? And this is how you repay him? By lying about him? Well, I don't believe you.'

'It wasn't like that, Elana, please believe me.'

'Why try to destroy the memories I'm trying so desperately to hang onto? Is this some kind of sick attempt at trying to grab Rick's attention and make him jealous? And were you also hoping to use Luke in the same way? I saw loathing in Rick's eyes, so your little plan hasn't worked.'

Eve can't make eye contact, but I notice her tears have stopped. She's agitated, running her hands through her hair as if she's holding her head upright.

'Rick and I had a blazing row and he'd walked out. Niall was comforting me, but there wasn't anything going on, believe me. I wouldn't do that to you, Elana. I know how strong your marriage was and I envied that.'

'Enough to stand there and tell me my husband kissed YOU? Eve, you are no longer welcome here. Any friendship we had is over.'

I walk off and go upstairs, locking myself in the bathroom. Washing my face in cold water, I scoop up handfuls of it in an attempt to wash away my disgust, but it doesn't help. As I dab at my wet face with a towel I look at the person staring back at me in the mirror. I don't even recognise myself, the haunted look in my eyes is painful to see and I know what I have to do next. I go downstairs and dial Rick's mobile.

'Rick, I'm going to ask you one question and if you have any conscience whatsoever you'll tell me the truth. What exactly did you witness? I need to know, because my life might be about to fall apart for the second time and I need you to think carefully about this. I'm only interested in the facts and not the jealous reaction of an angry man looking for an excuse to leave his wife.'

I can hear muffled background noises that indicate he's on

a motorway. The sound of a lorry's engine grows in intensity for a few seconds and then begins to tail off.

'I wouldn't lie to you, Elana. I walked in on them in the kitchen and they were standing up close, kissing. After that, Niall avoided me. Eve and I had another blazing row and she refused to talk about it, saying he was merely comforting her. But I know what I saw.'

The only sound I can hear is my heart shattering into tiny little pieces, as real as if it is made of glass and has fallen to the floor. Gushes of pulsating blood squeezing through arteries pound away inside my head. My Niall, my lovely Niall was unfaithful to me.

I press disconnect and throw down the phone, letting anguish overtake me.

Chapter 38

Elana

I'm Broken and in Pieces

When you're a mother you can't give in. You can't run and hide because the bottom has just fallen out of your world. You have to paste on a smile and function. And that's what I did. I sat Maya down and asked if she'd like to go and stay overnight with Grandma Carol and Granddad Philip, as a treat.

Philip was surprised when I made the call, but sensed an underlying problem. He was kind enough not to ask about it and when they arrived and I waved Maya off, she was so excited about the thin layer of snow on the ground that parting was easy.

'How much snow do we need to make a snowman, Granddad?' I heard her asking as they walked up to the car. I shut the door, unsure of how much longer I could remain standing here without dropping to the floor.

I lay on the sofa, trying to sort it all out in my head, but it's a jumble. Images of Niall when he was here, laughing together, loving together. We were like one; there were no secrets between us. How could there be? Wouldn't I know if he'd really been unfaithful to me? But what if it was true? Was it just one kiss, or one of many? Was it a kiss that meant something? But, surely, every kiss means something, because it indicates that some sort of a connection has been made? Was it a kiss that led to something else?

Hours go by and it's wine o'clock, but after three glasses I'm stone-cold sober. I try coffee next, but even the caffeine can't help mask the pain. I can't be alone right now. But I can't ring Mum or Dad – how can I admit what's happened? I no longer have a best friend and reaching out to anyone not within my inner circle isn't an option. Everyone knew us as a couple, a happily married couple. This is Niall's memory I'm in danger of dirtying, of degrading, when I'll never know for sure what actually happened.

I cast around for my phone and eventually find it, at the side of the chair where it had landed. The corner of the case is broken but it's still working. I look through my contacts and ring the person I want to speak to more than anyone else right now.

'I need help. Can you come?'

***

It seems like hours since I made the call, as each minute stretches out endlessly. I'm too tired to think any more and too depressed to do anything. When the doorbell rings I'm not even sure I can face anyone and my feet head slowly towards the door, my hand hesitating before I open it.

Luke stands there, his face registering concern as he takes one look at me and steps inside. His arms are suddenly around me as he half-walks, half-carries me back into the sitting room. It's gloomy, as only one side light is switched on, but even in the shadows I can see the look of shock on his face.

'It's okay. I'm here. You don't have to say anything, just sit for a while.'

I couldn't talk even if I wanted to and as he eases me down onto the sofa, he sits next to me with his arm around my shoulder. Eventually I drift off into a fitful sleep, a jumble of the past replaying in my head like an old film you've watched so many times the familiarity is comforting. When I wake I'm slouched against Luke's chest, his arm still wrapped around me and the other holding my head up a little.

'Sorry. That can't have been comfortable for you. How long did I sleep?'

'It's half-nine now, so about an hour and a half. You were shattered.'

He doesn't ask what the problem is. I don't think I can tell him. I thought it would be easier if I shared it with someone who wasn't a part of my life before, but once I say those words it makes it real. It won't be Rick or Eve telling their lies. It will be me, Niall's wife, giving it credence. But I still don't know what really happened.

'How much wine have you drunk?'

Luke takes in the half bottle standing on the table and the empty wine glass. 'Was that it, or was there more?'

I shake my head. 'Three glasses. I'm not drunk.'

'Where's Maya? I assume she isn't here?'

'No. She's ... with family.' I can't say Niall's name; can't even say she's with Niall's parents.

'There's no rush. I'm not going anywhere.'

There's comfort in the gloom, comfort too in having Luke's arm around me. Inside my head I'm screaming 'Why me?' And why now? Just when the pain was finally becoming almost bearable. Luke's hold tightens slightly, as if he can feel the pain radiating out from the centre of me. My precious, wonderful Niall – all my memories now tarnished with doubt. What was real? Did I simply see what I wanted to see and remained blind to what might have destroyed us? But our marriage wasn't like so many others, what we had *was* real – I know it!

In the early hours of the morning I think we more or less took it in turns to sleep, our heads back against the sofa, but still sitting close together. Luke's own gentle snoring finally wakes him with a start and he apologises.

'I wasn't sleeping,' I admit. I had been watching him, though, wondering how he instinctively knew what not to say. That requires maturity and I can't take that quality away from him, even though he's young in years.

'It's nearly three. You must be shattered.'

'No. Wide awake. I need coffee.'

I get up and stretch, my body slightly stiff from the unnatural position I've been sitting in for several hours. Luke follows me out into the kitchen as I go through the familiar actions.

It's only when my back is towards him that I can begin

speaking. I don't want to look at his face, catch his reaction, or see what might be reflected in his eyes.

'Rick told me that he walked in on Niall kissing Eve.'

The silence is earth-shattering, because there is nothing Luke can say in response to that.

'What hurts—' I take a deep breath as tears begin to form. 'What hurts is that I'll never know the truth for sure. Eve is saying very little, other than that Niall was comforting her and Rick can only repeat what he saw, or thought he saw. How can they destroy all of my wonderful memories, knowing full well nothing will ever be the same again? Was it just a meaningless kiss or a kiss filled with emotion? Would you kiss me out of sympathy, or empathy? Does that happen? What if it was a loving kiss?'

I spin around and he looks as white as the wall behind him. Shocked, appalled and speechless, as I expected.

Chapter 39

Elana

Facing Up to the Impossible

Diary Log – day 504. 6 days to Christmas. I feel that something inside of me has died. Stopped working, like the mechanism of a clock that will never tick again. I'm writing this as the last entry because … because … because if it's true, do I hate you, Niall? If it's not true, is that element of doubt always going to tarnish our past, because I will never know for sure? Maybe this is the wake-up call I needed and I have to let go now, in order to preserve my sanity. My heart wants to love again and I think it's time I allowed myself to do that. I can't waste the rest of my life by constantly looking back. It really is time to say goodbye.

I stop typing and start whispering. 'I'm going to delete this file now, my darling. It hurts too much to re-read what I've shared with you since you died, and if I don't stop myself now, then my life is over. I can't do that to our daughter. Just one word from you and it would all be so very different. But I'll never know for certain what happened, until I'm with you once more. I want to be with you, but I know that isn't an option. I want everything to be as it was and I'm scared, so scared. Scared for me, scared for Maya and scared for you.'

My finger hovers over the delete key and the pain in my chest is like an explosion taking place. It's a real, physical pain like nothing else I've ever experienced before. One key, one touch and then I vow never to look back again. Ever.

Delete.

***

'What time is it?' Luke stirs as soon as I walk back into the sitting room carrying two mugs of coffee. It's five a.m. but an inch of snow lying on the ground and a pale-grey sky that is almost luminescent, makes it feel later.

'Five. Here, you probably need this as much as I do.'

'Sounds like you're ready to talk. You scared me last night, you know.' He swings his legs around into a sitting position as I put the hot drinks down on the coffee table in front of him.

'I scared myself. You don't know how strong you are until you are tested. Failure is always one of the possible outcomes. I'm tired, Luke. Tired of trying to make everything perfect when it isn't, it's broken and the pieces can't be put back together.'

I settle myself down next to him, the gap between us re-establishing our normal comfort zone.

'I want to thank you for getting me through the worst night of my life. You see, I thought I'd already had that and took a sort of pride in the fact that I'd survived the worst imaginable thing that could happen. I thought that pride was a sense of self-esteem, of dignity, honour maybe. I played life by the rules and even when it took something from me that I truly loved, I behaved with decorum. I took it on the chin and refused to be beaten.' The laugh that escapes my lips is one filled with bitterness. I can see Luke recoil slightly, a look of bewilderment reflected in his eyes.

'Now you're scaring me again.'

'I don't mean to, I just want to let you know that last night meant something. When I was feeling desperate you were the one I wanted to turn to, the only one. At first I reasoned it was because no one wants to turn to their parents and I've fallen out with my best friend. I convinced myself I rang you because everyone else I knew was too involved in my life to go through another crisis with me. Well, who am I kidding? I called you, Luke, because I like having you in my life.'

His jaw visibly drops and he starts to speak, but immediately stops, a lonely 'but' hanging in the air between us.

I've just deleted what feels like the whole of my adult life with one swift press of a button. That might have been reckless, but this move is a considered one, albeit also a brave one.

As I look across at him and our eyes speak without words, I have no idea what is going to happen next.

Chapter 40

Luke

Someone Else's Pain

I hate landing Greg in it, but there's no way I can just head off to work and leave Elana alone. I text both him and Dad, saying I need to take the day off because of a personal matter. I acknowledge it's last-minute, but Dad immediately texts back to say he'll cover it. Greg prefers to work with me, but it's only one day. I hope. Within five minutes my mobile rings and it's Mum. There's no way I can't answer it, but I'm not sure what to say.

'Hi Ma.'

'Luke, are you okay? What's gone wrong? It's not Joe, is it?' She's holding her breath.

'No, Ma. This isn't family stuff – it's a friend in need. Look, I can't talk at the moment. If it wasn't serious, I wouldn't be letting you down.'

'Just be careful, my son. Don't get pulled into something just because you have a good heart. Let's speak when it's more convenient. If you need anything, remember that I'm here to help.'

I can tell from her voice that she thinks I'm in some sort of trouble. I suspect she assumed Anita and I had a row over money. At least admitting it's about a friend buys me some time.

Elana said some weird stuff in the early hours of this morning and I wondered if she was telling the truth about how much she had actually drunk. It was totally out of character, and shortly after six a.m. I managed to encourage her to go and lie down on the bed. She hasn't moved since and it's just after eight.

I still don't know the full story, or why Elana would send Maya to be with Niall's parents? From what I saw at that dinner, it seemed they were only just rekindling their relationship. Why didn't Elana's parents take Maya? Surely they would have wanted to help if what Rick said is true? I mean, Elana is clearly devastated.

Geez, I have so many questions and yet it's none of my business, really. But I care enough to want to be here for her, no matter what. My phone bleeps, then bleeps again and again. It's Lisa and she's furious, accusing me of standing her up. No! I totally forgot we were meeting up and she didn't deserve that. I haven't the heart to text her back at the moment, so I switch off my phone. I'll have to deal with that later.

I wonder if this will push Elana over the edge and into some sort of nervous breakdown. If it's not true, then what possible reason would Rick have for saying that? I grab a coffee and go through into the sitting room to think it through.

Then I remember what Maya said the day she drew *I'm sorry* in the dust on the table. She said it was the message her dad had given her. Did she tell Elana, and could the message be referring to this revelation? Anyway, it's pretty freaky a young child saying she talks to her deceased father. I mean, that can't be normal, can it?

I glance across at the fireplace. The letters Maya has been leaving for Santa might simply be things she would like to add to her wish list, but something tells me that probably isn't the case. Then I remember the time I was on the roof and I heard Maya talking to Santa about her dad. I thought it was odd, but never mentioned it to Elana. My head slips back against the cushions on the sofa and I let my mind wander. Remembering that vivid blue, wintry sky and standing there looking out at the view. I was thinking how lucky these people are to live here. Maya's words were a whisper that echoed up the chimney stack, which acted like a funnel. It was something she wanted Santa to do so her daddy wouldn't think she'd forgotten him. She'd said 'you can't send presents to people who are in heaven, even though you can still speak to them'.

I put the coffee mug down and walk over to the fireplace. The ledge is towards the back and it isn't much of a reach to find the little pile of folded paper, but for a child of Maya's size it must be a little awkward. As I withdraw my hand, I see there are now five in total, but not all of them have the same handwriting. Now I have a dilemma. Elana has decided that a child has the right to their privacy, but what if the answer lies here in my hand and it means I can help in some way?

I sit down, feeling it's the right thing to do, simply because it's not something Elana feels comfortable doing. Whatever I see, if it's obvious it has nothing at all to do with what's going on here, then I'll simply put the letters back on the ledge.

I lay them out on the coffee table in front of me. Four are clearly in the same handwriting and then there's one that looks totally different. I open the one with a heart drawn beneath the words 'To Santa'.

My pulse quickens as I read it.

> *Dear Santa,*
>   *Please give my Daddy a hug from me so he isn't lonely this Christmas. I do miss him but I know he's safe in heaven. All I really want is for Mummy not to be alone any more. And did you get the letter we posted?* *Luv Maya x*

I shouldn't be doing this. With a feeling of guilt, I open the second letter, written in the same dark-blue felt-tip pen.

> *Dear Santa*
>   *I have a snow globe for Mummy, but really she wants a visit from Daddy. She's very sad, can you tell Daddy? And I don't want a big piano now as we don't have any money for lessons. Luv Maya x*

It's heart-breaking reading the carefully formed words that are really very neatly written, considering she's only six years old.

Dear Daddy

I hope Santa gives this to you. I forgot your message for Mummy and I've been waiting for you. Are you cross? Luv Maya x

Wow – Elana needs to read these. I open the last one in Maya's handwriting with a sense of trepidation.

Dear Santa

Can Mummy have something special if I don't have any presents this year? Mummy works very hard and misses Daddy all the time. I will be extra good. Thank you. Maya x

This is crazy; Elana needs to sit down and have a good talk with Maya, because it's rather bizarre that she believes Santa can talk to dead people. Heck, it's odd that she seems to genuinely believe that her daddy still talks to her. This could get out of hand. There's one letter left. It's in pink felt-tip pen and the handwriting is very different. Not so tidy, but equally as legible.

Dear Santa

Please can you make my mummy and daddy happy again? Oh, and I'll be good. Maya said I need to tell you that. Amelie Jane x

What has Maya been telling Amelie? I refold the letters and place them in a neat pile in front of me. I've heard Rick and Eve arguing, so it's likely Amelie might have overhead something, too. Kids worry and when they start hiding things, or keeping secrets, then that's a warning sign. A movement in the doorway draws my attention and Elana is standing there, wrapped in a soft, lilac-coloured bathrobe.

'The letters,' she speaks, softly. 'Of course. I wasn't brave enough to look. Should I be worried?'

I pat the sofa, encouraging her to come and sit down next to me. She looks exhausted and her face is very pale.

'You need to read them. There's one from Amelie, too.'

Elana jumps, almost as if I've pinched her and she looks at me, appalled.

'What does it say?'

I pull out Amelie's letter and pass it to her.

'Great. I don't need this at the moment. What else? Haven't I suffered enough, already?'

She holds up the carefully folded piece of paper, as if talking to someone *up there*. I take it from her and put it back down, then hold her hand in mine.

'Hey, come on. Clearly Maya thinks Santa can grant wishes and it says a lot that they both wanted to put someone else first. What great kids!'

She shakes her head.

'It means they are both unhappy, Luke. And it means I'm failing Maya, because she's holding things back when we should be talking them through.'

Damn it. I shouldn't have meddled and now I've added yet another problem into the mix. However, my gut instinct is telling me that there's no point in glossing over this, it's important.

'That might be partly down to me, I'm afraid.'

I tell her all about overhearing Maya talking to Santa, then as much as I can remember about our little chats. When I get to the bit about the message written in the dust, Elana looks as if she's going to faint. Her head falls forward and she sinks lower, almost scrunched up into a ball. When she finally pulls herself back up into a sitting position, she looks fraught.

'I'm undoing the ties with Niall one strand at a time and each one that is severed is like a knife wound to my heart. Once cut, you can never go back. It's as if Maya is trying to keep him alive and I can't cope with that now.'

'Elana, there is no going back, you can only move forward.'

'You have no idea how much I want to let go. If I could just speak to him one more time, just to get things straight. And now—'

Her words simply tail off and even though I lean forward a little, encouragingly, she remains silent. I put an arm around her shoulders and seconds later she sinks into me. It's the first time in my life that anyone has really needed me and I find myself wanting to fix everything for her.

'You're right, Luke, I have to sit Maya down again and tackle this head-on. We talked things over straight after Niall died, of course, but she was barely five at the time. After the initial upset, she seemed to adjust and for her it became all about the occasional sad moments – times when she was suddenly very conscious of his absence, like at Christmas. I had no idea some of these other things were happening. I don't know why she hasn't talked to me about it.'

I put my chin down on my chest, then tilt her chin up so that I can look into her eyes.

'This isn't your fault. It's been a tough time for you, too, and laying a guilt trip on yourself won't help matters. Talking to Niall is Maya's coping mechanism, as she's obviously dreaming about her daddy and the past, but there's no harm done.'

Elana adjusts her position, bringing her head up in line with my own.

'I have to start over again and I can't keep slipping back like this every time something goes wrong.'

Chapter 41

Luke

Wanting Something Doesn't Mean it Can Happen

I keep finding myself wanting to kiss her, to wipe away the tears when I see her eyes getting bright and filling up. She's up and down: one moment sounding a lot like her old self and the next seemingly overcome. It's hard watching what I say, trying not to make it worse.

Elana goes off to shower and dress, leaving me in the kitchen to sort breakfast. I don't think either of us is actually hungry, but it's mid-morning now and at least sitting around the table will be a distraction. To be honest, it feels as if someone has just died. Is this a normal part of the grieving process, I wonder? Just when you think the worst is behind you, it starts all over again. I want to tell Elana that I feel confused about what's happening, but she's way too fragile to question. Does she have any reason to think that what Rick said is true?

She walks back into the kitchen looking and smelling really good. In a long, fluffy cream jumper and leggings she manages to wear with style. She looks like something out of a clothes advert on TV. Her hair is shiny, the blonde mass of curls refusing to be tamed and giving her that very natural look. The only hint that anything is different today is the pallor of her skin.

'That feels better. What's on the menu?'

I turn, surprised that the tone of her voice is different, almost upbeat.

'Scrambled eggs and toast, I'm no chef, that's for sure! You sound ... better.' I catch her gaze and she gives me a weak smile.

'Having you here makes all the difference. I just hit a low point, but you know what they say, the only way is up. I realise there is nothing at all I can do about Rick's accusation and I can't let it drag me down.'

I dish up the eggs and quickly butter the toast, carrying the plates to the table.

'This looks good, thanks.'

She stares down at the plate, picking up the smallest piece of egg she can find and placing it in her mouth. I follow suit, knowing neither of us really wants to eat. Do I simply play along and see how the day pans out? What if she's still acting erratically later, when Maya returns? Is she safe to leave on her own?

'Luke, I don't know what you're thinking, but please stop frowning. I was having a wallow, feeling sorry for myself. I didn't want to involve my parents in this for obvious reasons and I really appreciate you being here for me.'

I put down my fork and sit back, trying to look relaxed.

'So you're okay now? You'll sit down with Maya, have another talk and this little episode will be over? Just like that.'

Why am I giving her a tough time? We could simply have breakfast and I could be on my way. It's obvious the mini crisis has passed. Why do I feel disappointed?

'I dragged you over here and you were good enough to come. I wasn't thinking straight because I was so tired and emotionally distraught, but you should be at work. You have a good heart, Luke. I'm very grateful to you and I don't know how to repay your kindness.'

Is she dismissing me? It's clear neither of us is going to eat any more, so I clear the plates away – most of the food still undisturbed on the plate. I feel used because I wanted Elana to need me for more than just a listening ear. Once again, what a fool I am. I hear her chair being pushed back, but I can't face her and I remain with my back to the table. I have to make my excuses and get out.

'It wasn't just kindness—'

'I'm glad, because I needed you here.' Suddenly she lays her head on my shoulder, her body pressed against my back. Her words are merely a whisper, warm and comforting. 'I didn't want anyone else, I wanted you.'

I close my eyes. Stop there. Don't say another word, let me have my moment before it's spoilt and you go on to say, 'Thank you, Luke, now you can go'.

'I meant what I said. I like having you around,' she adds.

This time her words give me a sense of real hope and as I turn into her, she melts into me. Before I can even think about it her lips are on mine and her body presses into me.

Her mouth is soft, her kiss gentle and I have to restrain myself, as I want to lift her up in my arms and carry her upstairs. My heart is beating so fast I'm sure she can hear it and that old, familiar sense of desire begins to build. But this is different. Normally I'm in control, but with Elana I just want to lose myself in her. I force myself to draw back and slow it down. As I pull away she looks at me questioningly.

'Did I misread the signs?' She sounds hesitant, fearful.

'No.' I clear my throat, in an attempt to calm myself down. I want her more than I've ever wanted any woman before. But if this is just lust on my part and a knee-jerk reaction on hers, then it's not just wrong, it's disastrous. 'I mean, I'm just surprised. I don't think you're in the right place at the moment, Elana, and I'm not sure I can control my feelings for you.'

She smiles, colour finally coming back into her cheeks.

'That's all I needed to know. I'm in exactly the right place and I think you are, too.'

Chapter 42

Luke

Feeling Alive

When Niall's parents bring Maya home shortly after lunch, I greet them at the door. Maya steps over the threshold first, seemingly unsurprised to see me.

'Hi Luke, the snow's all gone and I didn't get to build a snowman! Where's Mum?'

'Hi Maya, your mum is in the kitchen baking you some cookies.' She scoots past me, as I smile awkwardly at Carol and Philip.

'Come in, don't mind me. Elana's hands are covered in flour. I'm here doing some painting.' It sounds lame, but they take it in their stride and don't seem at all upset to see me here. I make myself scarce, heading off to the room beyond the utility to measure up the floor. When I return to the kitchen Elana and Maya are alone, laughing and chattering away as they lift the cookies onto a wire rack to cool.

'I don't think Maya needs any more sugar,' Elana smiles at

me over her shoulder, pulling me into the conversation. 'Seems she had a great time and was thoroughly spoilt.'

'Hmm, those cookies look good.'

'Shall we let Luke have one, Maya? What do you think?'

Maya laughs, the carefree sound of a child's happiness filling the air and Elana and I exchange glances. It's time for me to go so they can have their chat.

'I'd love to take one with me, if you can wrap it up. I need to get back to work.'

Maya makes a little parcel, wrapping two cookies up in some kitchen towel. 'There you go, Luke. In case you get hungry later.'

Elana sees me to the door and all I want to do is pull her to me and kiss her again and again and again. I can see that she feels the same. She puts out her hand to fleetingly touch my shoulder. She trails her fingers down my arm. For a brief second she entwines her fingers around my own and there is a look in her eyes I have never seen before.

'Come back soon,' she whispers and I nod, then turn and walk away.

***

What just happened? This is crazy. Think, Luke, think. Elana isn't some young woman shopping around for a partner. She's a widow with a daughter, trying to sort out her life and what can you offer her? You're a mess and your life is a mess. You can't support her because you have nothing except a load of bills and a ton of responsibility that isn't going to disappear overnight. As I walk up to the car, I reach into my pocket and pull out my phone to turn it back on. There are over a dozen texts from Lisa. I groan.

'Hi, Luke.' Rick walks past me carrying two suitcases.

This is incredibly awkward. I don't want him to think that Elana has been talking to me about his accusation, so I feign ignorance.

'Off on another trip to London?'

He shrugs.

'Might be a long one this time. You still working inside Bay Tree?'

'Finishing up now, just a couple of small jobs left to tidy.'

He opens his car door. 'Is Elana alright.'

The fact that he's trying to get information out of me isn't good. He's no doubt feeling guilty for the trouble he and Eve have caused Elana.

'She's just come back from her grandparents' house. They're both home.'

'Good. Well, see you in January. Eve's looking forward to having the conservatory installed.'

I nod, then jump into the pick-up, deciding it's best to pull away and park up somewhere quiet to phone Lisa. Finding an empty lay-by I press return call before I can think of a reason not to do it.

'Hi, it's me. I'm really sorry. I wouldn't just stand you up like that, but I had to deal with an emergency.'

I blurt it out before she has a chance to get a word in. I can tell from the texts how upset she is about my no-show.

'You know, guys who are unreliable are a liability and I

don't have time for that. But I also feel you shouldn't be let off the hook. You can't treat people like this, Luke, and I thought you were better than that.'

Ouch! But I deserve it.

'Look, a friend had a bit of a meltdown. We were up most of the night and I'm only just able to walk away now.'

'And you couldn't even stop to text me, to save me hanging around looking like a total fool? It was embarrassing, Luke. I like you, but I won't be messed around.'

This isn't going to be easy, but I can't explain because it would mean betraying a trust. Or do I mean acknowledging my feelings? Either way, I can't start anything with Lisa after everything that's happened in the last twenty-four hours.

'Look, Lisa, I've tried to be straight with you from the start, so I hope you can see that I never intended for this to happen. What it has done is made me realise that the timing isn't right for me to think about dating again. That's why I was being cautious in the first place, to be honest. I have too many problems to juggle and until everything is sorted out I can't make any plans. You're a lovely lady who deserves more than I can give at the moment. I'm being pulled in too many directions and struggling to get the balance right. You deserve much more than that.'

A sigh drifts down the line.

'I feel sorry for you, Luke. If you get yourself sorted, give me a call. I'll tell Cheryl to back off. It's a pity, I will admit. You're an interesting guy and I think we had some sort of connection.'

I feel like a heel. I can hear how disappointed she is and I hate the thought that I've hurt her, as that was never my intention.

'Life is all about timing. At the moment I'm a bit of a walking disaster, I'm afraid. Best avoided.' I laugh, hoping to lighten the moment.

'You're funny, Luke. Most people get depressed when they're going through tough times.'

'I've learnt that every time you fall you have to bounce right back up again.'

'Well, keep bouncing and ring me any time. I enjoy talking to you, even if you have turned out to be a bit of a let-down.'

In a way I wish she'd simply gone into ranting mode and put the phone down on me. That's what I'm used to, as it never takes much to send Anita into a rage. The fact that Lisa was so understanding and mature about it impresses me. Not that I'm used to giving women bad news, but I bet that's not a common reaction.

Anyway, it's all true. I am in a mess and now I have a new problem. Elana isn't in love with me, but I'm in love with her. I'm a quick fix, something to heal her broken heart and divert her attention from the pain. But I know I can never be the man in her life, because she's way out of my league. I'm going to get my heart broken and yet I can't help myself. When she kissed me I knew it was for all the wrong reasons, but knowing that doesn't make any difference.

***

When I walk into the office Dad immediately picks up a clip board, acknowledging me as he walks past to leave me alone with Mum.

'Long night?' Mum's eyes scan my face searching for clues.

I sit down next to her desk, suddenly feeling very tired and a little deflated.

'Is it Mrs James at Bay Tree Cottage?'

I nod. 'Her name is Elana. How did you know?'

'Every time anyone called her "the widow lady" it annoyed you. I could see it on your face. I've never known you not to come into work for personal reasons, so I put two and two together. Am I right?'

There's no reason to deny it and no point in trying to lie. Mum knows me only too well.

'It's complicated.'

'Relationships always are, my son. Is this a shared problem, or are you just being supportive?'

It's a leading question and we both know it.

'Elana has had a tough time, on top of which she has a six-year-old daughter, who claims to speak to her deceased daddy. Then she received some bad news and it was all a little too much. She's a strong lady, Mum, but there's only so much anyone going through a grieving process can take. I feel bad for her and when I received the call I had to go.'

Mum lays her hand on my forearm, which is resting on the desk. The warmth is comforting and reminds me of my boyhood, the way she'd comfort me whenever anything went wrong.

'Does she know you have feelings for her?'

Her eyes search mine and I know what she's thinking. She doesn't want to see me get hurt again.

'I don't think she's in a place where she can see anything very clearly at the moment. I'm happy to be there for her whenever she needs me, no strings attached.'

Mum sighs and sits back in her chair, looking weary. I hate the fact that she worries about me so much, but she'll worry more if I keep things back.

'You know the risk you are taking? Everything passes with time, even the pain of losing a partner. Being a crutch is all well and good, but when feelings are involved that's a warning sign, Luke. A relationship has to be a two-way thing, or it isn't a relationship. How will you feel if you let her into your heart and then suddenly she moves on with her life? You're worried about her, but I'm worried about you.'

'I'm not repeating an old mistake, Ma, honestly. Elana is nothing like Anita.'

Mum gives a tired, jaded little laugh.

'You are two people who are each going through emotionally painful times; that alone will serve to give you a sense of connection. But what else do you have in common, because once the healing begins what will there be left to cling on to?'

'Ma, I know what I'm doing. I'm no longer that naive young guy. Being needed, useful, is making me feel good about myself again. Anita ground me down so low I felt worthless. I know this can't go anywhere, but it's what I need at the moment. I feel like a decent human being again, instead of someone only capable of causing their mother to worry herself into an early grave. So stop worrying about me, Ma, until there's something to worry about.'

'If you say so, my son. Just, please, don't go falling headlong into this without sparing a thought for yourself. How are you going to feel when Elana begins to pick up the threads of a normal life again, if she doesn't choose to do that with you? You aren't a taker, Luke, and there are times when that isn't a good thing.'

Here endeth the lesson and I know Mum has seen through my reassurances. She doesn't know Elana, but her instincts are good enough to set alarm bells ringing. The truth is, I can't help myself and whatever price I end up paying is irrelevant. For the first time in so long I feel alive and it's a feeling that is every bit as euphoric as a drug.

Chapter 43

Elana

A Head Full of Worries

It's all lies. It must be. Rick needs an excuse to walk away from Eve and Amelie, and he's desperate to find something to ease his conscience. Niall was a thoughtful and caring man, so I'm not surprised to learn that he comforted Eve if she broke down in front of him. Was she jealous that our relationship was so strong, when her own marriage was beginning to fall apart? I believe that Eve was trying to make Rick jealous and Niall was the man she used to do it. She obviously knew Rick was there and about to walk in on them, so she kissed Niall. Why is it suddenly so important to Rick now, when Niall isn't here to tell his side of the story? Their relationship has continued to deteriorate and I suspect Rick has had enough. He's using Niall, and maybe even Luke, as his excuse to walk away from his family – how can he do that?

My head aches from constantly going over and over those final months with Niall, trying to find a hint that he wasn't satisfied with me. But nothing was different about him, only the stress from working long hours, either at work or on the cottage. If anything had been wrong he simply wouldn't have been so committed; you can't fake things like that. We were both doing everything possible to make our future easier and to turn this into a wonderful family home. I feel bitter that Rick and Eve are selfish enough to drag us into their misery. Why would they do that, now, of all times?

Maya saunters down the stairs.

'Mum, can you please ask Luke if we can light the fire now. Please, Mum, please?'

It's hard to switch from one train of thought to another, but I can't put this off any longer.

'Let's go into the sitting room, darling, we need to have a chat.'

Maya skips through ahead of me, flopping down into her favourite bean bag. She's all legs and arms, and as if it's a total surprise, I realise just how much she's grown in this last year.

'I'll ask Luke about the fire, I promise, but don't get your hopes up. Why is it so important, Maya?'

Her little face puckers up as she considers her answer.

'You know that book, the one you read to me last year? It said that you throw your letters on the fire and when the smoke goes up the chimney that's how Santa gets your messages. It's too late to send them by post now and I'm worried, Mum. What if he doesn't get them?'

'Oh, darling. If there's anything you want Santa to know then you only have to tell me and I'll make sure it's delivered in time.'

Maya shakes her head.

'No, Mum. Then it wouldn't be a surprise for you, either.'

This is awkward because I can't let her know I've read the letters she's been writing, or that I'm also aware of Amelie's sad request.

'Do you know what I'd really like, much more than any surprise?'

She sits forward, her face now relaxed and smiling.

'What?'

'I'd like to talk about Daddy. Would you like to do that?'

Her forehead wrinkles and I can see she is torn.

'But I don't want to make you sad, Mum, and it always does.'

'Oh my darling, I love talking about Daddy and of course it's going to make us sad, because we miss him. But there's nothing wrong with feeling sad as long as it's not all the time. Daddy wants us to be happy, and we also have lots of wonderful memories to make us smile, don't we?'

Maya rocks back and forth, her arms cradled around her legs.

'Yes. He said that he's never far away and he's watching over us.'

My heart beat increases and a lump rises in my throat. That's almost word-for-word one of the lines from a children's book on dealing with bereavement that we read shortly after Niall died.

'Even though Daddy is in heaven he will always love us, Maya. I often dream about Daddy, and I expect you do, too. All those lovely memories we have of Daddy get replayed in our heads. A bit like watching a DVD. It's a very special thing. But Daddy can't really be here with us any more. He's simply in our hearts and in our memories.'

The frown is back.

'But he lies down next to me on the bed and we talk, Mum.'

I go and sit next to her on the floor so I'm at the same level, taking one of her little hands in mine.

'That's lovely, darling. But Daddy isn't actually there, you're simply dreaming.'

She withdraws her hand, looking at me with a shocked expression on her face.

'No, Mum, you're wrong. Daddy talks to me about school and you.'

I sigh. She's a child with a very vivid imagination and that's not something I want to curb, but how do you explain the difference between fact and fantasy to a six-year-old?

'When we fall asleep our heads are full of everything that has happened during the day, so it all gets jumbled up with old memories. That's why in dreams we often find ourselves doing something we've never done before, or having conversations that have never actually taken place. It feels like it's real, but it's not. That's fine, darling, but we have to remember there is a difference between a dream and real life.'

'But I'm not asleep when Daddy is here. You don't understand, Mum. I wish he'd visit you too, then you'd know for sure.'

She's getting frustrated and I wonder if maybe this is something that will pass in time, like all phases children go through.

'Does it make you happy?'

Her eyes open wide and a broad smile sweeps over her face. 'Oh, yes, Mummy. But I do wish you could see him, too. I told Daddy that.'

'Maya, you know that you can always talk to me about anything, don't you? I will ask Luke about the fire, but Santa is very busy making sure all the right presents go to the right homes. So if you want to talk about anything else, anything at all, that's why I'm always here for you. Do you understand?'

Maya rocks herself back into the bean bag, her attention beginning to wander.

'Should I tell Daddy it's okay if he talks to you, too?'

It's so difficult to know what to say, as I don't want to undermine something that, quite clearly, is important to her at the moment. Letting go of someone isn't easy as an adult, so as a child it must be almost impossible to understand.

'Yes, of course. But he's always in my heart and I think of him every day, Maya. Nothing will ever change that.'

'He said Luke is doing a grand job. I love our cottage, Mum.'

Her words send a chill through me. Maya doesn't use the word *grand*, what child does? It was one of Niall's favourite words. It stops me in my tracks for a moment, then I realise it was so much a part of him that Maya would have picked up on that.

'I'm glad to hear that, darling. It feels really cosy, now, doesn't it?'

'Yes and I like Luke, too, Mum. He makes us both laugh, doesn't he?'

What don't children see? Much more than we often give

them credit for, so I'm going to have to be very careful here. Luke is a very special person, and yes, I'd like to be more than just friends. Maya is right, we are both very comfortable whenever he's here. He seems to fit right in as if he's always been around. Then I remember that he's very young; I feel like I'm a hundred years old and have the weight of the world on my shoulders. Is it wicked of me to accept comfort from him and pull him into our lives? He already has so much to deal with in his own life and here I am, thinking only about what I need. Of course I miss having a man in my life, being loved and feeling wanted, needed. What woman wouldn't? But this can't be just about me. Luke deserves to be with someone of his own age, not a widow who is ten years older and carrying a lot of very heavy emotional baggage. My conscience is ringing a warning bell. I just hope I'm capable of doing the right thing.

Chapter 44

Elana

Wishful Thinking

The mobile kicks into life.

'How are you, today?'

Luke's voice wraps itself around me like a hug and immediately a smile takes over, smoothing away my worries.

'Five days to Christmas and I ought to be panicking and making last-minute shopping lists, I suppose, but instead I've been working. We had a difficult start to the day as Maya wants Amelie to come over and, to be honest, I still can't face talking to Eve. I want to thank you for dropping everything to come to my rescue. You're a gentleman, Luke. And you forgot to take your envelope with the cash in that I put on the side for you. If you're free to pop round tonight, why don't you stay for dinner?'

He chuckles and I realise that all came out in rather a rush, but hearing his voice really perked me up.

'Money and dinner. Who could refuse?'

He sounds upbeat, so I guess his friend Greg didn't give him a hard time about not showing up on the job.

'What are you going to do about Eve and Amelie?'

I sigh.

'I can't avoid Eve forever, but it really hurts, Luke. I feel like I've been stabbed in the back. I'd prefer never to speak to her again, but I have to think about Maya. She's too young to understand what's happened, and then there's little Amelie. It's always the kids you feel sorry for, isn't it? I mean, what sort of Christmas are they going to have?'

'Look, you can tell me to mind my own business, but unless Eve is suddenly going to move out, you can't avoid seeing her. Maya and Amelie will want to continue to spend time with each other, so somehow you have to at least re-establish contact. How about tonight, after dinner, I knock on Eve's door and invite Eve and Amelie round? The kids can play and you can sort out some ground rules for how to move things forward. Like it or not, you live on each other's door-step and being so isolated doesn't help matters. What do you think?'

I think that you are one of the kindest, most caring, guys I've ever met.

'I'd appreciate that, Luke. The last meeting with Eve didn't go well and I've been dreading bumping into her, to be honest.'

'I know and that's only natural. What time shall I come round?'

'About six? We'll eat first and then do the deed. Besides, Maya has a question to ask you.'

He laughs, and an image of his face flashes into my head, sending a flush of colour to my cheeks.

'See you tonight.'

***

'Luke, can we light the fire? Please?'

'Maya, let Luke at least step inside before you start questioning him. Sorry, Luke, it's all Christmas craziness here tonight.'

We exchange brief glances before Maya is pulling him off in the direction of the sitting room. I head into the kitchen to stir the Bolognese sauce.

'Mum, Luke says we can!' Maya comes dashing out of the sitting room, literally shouting at the top of her voice. Competing with Slade, and Noddy Holder belting out '... everybody's having fun—', she demonstrates that she has an amazing set of lungs.

'Don't shout, darling, I did hear you. You sure it's okay, Luke?'

He appears behind Maya, his warm smile making my heart quiver just a little.

'I'm sure it will be fine. It's been dry and, unusually for this time of year, there haven't been many frosts. That's what really upsets drying mortar, as the ice crystals do the damage. I think we've been rather lucky with the weather and I'd say it was time to throw on some logs.'

Maya literally jumps up and down on the spot, clapping her hands in pure joy. She doesn't notice the look that passes between Luke and me, as we think about the little letters sitting on the ledge. He cocks an eyebrow and I nod, giving him the go-ahead.

'Right, Maya. Let's go and take out the lights Mummy draped around the logs and find some fire-lighters.'

As I lay the table and listen in on the excited chatter coming from the sitting room, I realise that's what makes this cottage feel like home. Much more than the beautiful new floor, and more than the Christmas ambience that I've tried so hard to create for Maya. Home is about the people in it and the memories to be made. Is it going to be possible to make new memories here with another man without feeling like I'm hurting Niall? And will Niall understand my reaction to Rick's allegations? Listen to me – I'm doing what I'm trying to encourage my daughter not to do. To think that Niall is still here with us and that he will be a part of our lives going forward. Of course he will always be in our hearts, but the memories we make now will be solely ours.

'Penny for them.' Luke appears behind me, moving closer but stopping within reach. He wants to know where my comfort zone is and he's hesitant. I step forward so that there are merely inches between us, finally staring up into his eyes.

'You're very kind, Luke. It's so important to Maya that those letters go up in smoke in time for Santa to get the messages.'

'I know. I hear you had the talk. Maya said that Santa can only think about presents in the run-up to Christmas. Just in case I didn't know that.'

We laugh, a child's-eye view reminding us that there is still magic in this world, no matter how serious it all becomes.

We want to touch each other, but we daren't. This is not the time and the place, and we both know that. But the longing is so tangible that it wraps itself around us, tying us together like an invisible web. The smiles drop and it's passion I see reflected in his eyes. He coughs, then turns, walking back into the sitting room and calling out, 'Maya, can you see any flames yet?'

If I open up and let Luke into my heart, I know that he would love Maya as his own and that both Maya and I would welcome Joe into our lives. Could it be that simple? Is age meaningless when it comes to love?

As I start dishing up, my head is full of mixed emotions, as if it's in overdrive. Thoughts and feelings tumbling over each other in quick succession. I shout out to Maya and Luke that dinner is ready, and as I carry the plates to the table I stop, mid-step. Maya and Luke appear, also stopping in their tracks as they see the expression on my face. We all stare at the table and they, too, realise what I've done. Niall's place is laid ready for Luke to take his seat. I snap out of my reverie and put the plates down.

'Come on, guys, don't let it get cold.' My voice is too high and bright, like I've had a quick blast of helium, but they both take their seats and the moment passes. Maybe we are all ready to move on.

'Delicious, Mum!' Maya's mouth is half-full and I put up a finger, to remind her not to speak when she has food in her mouth.

Luke looks a little uncertain; his eyes stray across to the other empty chair, the one he usually sits in. I pretend not to notice, but in my chest a sense of anxiety flutters, unbidden. New memories, Elana, new memories – that's all.

Chapter 45

Elana

Someone Else's Misery

Luke returns from next door with Eve and Amelie trailing behind him. Amelie is excited, cannon-balling through the door and off in search of Maya, totally unaware of the awkwardness between the adults.

Luke bends to undo his shoe laces and Eve gives me a nervous glance.

'Thank you, Elana. Amelie has been going on and on, wanting to come over and see Maya.'

If she's expecting me to pretend nothing has happened, then she's in for a shock. I can't do that, but I won't let this affect our daughters.

'It was Luke's idea,' I confirm. 'Come into the kitchen.'

We sit around the table, rather awkwardly nursing our drinks. Luke has beer and Eve and I opt for wine. He sits between us like a mediator.

'I know this is awkward, and I'm not trying to butt in,

but there are two little girls in there feeling the magic of Christmas. Life isn't perfect and both of them have had a tough time. It's the same for me with Joe. My son deserves a proper family celebration and that isn't going to happen, so instead both my ex and I have to make it special for him in our own way. I believe that this year it will mean a lot to both Maya and Amelie if they can spend time together, rather than being kept apart. At least that's one thing in their lives that can function normally. Do you understand where I'm coming from?'

I don't answer, but Eve nods. They both turn and stare at me.

'First, I need the truth. Without that I'm tempted just to pack up some things and head off with Maya to my parents' house for the entire period.'

Luke looks surprised, and maybe a touch disappointed with my belligerence. Eve looks frightened but, once again, nods her head. He looks from one to the other of us, then picks up his beer and walks off into the sitting room. Obviously punches aren't going to be thrown, just possibly some rather harsh words.

Seconds pass and I know she wants me to say something, anything, but I keep silent. After a few minutes that seem to stretch out like an eternity, she begins.

'It was a mistake. A silly, terrible mistake, Elana. Yes, it happened, but there was no intention ... I mean, it wasn't meant to happen. I was distraught, as it was the first time that Rick had threatened to walk out on us. Niall knocked on the door and took one look at me, then followed me back inside. He walked forward, I turned and he put his arm out to comfort me, that's all. I heard the click of the front-door latch and as I turned to look over Niall's shoulder to see who it was, our faces made contact. He jumped back immediately, but it was too late and Rick had already turned and hurried back outside. Niall looked at me in horror, Elana. Horror. I didn't do it; I mean I didn't get it in my head to kiss him, or anything. It wasn't like that. Please, please believe me.'

Once more the tears run down her face, but I'm too emotionally drained to react.

'And that's it? There was no lead up to it before or any repeat of it afterwards?'

She pulls a tissue from the sleeve of her jumper, swiping it across her eyes and then mopping up the little collection of glistening wet before it drops off her chin.

'Niall wasn't interested in me. Before, or after. In fact, after that he never knocked on the door again. I only ever saw him briefly if I was dropping off, or picking up Amelie from here. We were both shocked and embarrassed, Elana. Trust me, it wasn't planned or intentional.'

If this had happened to me, with Rick, would I have told Niall? Explained what had happened, even though he'd probably never find out about it? The answer comes back with an unequivocal *yes*. So why didn't you tell me, Niall? Was there anything at all to hide?

'And Rick – why let him linger under a false impression? Were you hoping he'd be jealous and that would make him stay with you?'

Eve looks appalled.

'You think I used Niall like that? I did tell Rick what had happened, but he said I was lying and refused to listen. He thinks I was spinning a story and kept on and on about wanting the truth. The truth is that there is nothing else to tell. It's not that I won't talk about it, at all. It's simply that he wants to believe there's more to it. He wants me to say that I stopped loving him a long time ago, but that's simply not true. I just want things to be right between us again, but I know he hasn't been happy for a while.'

The irony of this situation is not lost on me. I want this to be true, and for his own very different set of reasons, Rick wants it to be a lie.

'Luke is right, Eve. It's important that Amelie and Maya have their friendship to help them through the holidays. We're going to my parents' for Christmas Day to make it a family occasion, and unless you and Rick can heal this rift, it looks like you and Amelie are going to be in a similar situation. Thank God for grandparents. But, in between, our girls are both going to be thinking about the one person who is missing, so we need to make it as happy a break as we can for them. Can we do that?'

If you were a true friend, Eve, you would have told me what had happened at the time it occurred, and I would have believed you. This far down the road I'm still not so sure. The fact that both you and Niall chose not to say a thing leaves a tiny seed of doubt in my mind. But maybe that's because my pride is feeling a little wounded.

'Yes. This is about the girls and not us,' she agrees.

'I've been through hell, Eve, and you know that. I wanted this Christmas to be a little easier and now this ... it's hard not to be angry with you.'

She shifts in her chair, anxiety written all over her face.

'Oh, I know! I really do! This will always be the biggest regret of my life, because I know I've lost your friendship and trust.'

Luke reappears, his face registering that he heard Eve's words.

'Did you tell Eve about Amelie's letter to Santa?'

'I'm just about to. I can only hope our kids grow up with a positive attitude to relationships after what we've put them through.'

Luke walks over and places his hand on my shoulder.

'We have no control over death, Elana. There's nothing you could have done to change that.'

My heart cries out in the hope that it was an image of Maya and me in Niall's head in that split second when his life flashed before his eyes. I couldn't bear to think that wasn't the case as he took his last breath and I don't think Eve will ever really understand the damage she's done. For that, I can never forgive her.

'Daddy, my letters to Santa went up the chimney tonight. I asked Luke to check and he used the poker to run along the ledge thingy. There were only a lot of black curly bits that floated up into the smoke, so they're really gone! Mummy and Aunty Eve were very sad again tonight. Amelie said her daddy isn't coming home but he's not dead, like

you are. I tried to tell Mummy that you still come to talk to me but she didn't understand. Please talk to her yourself, Daddy, because she thinks you're gone and I know you aren't. I love you, Daddy, a zillion billion and one.'

Chapter 46

Luke

Life is a Rollercoaster Ride

It was one of the worst nights of my life and yet, within it was a moment of the purest joy and happiness I have ever felt. Maybe I'll never get to feel that again and I now know the real meaning of bittersweet – two such powerful opposites, drawing you towards a precipice.

I knew Elana wanted to believe what Eve told her, but how can she ever really know for sure? Eve is devastated to have lost the trust of her best friend and I can't see how that bridge can ever be rebuilt. Rick isn't coming back and he's already made that clear, so Eve broke the news that Hillside View will go on the market as soon as the conservatory is finished.

It's strange, when I first came to work on this side of the valley my life was in a mess, and these two families represented everything I wish I'd had. Looking in on their lives, they seemed to have it all, albeit Elana was a widow. I just assumed she'd pick her life back up, having been left in a position where at least she didn't have money worries to add into the mix. And Eve, well, she had the perfect home, husband and family. I find myself shaking my head; having seen their pain I wonder why life is so damned hard at times.

When Eve left and Maya was safely tucked up in bed, Elana came downstairs looking exhausted.

'Do you think I have any chance of surviving this Christmas?' She half-smiled and I knew exactly what she meant. 'Keeping up a pretence that I'm on the mend and moving forward when my emotions are in a new state of turmoil, well, my parents aren't fools. They'll know something is wrong, but how can I give this any credence by repeating it? I don't want their memory of Niall to be tarnished by any element of doubt.'

As her eyes welled up she stepped forward into my arms.

'Don't do this to yourself, Elana. It's a form of self-punishment. You heard what Eve said and you have no reason at all to disbelieve her. Rick has his own agenda, surely you can see that? I think this might even be about something, or someone, else.'

Her eyes were bright with tears as she looked up into my own, questioningly, but saying nothing.

'You keep talking about moving on and yet you seem reluctant. Don't make this the excuse to stay in limbo, this changes nothing about the here and now.' Was I pleading my case, hoping our friendship meant something more to her, as it did to me?

I sensed her tensing up, fearing I'd gone too far and spoken out loud something that should have remained a private thought. She pulled away slightly and I smiled down at her, wishing it really was my place to wipe away those tears. And then I began to feel angry and I knew it was ridiculous and out of order, but I couldn't help myself.

'You've spent a long time talking to me about my hang-ups and giving me the benefit of the wisdom you say comes with age. Did it ever occur to you that some wisdom comes from actually living it yourself and that can teach you a whole lot in a short time?'

She sighed. 'I just feel like I've been bulldozed, Luke, and I don't know how long I'm going to feel this way. Life can grind you down, you know that. But if I was ten years younger I would probably bounce back a whole lot quicker. That's the difference between us and it's real. Nothing can change that.'

'You should know better than that, lady, and stop treating me as if I'm not an equal somehow just because I'm younger than you. This isn't some kind of cougar thing; feelings are what they are. I can't help the fact that I find you attractive and that it makes me angry you let your hang-ups hold you back. Sorry if that makes you feel uncomfortable, but it's the truth.'

'Oh, and now I'm supposed to say that I find you attractive, too, I suppose!'

She's mad, really mad.

'No, of course not. You're too—'

'What? Uptight? You don't think I long to be held in a man's arms again? That I don't miss what I thought I had? You want to step in, a guy who's made some very poor life-decisions and has a chip on his shoulder, to rescue me. I'm devastated by the thought that perhaps my husband wasn't faithful to me and all you can think about is how you feel?'

'I'm working through my problems and you're the one who is trying to run away and pretend everything is fine. I know you like me, and I really wish you could stop dismissing me like some insignificant annoyance. We're both adults here. You needed some work doing, I needed some money. More importantly, we both needed a little company because it's a long, lonely night when your head is full of fears.'

I stood, not sure whether I was more disgusted with myself or her. I was disappointed, that's for sure, but I refused to be lectured by someone who appeared to have less of a grasp on the state of her own emotions than I did.

Then she delivered the final blow.

'Do you want to know the truth, Luke? Until I can find the courage to slip this wedding band off my finger, I'll always be Niall's wife.'

She almost collapsed against me; I knew the anger between us wasn't really that, it was frustration and longing. A longing to escape the mess we both found ourselves in that wouldn't allow us to step outside it for even one moment, because everything was tarnished by it.

I held her for a while, neither of us able to move. I didn't want to let her go and, presumably, Elana was feeling the same way, too. What passed between our bodies wasn't passion; the heat was one of healing. Wounds that lay at our very core are seldom touched by words alone. But when two bodies cling onto each other out of desperate need, suddenly the loneliness isn't quite so bad. Eve had unknowingly put yet another barrier in our way, or had it only ever been wishful thinking on my part that Elana and I could ever have a viable relationship? I could feel the need in Elana, as she sensed the need in me, but whether it was our fate to be together ... who could know that?

What we shared last night will remain in my memory forever. At that precise moment the person Elana needed most in the world was *me*. I was powerful, positive and strong, while also feeling desolate at the same time.

I'm not due back at Bay Tree Cottage now until Elana can afford to think about replacing the windows. I have one last wooden strip to lay around the hearth still, but that's on order and goodness knows when it will arrive. It's a slim lifeline to hold onto, because I'm already feeling that the dream is over before it even began.

Chapter 47

Luke

Getting Real

Another day dawns with still no contact from Elana and, I'll be honest, all morning I've been working with one eye on the phone, hoping she would call. It's Friday and, with three days to go before Christmas, I expect she's out shopping like most other mums at this time of year.

When, eventually, my phone does starts vibrating, I snatch it up and hold my breath as I put it to my ear.

'Luke, I need you!' The uncontrollable sobbing isn't enough to disguise Anita's voice. It's like a blow to the gut.

'What's wrong? Is Joe alright?'

'Yes, he's fine. Can you come over? I really need to talk to you, now.'

Greg looks across at me and I shake my head, indicating it's not Elana.

'Okay. It will take me half an hour to finish this off and then I'll take my lunch break a bit early. I'll be there as soon as I can.'

'Thank you. You are my rock.' I wince. Rock? She's called me a lot of things, but that was never one of them.

'It's not Anita again?' Greg looks at me, exasperated.

'Yep. Sounds urgent, though, but it's not to do with Joe.'

'Don't get suckered, mate. She uses you.'

Greg doesn't understand that I can't just say 'no' to Anita. Her well-being is important to Joe and, whether I like it or not, I am involved with his mum and always will be.

When she opens the door she's clearly been crying off and on for quite a while. I should be used to this by now – it seems I attract tearful women like a magnet. She doesn't fall into my arms, which is a relief, but I do feel sorry to see her in this state.

I close the door behind me and follow her inside.

'What happened?'

There's no sign of Joe and she catches me looking around for him.

'Joe is at Mum's. It's Chris, we had a row and he walked out – it's over.' She starts crying again and I take her arm, lowering her into the nearest chair.

'I'll put the kettle on and you can tell me what happened.'

'Things were going so well, Luke. He said he loved me and he wanted us to get engaged. He met Mum and Dad, and that went well. It all looked so ... promising.'

It's hard to keep an edge out of my voice, reflecting the fact that she can't seem to understand why any of this should be even mildly upsetting to me. I mean, she's talking about bringing in a guy who would be like a second dad to Joe.

'He says if it wasn't for Joe our life could be perfect.'

'He said *what?*'

She nods, miserably.

'What are you trying to say, Anita? You aren't going to turn your back on our son, are you?'

'Do you hate me that much, Luke, to believe I'd do that?' The look on her face is one of horror. I immediately back down a little, working hard to get myself under control.

'No, of course not. I'm sorry, it's just been a tough few days. Whatever our differences, you've always been a great mum to Joe, Anita, and I appreciate that.'

That signals another round of fresh tears, but I let her sit and cry, thinking that's probably for the best. Eventually she's bound to quieten down.

I sit, staring at the mugs of steaming tea on the coffee table between us, as if I'm some stranger who has walked into an awkward situation.

'It's never going to work with anyone else, is it?' Her voice is almost a whimper. 'I just thought there was more to life than this ... I didn't realise I already had a good man until I let him go.'

I freeze.

'I mean, you always put us first and instead of appreciating that, I saw it as being trapped. I couldn't let go of the life I'd had before and yet there you were, taking on this huge responsibility without a second thought. I let you down, Luke, and it's taken this for me to see that. Can you ever forgive me for the way I've treated you?'

I glance across at her, feeling shocked. Is that all it takes to make someone do a one-hundred-and-eighty degree turn?

Linn B. Halton

'It was a time of adjustment for both of us, Anita. If we'd planned it then maybe things would have worked out better. I wouldn't change a thing, though, because Joe is the best thing that has ever happened to me.'

She's calmer, even reaching for the tea and taking a sip.

'I was a dreamer, Luke. I thought everything was going to be perfect and I didn't realise that having a baby around means nothing is ever going to be the same again. All my friends were envious of me, but I was envious of their freedom. Crazy, isn't it?'

I'm so taken by surprise, I don't quite know what to say. Up until now everything has, according to Anita, been my fault and, eventually, even I came to believe it. Should I have known better, been the more responsible one? Anita repeats my name.

'Luke, Luke. I'm sorry I kicked off when you gave up your IT career to join the family business. It was wrong of me. You did what you had to do and I understand better now that family comes first. Joe has finally taught me that.'

It's as if I'm talking to someone I don't know; this certainly is a new side to Anita I've never seen. She'd once screamed at me that I'd robbed her of the best years of her life, the years she should have been partying with her friends and having fun.

'I'd ... um ... better get back to it. Greg will be wondering where I am. When is Joe coming back?'

'Later this afternoon. Why don't you come round for tea, straight from work? Joe would love it and you'd have at least an hour before his bedtime. You could bath him; you know how he loves splashing around.'

308

A part of me wants to say 'no', but another part of me longs to be the dad I want to be to Joe and grab this unexpected opportunity. Anita is making a peace offering and I'd be mad to turn it down.

'Great, I'll see you later, then.'

***

'Have you totally lost your mind? Mate, I'm so disappointed in you. She's trying to suck you back into her life. What about Elana?'

Greg leans on his shovel, looking at me and shaking his head.

'This is a major turnaround for me and I can't expect you to understand until you have kids of your own. When Joe was first born I was there every evening, walking him up and down, giving him his bedtime bottle and involved in every aspect of his life. Then suddenly everything changed – just like that! Six hours a week is nothing; it's a couple of hours at a play centre, or maybe at the indoor water park and a quick visit with my parents so he doesn't forget who they are. It's hell, Greg.'

'I've seen her in action, Luke, and I can't help thinking there's a catch. Now this new guy is out of her life it's too convenient to drag you back in. Just watch yourself.'

I know he means well, but it's too complicated to explain.

'Having a baby makes you grow up really fast, Greg. Maybe a couple of years have made all the difference and it's a sign of maturity. She's a really good mum to Joe and I can never forget that. I think she's just come to her senses and wants me to be more involved in Joe's life rather than pushing me away. There's nothing between us now, other than Joe.'

'Okay, ignore me. The only thing I've learnt watching you is that I definitely won't be having kids for a long time, mate. It's all hassle, from what I can see.'

'But that's just the point, Greg. It isn't. Joe is amazing and he reminds me what life is all about. Your time will come and when it does you'll feel exactly the same way. I want my boy to be proud of me and I need to keep things between Anita and me amicable for the future.'

'Yes, well, I don't think amicable is exactly what Anita has in mind.' Greg gives me an unrelenting stare.

Chapter 48

Luke

A Whisper Away … and it's Gone in a Flash

'What's wrong, Luke? I can tell something is up. It helps to share, you know.' Mum tries her best to sound light-hearted, but worry is written all over her face.

I feel as if I've had to choose between Elana and Joe, which is ridiculous, of course. If Elana knew the strength of my feelings for her she probably wouldn't let me in the house ever again. 'Just life.' The silence hangs heavily in the room and Mum puts her head down, pretending to be busy updating a job sheet. I know she's really waiting for me to open up.

'You know,' her hand travels across the page, her writing legible even from here, 'sometimes we over-complicate things. It's a part of the human condition.'

I laugh, wondering if my generation will ever be as good at parenting.

'Believe me, Ma, this isn't my doing. Not this time.'

'Is it Elana James?'

'No, it's Anita.'

'Well, that's a surprise. Is this bad news?'

'Not really. She wants me to spend Christmas with her and Joe. The guy she was seeing is unexpectedly out of the picture. I know you're expecting me at yours, so I told her I'd think about it.'

'So what's holding you back? Clearly it's not your father and me; you know we only want what makes you happy. Is it Elana James?'

I toy nervously with the paperweight on her desk, moving it around as if it were a chess piece.

'No, but I wish it was. I thought maybe something was developing between us, but I think she just needed a little support. No harm done and I was glad to be of help.'

Mum sighs.

'Oh, my son! You have to start thinking about what you want for a change. I don't know Elana, other than what little you've told me about her, but I do know my son. Helping someone out is a wonderful thing to do, but if you end up fooling yourself about how you feel you will get hurt. What is your heart telling you to do?'

This time the laugh I let out is one of pure frustration.

'I wish I knew! Spending Christmas with Joe would be top of my wish list if I had one. I mean, this Christmas he knows a little about what's going on and just to be able to be there when he wakes up—'

'You'd spend the night?' She sounds shocked.

'On the sofa. Anita said it would be a lovely memory for us all and she's right.'

'Then that's what you must do. Just tread carefully, Luke. Make sure everything you do is for the right reason and not purely for Joe.'

She stares at me, holding my gaze long enough for me to get the message.

'Yes, Ma. I won't let Anita walk all over me. We'll never get back together as a couple. I'm doing this for Joe and for myself.'

'Then, everything will be fine. I'm happy for you, Luke, because I know how much this means.' The look on her face doesn't mirror her words and I hate the fact that I'm still a constant worry to her. So much for being a mature and responsible adult, then. No wonder I don't inspire a woman like Elana to think that I'm a real candidate when it comes to picking a new partner. I mean, it's not just about her, but also about Maya and what she would need from any future male influence in her life.

***

As I walk back to the pick-up my phone starts vibrating and when I check the caller ID it's Elana. My stomach does a somersault, but I manage to keep my voice even.

'Hi, how are you doing?'

'Sorry I haven't been in touch after the other night. I had a lot of soul-searching to do. We're heading off to Mum and Dad's tomorrow for a few days. We won't be back until the twenty-sixth. Maya was a bit disappointed at first, you know, not being here Christmas morning, but I've convinced her it will be fun. I just need to get away, sort my head out. The thing is that we have a couple of presents for you and Joe, nothing big, just a little thank you. As we won't be having Christmas morning here, we're going to open a present each tonight and make a bit of a thing about it. I wondered if you fancied coming over to join in. Maya specifically asked me to give you a ring, and to tell you we've made gingerbread builders.'

My heart leaps in my chest. Maybe it's not the romantic invite I've been longing for, but it means they've both been thinking of Joe and me. It means a lot to know that.

'Gingerbread what?' I have a stupid grin on my face and I'm only glad Elana can't see it.

'Builders. They're holding hammers, it was Maya's idea. Some of the hammers look more like funny-shaped balloons, though.'

We exchange laughs and there's no way I can decline.

'I'll pop round after work.'

'Oh, I wasn't sure if you'd be off today.'

'No, it's our last day, but we'll be finishing early because everyone is looking forward to nine days off. Not a lot is going to get done, that's for sure.'

'Well, come over as early as you like. I have a casserole in the slow-cooker. We'll look forward to seeing you later, then.'

I almost said 'that's a date', but managed instead to change it into 'that's great'. Is she reaching out to me, or is this a peace offering?

The minute we disconnect I panic, wondering what on earth I can take with me. There's no point asking Greg for present-giving advice and I can't ask Mum, as I'm not sure she would think it was a good idea to go. Instead, I leave the little party going on at the office as surreptitiously as I can and head off to the shops. It can't be expensive, but it has to be thoughtful. Maya is easy, as one of the first things I spot is a bright-pink journal made with handmade paper, and a little lock and key. It has a fairy on the front and that makes it extra special. Looking around for something for Elana is much harder. A lot of the items are Christmas novelty things that look rather cheap. Then I see it – a solitary little musical box, about six inches square. Standing on the top is a model of a small bay tree, standing quite proud. When I pick it up and turn the small winder underneath, it plays 'I'm Dreaming of a White Christmas' and the bay tree spins around. I leave the shop with two perfectly packaged presents, feeling pretty pleased with myself.

'Mum, Luke's here!' Maya holds the door open for me to step inside, while shouting over her shoulder. 'We lit the fire, Luke. Just like on Christmas morning.'

To my dismay I realise it's holey-sock day again and Maya and I both stare down at my feet.

'Mum might not notice,' she whispers, laughing, and I follow her into the kitchen.

I feel awkward, like a visitor again, and I stand, presents in hand, waiting for Elana to finish stirring the casserole. The smell of beef and red wine makes my mouth water.

'Luke, can you pop the kettle on, or do you want something stronger? I wouldn't mind a glass of wine if you are happy to do the honours. I just need to sort out the veggies and dinner will be served.'

I place the packages on the side and sidle up to Elana to fill the kettle. Instantly she's made me feel at home and I love the way she does that with ease. She leans slightly towards me, while her hands chop off the tops of French beans, but by the time I realise she thought I was going to kiss her cheek, the moment is lost. Luke, you just don't have that polished, smooth approach that older guys seem to exude. It's what a woman like Elana surely expects. Instead, I shoot her a smile and the one I receive in return is heart-felt.

'We're visiting Grandma and Pop for Christmas, Luke. And we're going ice skating tomorrow at an outdoor rink. I've never been before.'

Maya is already seated at the table, obviously keen to get dinner out of the way and move on to the present-opening bit.

'And my present is hidden in the utility room. I'm not allowed to go in there until later.'

'Oh, well, I can't wait to see what it is now – I'm intrigued. Is it something from your Christmas list?'

We both turn to face Elana, who swipes her forearm across her forehead to shift a stray tendril of hair.

'No, it's not on Maya's list but I know she's going to be very happy when she sees what it is.'

Maya claps her hands and then slaps them lightly on her cheeks, rocking her face back and forth.

'I love Christmas, Luke. Is Joe getting excited?'

Elana flashes me a look, checking that Maya hasn't put her foot in it.

'Yes, he is. It's his second Christmas ever and this year he understands a little bit about what's going on. I can't wait to see his face when he wakes up on Christmas morning.'

Elana had turned back to the chopping board, but suddenly she stops. She spins around and our eyes meet.

'Family Christmas at Anita's,' I half-whisper. 'An unexpected invitation.'

She nods, her face semi-frozen before she recovers her composure and smiles, this time only with her eyes.

'I'm pleased for you,' she half-whispers in return, but Maya's attention is now focused on the Christmas cracker next to her plate.

I wonder if my news will kill the mood, but it's light-hearted and Maya's excitement is infectious. After the gingerbread builder experience, which makes them all look like they are about to club someone, we move into the sitting room.

'Bay Tree Cottage has a wonderful feel to it now it's almost complete,' I remark, filling the growing silence.

'No more dust,' chants Maya, skipping around. But it's more to do with her rising excitement than appreciation for the aesthetics. Elana nods, appreciatively.

'It's been a huge turning point for us, Luke, and it's all down to your hard work.' She raises her wine glass and we chink. 'Now, present time. Maya, can you please bring down Luke and Joe's gifts.'

I make my way back into the kitchen to collect my two little packages and Maya hares off up the stairs.

'It will take me two trips,' she yells behind her.

'I thought you said something small?' I question Elana, who appears behind me.

'I meant in price, not necessarily size.'

I study her face; relaxed, glowing and not a sign of a frown anywhere. This is the second when I know our moment has passed and I could kick myself for not taking it. That night after Eve left I should have taken her in my arms and refused to let go.

Maya comes rushing downstairs with a present the size of a small pillow in her arms. She starts laughing and so does Elana.

'What's funny?' I ask, puzzled by their reaction.

'Open it and see,' Maya squeals, holding it out to me.

I place it on the table and begin to unwrap it carefully, building the tension. There's so much sticky tape it seems to take forever and after a minute or so I start tearing at it. Out falls a virtual mountain of socks.

'No more holey-sock day!' Maya skips on the spot, laughing and jumping. 'And they're all the same colour. So you don't have to worry about matching them up.'

I burst out laughing. 'It's the perfect present, thank you so much, ladies. Do you mind if I put a pair on now?' To their absolute delight I pull off my socks and put on a new pair, consigning the old ones to the bin.

'Whose turn next, Mum?' Maya asks, unable to contain herself.

'Well, ladies, I'd rather like you to open these.' I place the respective packages in front of them and watch as Maya tears off the paper, and Elana carefully unties the bow around her gift.

Maya hugs the journal to her, shouting, 'Luke, I love it, thank you! Somewhere I can write down all the things I don't want to forget!' She runs across, flinging her arms around me and I bend to ruffle her hair.

'You're very welcome, Maya.'

She races upstairs, reappearing a moment or two later with a parcel wrapped in paper covered in snowmen.

By now Elana has the music box in her hands and turns the winder. As the strains of *I'm Dreaming of a White Christmas* fills the air, we all stop and stare at it. The little bay tree turns steadily and Elana's face registers sadness before she switches to smiley mode.

'Ah, it's lovely. Thank you Luke, but you shouldn't have bought us presents. We just wanted to say a little thank you for everything you've done. And this is for Joe. It's a Hot Wheels set. Maya chose it.'

I take the box and nod, appreciatively. 'He'll love it and I'll make sure he knows who it's from when he opens it on Christmas morning.' The thought sends a little thrill coursing through me. I'm going to be there when he wakes up and see the magic of Christmas through his eyes; I have to be grateful for that and not think about anything else. I clear my throat, trying to let go of a feeling of loss that's crazy and stupid.

'My turn!' Maya shouts and Elana waves her hands up and down, indicating for Maya to tone it down a little. 'Here's your present, Mummy.'

She carefully places her gift in Elana's hands. 'Don't drop it, or it will break,' she warns.

As the paper falls away from the snow globe, Elana raises it up in front of her, shaking it from side to side. The falling snow partially obscures the scene.

'It's you, me and Daddy,' Maya says, enthusiastically and I can see a fleeting moment of pain and love flash over Elana's face. She pulls herself together very quickly and takes Maya's hand, unable to reply and instead heads across the dining room.

'Come this way.'

Maya and I follow Elana over to the utility room and when she opens the door, the ceiling lights are twinkling, but there's no sign of a present. Then we hear it before we see it.

'Meow.'

Maya stands still, in total shock.

'Meow.'

Elana and I stand side by side as Maya drops to the floor and crawls on all fours towards the tiny little kitten.

'Hello kitty. I'm Maya. What's her name, Mum?' The tiny tortoiseshell kitten inches towards Maya and then turns to run away as soon as she puts out her hand.

'Whatever you want it to be. She's yours, darling.'

'I want to call her Baby Girl. Oh Mum,' Maya jumps up and rushes towards Elana, wrapping her arms around her waist. They stand hugging. 'Thank you, thank you, thank you. I love my surprise and I can't wait to tell Daddy about her.'

There's a second of silence as Elana composes herself.

'Daddy always said when the cottage was finished you could have a kitten and it's almost done. She's coming to Grandma and Pop's with us, as we can't leave her alone until she's a little bigger. You have to feed her and put down fresh water for her every day. At the moment she can't go outside, so we have to be careful not to leave the doors open. I expect she'll stay in here for a while as it's where her bed is, but gradually she'll discover it's a big wide world and there are lots of exciting places for her to hide and play.'

Maya is totally captivated and we leave her, crouched on the floor and content to simply watch her new little playmate.

I want to stay but I know it's time to go. There's nothing left to say and we both know it will just prolong the awkwardness.

As I step out into the night air, I take a really deep breath. Elana's hand brushes my cheek briefly before she begins speaking.

'Life isn't about fairytales, Luke, is it? It's about working with the hand you've been dealt.'

She leans in to kiss my cheek, but it's a fleeting one, and then she whispers into my ear.

'I'm glad you are able to have that family Christmas with Joe. Dreams can come true and you must never forget that.'

New Year's Eve

Chapter 49

Elana

All in the Line of Work

Baby Girl made Christmas for us all. That little ball of fluff was better entertainment than the festive line-up on TV, or the same-old games we play every year. Just watching Maya following her around, dragging cat toys across the floor while Baby Girl honed her hunting skills, made us all smile. We not only survived our second Christmas without Niall, but it passed very pleasantly.

The day after Christmas I steeled myself and finally slipped the wedding band off my finger. I realised that it was holding me back and Baby Girl was a reminder that a lot of things were about to change in our lives. New characters were going to come into it and that wasn't a bad thing, it just required adjustment.

Ironically, Maya and Amelie haven't been able to play together, as Eve and Amelie didn't return after the Christmas trip to visit Eve's parents. There's been no sign of any comings and goings at all. I will be relieved when their cottage goes on the market, though, as Maya keeps asking about Amelie. I think it's best she knows what's happening sooner, rather than later. Maya has had two play dates with another friend from school who lives about a ten-minute drive away, and that too is something that signals the changes to come. We'll get used to having new neighbours when the time comes and it will simply become another part of our fresh start. A new year, new beginnings.

Between Christmas and New Year I've been able to get quite a bit of work done. Baby Girl has been such a distraction for Maya and kept her fully occupied while they bond. It's like me and my shadow, funny to watch Baby Girl following Maya from room to room, as she moves around the cottage. Or Maya will sit up on her bed, reading, with Baby Girl curled up against her leg. It's been wonderful to see how close they have become and how that tiny little bundle has triggered a sense of healing within my darling little girl. She hasn't mentioned Niall at all recently and for that I'm very grateful because I was so out of my depth. I have no idea at all whether there is anything in it, or it's purely imagination. But there's always that tiny little element of doubt, isn't there? They do say that children see the world in a different way, their eyes unblinkered by what they have yet to learn. As adults we translate everything we see, tempering it with logic and factual information we have picked up along the way. Do spirits wander among us? If they do, I've yet to see any proof, but that doesn't mean it can't happen. I just don't want it happening to my daughter.

As I walk through the cottage it feels empty without Maya

and Baby Girl here, as if it's only a shell and the heart is missing. Instinctively my hand goes to my ring finger, gently rubbing the spot that is now bare.

I carry the mug back to the computer, feeling better for the short break away. I've been reading up on my notes and trying to get to the bottom of the conundrum that is Seth Greenburg. In all of the phone chats we've had so far I feel he's been evasive, always steering the conversation away from himself and focusing on Aiden's talent. I realise he's trying to steer the direction I take in this tell-all, wanting Aiden to come out of it as a working-class hero who survived a tough childhood. And yes, his raw talent was his saving grace, the thing that rescued him from the spiral of drink and drugs, but it seems to me it's still a fine line he's walking.

With a large part of the book now written in draft, the purpose of tonight is to experience the Aiden Cruise phenomenon when he performs live and to do that as a part of his audience. But I also hope to get to the bottom of why Aiden allows Seth to control virtually everything he does. Whether he likes it or not, he's a part of Aiden's story and I'm not prepared to exclude him.

After an hour I have a page of notes, questions I want to ask if the opportunity presents itself, but now it's time to get ready. How on earth I'm going to turn myself into a glam version of me, I don't know. I'm certainly not feeling at all presentable these days, although the trip to the hairdressers this morning did wonders for the hair. I toss my head, looking at the reflection in the mirror and thinking maybe, with a little carefully applied make-up, I'll do.

***

As much as thinking about Eve pulls me down at the moment, the minute I stand in front of the full-length mirror I know she was right. It might not have cost a fortune, but I look the part. The lace panel adds interest to my little black dress and Eve's fuchsia-red silk shawl, looped round in a cowl at the neckline, makes a statement. I fasten it on one shoulder with a silver brooch in the shape of an arrow. With the matching clutch bag and a dash of red lipstick to complement the nails, I'm done. Although how on earth I'm going to stand all evening in these heels, I have no idea. It's been a while since my feet have been inside anything that wasn't flat and comfy.

I hear a car pull up on the drive and when I look out I'm shocked to see it's a rather swish black limousine. A chauffeur, in a uniform and a cap, is walking towards the door. Any concerns that I'm over-dressed are instantly dispelled, and it's Eve I have to thank for that.

***

It seems the chauffeur, whose name is Brian, has been told to escort me everywhere. He doesn't leave my side from the moment we arrive at what is a veritable mansion, set in acres of parkland, in deepest Surrey. It's all a little overwhelming, to be honest, even though he does dispense with his cap. It makes him look more like a minder and it's hard not to laugh. People are actually looking at us, no doubt trying to work out whether I'm anyone famous; I just feel uncomfortable and try my best to avoid eye contact.

We bump into the dreamy Morton Wiseman, who looks every bit as good up-close as he does on the screen. Brian introduces us and we shake hands. I wish him a happy birthday, then Brian ably steers me left and right, until we find our seats. For a private party it's all rather large-scale and formal, but then who has a home with a purpose-built stage in a ballroom that can accommodate probably well over a hundred people? This is wealth – and some. Brian keeps up a running commentary, obviously having been briefed on what I need to know. When Aiden and his crew take the stage, I recognise most of the faces and Brian confirms there are a couple of guest musicians who aren't a part of the usual line-up.

I don't know if Aiden recognises me, but it seems every time my eyes are on him he's looking directly at me. Is he singing to me? At one point I feel there are only the two of us in the room and I have to admit, Seth has done a good job of getting Aiden to sell himself. He's charisma on a stick, literally. You forget the bad-boy stuff and all you see is a guy singing his heart out, loving what he does. And then, quite unexpectedly, I understand why Seth is so protective. The only place Aiden feels happy is on stage performing; it's where he doesn't have to pretend to be anyone other than the talented singer he undoubtedly is – but when the performance ends the nightmare begins.

'Ms James, Mr Greenburg has asked me to take you to meet the band as soon as they wrap up the show. This is the last number, so I suggest we start making a move towards the back of the room as it's going to get a little busy once everyone stands.'

I nod and follow Brian, feeling as if I'm being treated as if I was royalty. Seth has thought of everything in his desire to impress me. Hasn't it occurred to him that I'd feel *managed*, in much the same way he manages Aiden? The truth is the truth. However, I'm glad I came to see the band tonight because I can now really understand the magic that keeps the fans wanting more. Aiden is a powerhouse and his songs transport you to another place; his voice is a gift that makes you wish you could sing like that too. It wraps itself around you, drawing you in as if he's singing just to you and it means something more than a bunch of lyrics and notes. Often the words are sad, but the melodies are uplifting and you know it's all going to end well. Cleverly constructed, even the slow numbers grab your attention and inspire you to sing along.

'Will I get to meet Seth, along with the group?'

'I'm not sure, Ms James. Mr Greenburg didn't confirm whether or not he would be there. I can go and enquire as to his whereabouts, if you like?'

'No, that's fine, Brian. Thank you for being such a thoughtful guide. I'm sure he'll appear at some point in the evening.'

'Through here, watch your step. Aiden Cruise, this is Ms James.'

He turns and we shake hands; there's a tiredness reflected in his face that is nothing to do with his performance tonight. He's almost burnt out and I've seen it before. No wonder Seth is so worried; he wants this book written before anything else can go wrong. At the moment, Aiden has been behaving himself, with little bad press, but it's the first time in several years that there's been a hiatus as long as this. Before me I see a young man who is going through the motions. I already know that I'll get little from this interview other than polite, pre-arranged answers to the questions Seth knows I'm going to ask.

I glance around at the room full of very glamorous, and rather famous, people. I bet there are many out there who aspire to this, but from where I'm standing it seems to be a hollow victory for Aiden.

Chapter 50

Elana

Shining Brightly

In fairness, it's not that bad an evening and Aiden does relax a little. Brian disappeared after handing me over to Aiden, who then introduced me to every member of tonight's line-up. The people I'd already interviewed via Skype suddenly appeared to be a little more hesitant as I tried to strike up a conversation. I had no doubt at all that it was partly due to the fact that Aiden insisted on introducing me as 'Elana James, my official biographer'. It reminded them that anything they say might be used in the book and I realised he was probably acting under Seth's instructions. The man himself was noticeably absent, but I knew instinctively that questioning Aiden wouldn't gain me any answers.

We did talk briefly about his previous manager, when I was able to slip in a question. But Aiden only wanted to talk about the money that had allegedly gone missing just prior to having sacked him. As this is under investigation still by the police, I've already been warned not to include anything about it in the book. That came from the publishers, so I knew it was strictly off-limits.

As the night draws to a close my feet are killing me and all I want to do is slip off my shoes and curl up under a blanket. Aiden eventually escorts me to a different car, a Bentley this time, with a sumptuous cream-leather interior. He makes sure I'm seated comfortably before bidding me goodnight.

'Take it steady, driver. Ms James here is writing my soon-to-be best-selling biography, so keep the speed down. I'll say goodnight and safe trip back. Happy New Year, Elana.'

He places his hand on the driver's shoulder, giving it a pat, before closing the door.

As we head towards the motorway it's a relief to be away from all the noise and bustle. Glitz and glam is fine, in theory, but in practice I'm happy to pass on it. I've become a country girl who enjoys her home comforts more than the bright lights. It's not a world in which I'd ever choose to live and I can only imagine the pressure of being almost permanently on display.

'Did you get the answers you were seeking?' the driver asks.

Seth Greenberg's voice is unmistakable and I didn't see this coming. He purposely absented himself tonight and now he's going to grill me to find out what I've managed to uncover.

'I think you know exactly what I discovered this evening.'

'Enlighten me, please, Ms James.'

'It's Elana.'

'Then you must, of course, call me Seth. I'm interested in

what you have to say, Elana, and as we have a couple of hours to kill, what better way to pass the time?'

I have to applaud the man. He knew he couldn't control what people would say to me tonight, but he can assess the damage.

'On one condition.'

'Which is?'

'That afterwards you answer all of the questions you've been avoiding so far.'

He chuckles, clearly I'm more of a worthy opponent than he gave me credit for and this is a concession.

'What is said between us tonight is in confidence, Elana. What finds its way onto the written page is by agreement when it comes to what we discuss. Do I have your word on that?'

'Since there's no other way I'm going to get to the bottom of it, you have my word. But don't for one moment think that you can dictate to me what goes into the draft manuscript. All of the work I've done so far is already a part of the story and for that, it will be between you, Aiden and the publishers to amend as you see fit.'

'Fair enough. Please begin.'

I talk for about forty minutes straight, with hardly any interjection from Seth. I end up by telling him that I think Aiden is once more on the edge and I know that will come as no surprise to him.

He doesn't react in any way, and from the smooth drive, I'm guessing the Bentley belongs to him. It tells me a lot about this rather private man – he works hard but doesn't have problems spending his money on the trappings of wealth. Image is important to him. You don't spend two hundred thousand pounds on a brand-new Bentley to keep a low profile; you are making a statement and telling the world you are very successful at what you do.

What I don't yet know is whether this man has any Machiavellian tendencies. As far as I've been able to deduce there are only two reasons I can think of for the way he's taken over Aiden's empire. If the worst-case scenario is true, then this is about getting one last big pay cheque before he walks away and hands over the job to someone else. If, however, my gut feeling is right, then I wonder if I should be worried. We're speeding along on a motorway; it's pitch black outside and the early hours of the morning. People are either out partying, having drunk too much, or safely tucked up in bed. Should I be worried as a woman alone with someone who is little more than a stranger?

As if reading my mind, Seth turns slightly, to talk over his shoulder.

'We're coming up to a motorway service area, do you mind if I stretch my legs? We could grab a coffee. I like to take frequent breaks when I'm driving. No point in taking risks.'

I agree. I know how easily accidents can happen and how lives can be ruined.

'By all means.' I was already beginning to wish I'd visited the powder room before I left the venue. Seth is the perfect gentleman, opening the car door for me and offering his arm. He's well-dressed, as I expected, every inch of him immaculate. He's a little older than I'd first thought; seeing him up close

I notice his hair has more than just a hint of silver running through it.

'A rather surreal place to be visiting as a new year dawns, but life is full of unexpected surprises.'

His eyes flash over me in an appreciative way and for some reason it isn't offensive, merely acknowledging the effort I've made.

'I know tonight hasn't been easy for you, Elana. I appreciate you putting your trust in me. That it was necessary. Now let's meet back in the café area in about five minutes. I'm delighted you don't feel I'm kidnapping you and calling in here is my attempt at making you see that you are perfectly safe. Out of your comfort zone, I'm sure, but shortly I'll be escorting you over the threshold of Bay Tree Cottage, and by then you'll know everything.'

***

This man is a real gentleman; it isn't a facade he presents to get him what he wants and that is becoming very plain to me.

'The truth, Elana, is that I'm Aiden's father – the one who walked away and left his ex-wife alone to bring up their son. Of course, it wasn't quite as simple as that. Molly was always besotted with bands and she was my introduction into a world that was previously unknown to me. What I didn't know was that Molly was, well, there's no polite way of saying this, a groupie. In those days it was almost acceptable, but it goes without saying that it wasn't acceptable to me. Molly and I divorced, I gave her virtually every penny I had so that she could start a new life and we could go our separate ways.

'The theatre was always my first passion and I'm a natural-born organiser, so eventually I worked my way up to become a producer. Molly and I lost contact, she reverted to her maiden name and Aiden never knew he was once a Greenburg. To her I was dead, pure and simple, and to my son I was this unknown person who had abandoned him, leaving them with nothing. I'd like to say he had a good childhood, but you know that wasn't the case. But even with all the disadvantages weighing against him, my son's natural talent shone out. He might be a walking disaster at times, but you saw it for your-self tonight, he also has a talent so real it has to be God-given.'

I nod.

'Yes. It's tangible and that's the difference between someone being merely a good performer and a true star. The X-factor. Does Aiden know, I mean, is that why you came back into his life?'

'Yes, he does. I didn't tell him at first because I knew what his reaction would be. I could see what was happening to him. Every little struggle made front-page news and so I walked away from a very successful career to help get his life back on track. Gradually, I managed to distance him from the bottom-feeders, the people who gather close to grab what they can and then run off.'

I can see by Seth's body language that this isn't some story he's spinning for me. He's on a mission to safeguard his son.

'So it's true that his previous manager stole most of his money?'

Seth nods. 'That's pretty much what happened, and how much is recoverable is anyone's guess. Maybe nothing. Aiden was too off his head to know what was happening. He's better now, of course, clean most of the time, but he's worn down. He needs to take a break away from the public eye. The plan is to get him back into the studio, because that's where he's happiest. Usually when someone launches a biography they do a big publicity tour, but Aiden isn't up to that. To be frank, we need a big injection of cash to fund his next two albums and after that I'm hoping he'll be raring to get out there again. If he loses the spark the tour falls flat and then overnight it's all over. The fans can tell, you see.'

'I'm sorry, I don't understand. Surely the book won't sell if Aiden isn't there promoting it?'

What am I missing in Seth's master plan, because this looks like only half a plan to me?

'At the moment we've kept a lid on all of this; no one knows I'm Aiden's father, not even our inner circle. Molly has, once more, been paid off, but even she wouldn't hurt her son for the sake of a few thousand pounds. There is no one else to break the news. That's why we're breaking the news in his biography. If Aiden isn't around, I will be and now I'm the accepted front man this twist will have all his fans wanting the whole story. I face the fans, Aiden has his precious studio time to rediscover his passion, and in the meantime the money rolls in to fund it.'

'Pure genius. You must love your son very much to put yourself in the firing line. You're going to face some tough questions, Seth.'

'As parents we put everything on the line for our kids, don't we?'

His comment unnerves me, just when I was beginning to feel relaxed, compassionate, even.

'You know I have a child?'

'I know everything about you, Elana. You have no axes to grind, a reputable ghost writer with nothing to hide. If you come under investigation by the press they'll find nothing except a devoted, hard-working mother. I'm sorry if that sounds cold, but this is my son's life we're talking about. If anything breaks before he's made his escape, it will push him over the edge and I can't let that happen. I failed him as a child; I won't fail him now.'

I push away the coffee cup, tiredness no longer an issue as the caffeine pumps around my body. I'm wide awake and my head is spinning.

'I understand. This isn't going to be easy to write, but once I've pulled something together for this section of the book I'll send you a draft to look at. The Molly angle is going to be a tough issue, so I'll need your help to get that right. Obviously the facts are what they are, but there are legal implications. You can rest assured that nothing we've discussed will go any further until the publishers press the go button.'

'Appreciated, Elana. Professionalism is one thing, but I knew you'd bring a whole other side to this – compassion. We're entering into what is little more than a circus ring; I know the public will be getting value for money. My family will have to pay the price for the return we so badly need to give Aiden back his future. If we can do that in as dignified a way as possible, I'd be very grateful. I'm not trying to absolve myself of any blame and I'll stick to the truth. I was very young and you had to be there to understand how badly things were deteriorating in front of Aiden's eyes. All I'm asking of you is that you don't sell out; don't get pulled into off-the-record interviews and exposés. Whatever you are offered, I'll double it for your complete discretion and silence.'

I can't take offence, simply because this is the reality of the world in which Seth has to function. It's not a world I'd ever want to be a part of and I find it quite shocking.

'My contract and fee from the publishers covers that, Seth. I'm simply doing a job and I have no intention of becoming a part of the problem. I really hope this works out, for all of you.'

'I do, too. Thank you, Elana. Somehow I knew you'd understand.'

A part of me already suspected that Seth was Aiden's father and not some scurrilous, money-orientated control freak. For peace of mind I needed him to confirm that what he was doing was for all the right reasons. I knew from my research he'd had a very notable career before managing Aiden. But there was always that slight chance he had a personal agenda that wasn't in Aiden's best interests. Money didn't seem to be a motive, but you never know for sure. It seems to me that out of everyone, he has the most to lose when it comes to reputation.

Chapter 51

Elana

Letting Go of Something I Never Really Had

I arrive home exhausted, collapsing into bed without even taking the time to remove my make-up. It's light when the doorbell wakes me with a start. I have absolutely no idea what time it is until I check the clock and see it's after two in the afternoon. Scrambling to cover myself with my bath robe, I head downstairs, hoping my bed hair and smeared make-up don't make me look like a mad woman.

'Morning, this is a surprise.'

It's Luke and he's carrying a small strip of wood. As soon as he realises he's woken me up, he looks embarrassed, but I wave him inside.

'Don't mind me, it was a late one, as I expected.'

'Ah, I forgot it was the party night. If I'd remembered I would have left this until another time, but I happened to be passing and it's one thing less to carry round in the pick-up.

Don't mind me – it will only take a couple of minutes to fit it and then I'll leave you in peace.'

'No, it's fine. I'll pop the kettle on. I'll ... um ... just go and splash some water on my face, first. I'm glad you woke me, I had no idea it was so late!'

'What time did you get in?'

'Just after five a.m.'

I notice when he takes off his boots there are no holes in his socks and it makes me smile.

Luke makes his way into the sitting room and I walk off towards the utility. Yikes! What I see reflected back in the mirror is scarier than most Halloween masks. Freshly scrubbed, I run my damp fingers through my hair and at least look a little refreshed. I lean in – actually, my skin looks glowing. Maybe a glitzy night out was just what I needed to remind me I'm in the land of the living. And Luke is just a few feet away. Whoa there, lady – this isn't your style and you know it.

'Coffee's ready.' I look in on Luke and he's just straightening up, surveying the finished job with pride.

'Damn good job, even if I say so myself.'

We stand side by side looking at the trim around the fire grate.

'And the service is second to none. I mean, it's New Year's Day. Happy New Year, Luke. I hope it brings you everything you're looking for.'

When I turn to look at him, a good-natured smile on my face, what I see is a troubled look in his eyes. I frown, not sure why my innocent remark should cause him concern.

'Elana, is it my imagination, or are we having a moment, here?'

Oh no, I'm flirting and I don't even know it. Now get yourself out of this.

'To be honest, I think we've had a few moments, Luke, but it's all about timing, isn't it?' He nods, sadly.

Following me through to the kitchen, we sit opposite each other, toying with the mugs in front of us. It feels safer having this conversation sitting down. I wish now I'd run upstairs and thrown on some jeans, but here I am in my bath robe sitting opposite a guy who has no idea how attractive and wonderful he is. Wonderful for some young, unencumbered woman who can still look at the world through that hazy veil of love and hopeful expectation. Not someone who has been to hell and back, constantly fearful of what might happen next.

'So you are saying the timing isn't right?'

'I wish it was, but it's more than that, Luke. I'm no cougar and you are no toy boy. I'm hoping Christmas went well for you?'

'Much better than I'd hoped, given the circumstances. Joe was so happy and we all ended up at my parents' house the day after.'

He's such a great guy that he deserves to find happiness and the family life he longs to have. As much as I'm now ready and willing, it would be wrong of me to pretend the age difference between us doesn't matter. I don't want to be the voice of experience in a relationship. It has to be an equal partnership.

'The best lessons in life are learnt the hard way, I'm afraid.'

'You're pushing me away, but I think it might be for all of the wrong—'

I put up my hand.

'Don't say it, please. As you said, we've had a "moment"

345

and it's reminded me that life can be exciting and unexpected. If we'd taken it further while we are both so vulnerable, who knows what the fallout would have been? Ten years doesn't seem like much if you say it quickly, but that's a lot of living – years you still have in front of you when I've already been there and done that. You deserve to have the opportunity of building your future with someone who is experiencing it all alongside you for the first time.'

He's slouched in his chair, coffee mug as empty as his eyes.

'You know, Elana. You are a real lady. Even when it comes to letting a guy down, you do it in such a way as to preserve his pride. You deserve someone who will whisk you off your feet – show you what an amazing person you are and take care of everything for you. To be honest, I wish that was me, but I know it isn't.'

Our hands meet across the table, fingertips touching.

'Some moments are special, Luke; a few wistful seconds that raise a smile and a warm feeling whenever life makes us sad. You will always be my moment to treasure.'

As our eyes meet we both start laughing. I follow him to the door; he turns and wraps his arms around me, hugging me so tightly it takes my breath away. When he pulls back it is with reluctance.

'I think I'll get Dad to put someone else on the conservatory job next door. It's just easier if I'm not around, if you know what I mean. But if you ever need me, I'm a phone call away. Always.'

I close the door, slumping back against it, feeling drained and in shock that I've just let Luke walk out of my life.

1st December, eleven months later—

Sometimes you have to get a little lost in order to eventually find the right path.

Chapter 52

Elana

The Perfect, Gentle, Man

'Mum, you need to hurry up. What's taking you so long?' Maya's voice drifts upstairs, disturbing my deliberations.

Seth is taking us out for a pre-Christmas surprise, whatever that means. What on earth do I wear? It's a cold day, the early-morning frost still hasn't fully melted and the valley looks crisp and almost snow-covered. Something warm, I think. Pulling on some skinny jeans and a thick, cable- knit jumper, I quickly run the brush through my hair. Hearing the doorbell and voices, it's clear Seth has arrived and I can hear them chattering away quite happily.

'I'll be down in five, just sorting my make-up.' I hear a muffled response from Seth, as Maya has probably taken him into the sitting room.

Lowering myself onto the stool in front of the dressing table, I begin applying a little foundation cream. As I add a touch of colour to my cheeks and begin applying mascara, I reflect upon the changes that brought us to today. Seth's friendship becoming a part of our lives has been a total surprise, and looking back he just seems to have stepped into it without any particular motive. Other than loneliness, which is a common denominator for so many people out there. Admittedly we had a lot of contact in the run-up to the launch of the book and lots of face-to-face meetings here, but even after that he still kept coming around. He treats Maya as if she is an adult, which she loves, and I realise that he's a man used to dealing with people. He puts everyone at ease without making a big deal out of it. He ensured I walked away with a big bonus, enough to finish the work on the cottage. Just knowing the money is sitting in my account is a relief, although when exactly I'm going to have time to progress that, I have no idea.

When the revelation that Seth was Aiden's father hit the news, the press was merciless in their pursuit of an in-depth interview. Seth dealt with that in a very controlled manner, presenting the facts and never, as far as I was aware, laying any blame at the door of his ex-wife. But he also didn't make excuses for his own actions, accepting that people had the right to their own opinions.

Aiden is still in the recording studio, having released a new album, which is doing well. Instead of touring, he's now producing an album for one of the hot new bands tipped to be big in the charts next year. Seth seems a lot less concerned about him these days and I think being out of the spotlight has given Aiden back a feeling of control. Maybe record-producing is the way forward for him and it could be his saviour.

At first I thought Seth's attention was merely gratitude. Then came the deliveries of flowers, chocolates and, ultimately, an invitation to dinner. He slid into our lives with ease, doing what he does best and that's to smooth out life's little wrinkles. I've since picked up two more ghost-writing jobs off the back of Seth's recommendation and work is coming at me from all sides. I'm content, really, without having made any particular effort; life just seems to have settled down.

'Here she is, looking gorgeous as ever.'

Seth steps forward, taking my hands and raising them to his lips.

'Are you ladies ready?'

'Well, I've been ready for ages, Seth, so as usual it's Mum holding us up.'

'Sorry, darling. Will you be warm enough in that, or do you think you should wear something a little thicker?' I glance at her thin, woollen tights, little black shorts and electric-blue sweatshirt, thinking she looks like one of the kids from a TV programme. When did my daughter turn into a style icon?

'Stop fussing, Mum. I'll be wearing a thick coat and boots. Do you think you're going to be warm enough?'

I raise an eyebrow, conscious that Seth has turned away and is smothering a laugh.

Maya is looking, and sounding, more and more like a mini-me than ever, these days. She's very opinionated at times and rather bossy – always quick with a reply to everything.

We don our coats and boots, Seth checking his watch. 'Well, I guess we are ready, then.'

As I'm locking the front door our neighbours, Grace and Martin, walk down the drive and we wave out.

'Morning Maya, Seth, Elana. Off somewhere nice?'

'It's a surprise,' Maya informs them.

'Well, stay warm. We've just walked down the hill and into the village. Once you're moving it's not too bad, but if you stand still for a while the cold really sets in.'

I watch as they descend the path to Hillside View, fleetingly thinking about Eve and Amelie, and wondering what's happening in their lives now.

Seth places his arm around me as we walk up to his car, Maya several steps in front of us.

'I hope you like ice skating,' he whispers. I look at him and smile.

'Maya will be delighted. Thank you, Seth.'

He squeezes me gently and opening the car door, takes my arm as I sink into the back seat.

'Your chauffeur is at your service, m'lady.' Maya and I both laugh; he says that every time I get into the car and it reminds me of New Year's Eve. Maya, as usual, sits next to him in the front and they chatter as we head into town, towards the Christmas outdoor skating rink.

I switch off from their conversation as Maya asks a lot of questions and Seth, being very knowledgeable, is good at giving detailed, yet easy to understand, explanations. Maya asks Seth which are his favourite places to visit in London and she's fascinated as he talks to her about the museums and art galleries. My thoughts drift off, who knows where, but suddenly Seth's head turns slightly and Maya spins in her seat, to face me.

'Did you hear, that, Mum? Seth says today is special.'

'Special?' Clearly, I've missed something.

'You'll have to wait and see. First things, first.' He gives one of his enigmatic smiles, that kindly face instilling a sense of everything being right with the world. I doubt there is anything with which Seth couldn't cope, or resolve quite satisfactorily. His charm and the way he interacts with people seems to make every little plan fall into place. He's the equivalent of a meditation session, inspiring a sense of tranquility.

'Well, I can't wait to see where we're going.'

Maya's excitement is building and when, eventually, we park she's already ahead of us.

'We're going to the outdoor ice rink, I know it!' She exclaims. This time last year she would have been dancing around and throwing her hands up in the air, but now she's more dignified, befitting the actions of a seven-and-a-half-year-old. Why do they want to grow up so quickly?

'I wish I had my own ice skates, Mum.' Maya's voice borders on that girlie-whinging tone. The *I want it now* one.

Seth glances at me for my reaction, more than ready to whisk her off to the shops immediately.

'I think that's something for Santa's list, maybe.'

He nods, acknowledging my wish that Maya doesn't think she can simply ask and have whatever she wants, when she wants it.

'Mum. Santa doesn't exist and it's pretty silly trying to keep up the pretence. You're old enough to know better.'

Seth smiles at me and I grin back at him.

'So I like a little Christmas magic, who doesn't? A bit like making a wish when you blow out the candles on your birthday cake – what harm does it do?'

'But it doesn't mean anything, Mum. Honestly, sometimes you are so embarrassing.'

She walks off, leaving Seth to take my arm and we follow her, shaking our heads and trying not to laugh out loud.

'You're not alone in enjoying a little Christmas magic, Elana. I hope I can make today rather magical for you both.'

As our eyes meet he hugs my arm a little tighter and I feel content. His friendship means a lot and I know how much he looks forward to his visits. Whatever treat he has in store after the ice skating, I know we'll enjoy it. He always seems to find just the perfect little restaurant to visit, the very best places, where it's an experience to remember. Seth doesn't do mundane, or make-do, he likes to celebrate life by making every moment count. Wealth makes that more attainable, obviously, but it still requires a lot of thought and effort on his part. There's a lot I admire about this man, whose professional persona tends to mask that very caring disposition.

Chapter 53

Elana

Life's Missed Opportunities

This is Maya's treat and I refuse to be coaxed into ice skates, preferring to let Seth and Maya share the experience. Having a quasi father figure in her life is exactly what she needs at the moment; someone I can trust to say the right things when those awkward questions pop into her head. Seth is not only diplomatic, but he seems to understand she feels something is missing in her life. It's reciprocal, he assures me, as it allows him to switch off a little from work. As he said, once, what else does he have to do? I felt sad for him, thinking that if things had been different maybe he would have grandchildren by now.

Watching them whizz around at much faster a speed than I'd ever manage to achieve, it's wonderful to see them laughing and enjoying themselves. She insists on letting go of his hand and while I hold my breath for a split second, I realise his arm is hovering, ready to reconnect if needed.

I sink down into the chair, feeling happy and content, putting my head back a little and closing my eyes. The warmth of the winter sunshine isn't strong, but it's pleasant and it's nice to relax and listen to the busy vibe around me.

'Elana?'

Hearing someone up close say my name and sounding rather shocked, makes me immediately open my eyes. I look up to see Luke and Joe standing, hand in hand, before me. Joe is no longer a shy toddler, but looks at me curiously, then glances back up at his dad.

'Luke? And Joe, what a little man you've become!'

Joe stares at me with seemingly no sense of recognition.

'Joe, this is Elana. She makes the best gingerbread in the world.'

Joe smiles, and I jump up, my stomach suddenly doing somersaults. Luke steps forward and I accept his kiss on the cheek. He looks flushed, but gives me a dazzling smile.

'Well, this is a surprise! How are you?'

His words come out in a rush and it's clear he's pleased to see me. We make eye contact and my heart misses a beat. It's been a long time and it feels like forever.

'Good, and you?' It's inadequate, but it's all I can manage while I collect my thoughts.

'Great.'

Now it's awkward. We are looking at each other expectantly, but the silence grows. Joe lets go of Luke's hand, taking a step forward to press up against the guard rail and watch the skaters.

'You're the last person I expected to bump into today,' Luke's smile just seems to grow in intensity.

'Same here. You look good. How's Lisa?'

'No idea, but hopefully she found Mr Right.' His smile is dismissive.

'And Anita?' The moment I finish speaking I wish I could rewind.

'Good, I think.'

Rewind. Rewind. Let me start again.

His eyes wander across to Joe, and then he looks back at me.

'She got back together with Chris and then went to live in Italy when Chris's firm moved him out there. It was a big step for her, leaving Joe with me, but her mum takes Joe over to stay during the school holidays. We figured it was the best arrangement, as I get quality time with him every evening and weekend. My mum does the ferrying to and from nursery while I'm at work and she treasures her time with Joe. So everyone wins. I couldn't begrudge Anita her happiness and she's a different person now. What's good for Anita is also good for Joe. Besides, we're having a great time – aren't we buddy? Just us two guys taking care of each other.'

My heart is thumping as I take in what he's saying. So maybe it really is still just Luke and Joe. I feel sad for him, but clearly he has moved on and is in a happy place now. He looks amazing – there's even an air of confidence about him that wasn't there before.

'Sorry, I didn't mean to— You look happy now and that's all that matters.'

'Is Maya skating?'

'Yes, we're here with Seth. You remember Seth?'

'The agent guy? I read some of the headlines after that book came out. Quite a story. You handled it well. I even bought a copy.'

'You did? Well, it was certainly a turning point for me and now I'm so busy there aren't enough hours in the day.'

He shifts, scuffing the toe of his shoe against the rough concrete floor, making no attempt to pick the conversation back up.

'How's business?' It seems like the safe thing to say.

'Good. Dad decided to take early retirement. He hasn't been well and he's taking things easy. I run the family business and am office-based now. We've taken on five new guys and we're expanding the area we cover. I've even installed a new computer system to automate job allocation and it keeps our customers updated by text prior to their work commencing. Focusing on customer satisfaction and communication is getting us a lot of word-of-mouth recommendations.'

I can hear the excitement in his voice; he's taking it to the next level and has found something that makes him feel as though he's doing something worthwhile.

'It's great to hear you're putting those IT skills to good use, Luke. You sound like you're in a good place and you deserve it.'

Suddenly Maya's voice is behind me and I turn to see Seth and Maya standing the other side of the barrier, talking to Joe.

'Joe won't remember you, Maya, as he was too young. Hasn't he grown?'

'Yes, Mum. He's really big now. Hi, Luke.'

Luke moves forward and hi-five's with Maya.

'And look at you. You'll soon be taller than your mum.'

Seth is watching with interest.

'Sorry. Seth, this is Luke. He did some of the work on the cottage and now runs the company following his father's retirement.'

The guys lean in to shake hands.

'Congratulations, Luke. Always best to start from the bottom up. Makes running things a lot easier if you know what goes on, on the ground. Are you skating today?'

Luke nods. 'Yep. It's Joe's first time.'

It's awkward and I look at Seth, hoping he'll jump in.

'Well, I think these ladies might be a little hungry by now, so we're off to eat. Enjoy your first go at skating, Joe. It's great fun!'

As Seth and Maya head off to the disembarking point to take off their skates, it leaves Joe, Luke, and me alone to say our goodbyes.

'It was nice catching up,' Luke jumps in before I can think of anything suitable to say as a parting comment.

'Yes, and I'm so glad it turned out well for you in the end.' My heart is beating so loudly I wonder if he can hear it, too.

Luke hesitates, then Joe grabs his hand. 'Can we skate now, Daddy?'

I laugh, 'Go on, don't keep the little guy waiting.'

'Goodbye, Elana. Glad we bumped into each other. You look amazing, as always.'

I make myself turn and walk away. If I let him lean in for a goodbye kiss I'm going to throw my arms around him and make a complete and utter fool of myself in front of everyone. Keep your back straight, Elana, and put one foot in front of the other. Just keep walking. Luke will always be the biggest regret of your life, but don't make it even worse by upsetting his new-found happiness.

Chapter 54

Elana

What More Could I Wish For?

'Where are we going?' I glance across at Seth and notice that Maya is looking up at him expectantly. He smiles down at her and they exchange a look, which excludes me.

'Somewhere very special indeed and it's only a short walk away. Ladies, step this way.'

We walk past the modern shopping-centre complex and beyond, to the small back streets that were the original centre of this once small market town. The old buildings are quaint and full of character; most are either antique shops or up-market boutiques now.

Seth stops in front of a small, French restaurant with the quaintest shop front. Either side of the door are two enormous planters with beautifully clipped bay trees. Even in December, the window boxes lining the windowsills are full of winter greenery, some covered in red berries. It's simply enchanting and I watch Maya's face as she takes in every little detail.

'Are we having lunch here?' She asks, excitedly.

'Oh,' Seth bends down to Maya's level, 'it's a little more than just lunch. Shall we go inside?'

He stands, but before he can reach out for the door, a waiter appears. He's dressed in black, with a crisp, white cotton apron tied around his waist reaching down to a foot above his ankles. He sports a handlebar moustache and his pin-tuck shirt is reminiscent of a time long gone. We head inside and it's simply perfect. Empty, but perfect.

It's nearly one o'clock and you would expect a restaurant as up-market as this to be buzzing. Instead, it's empty, which serves only to emphasise the elegant wood panelling and stripped oak floorboards. Miniature chandeliers grace the ceiling, showering little prisms of light in gentle cascades onto the tables beneath them.

Aside from the waiter walking ahead of us, we are the only ones here. I glance at Seth, who simply smiles and nods, indicating that we should continue walking.

Another two waiters, similarly dressed, appear to seat us at our table. It's towards the back of the restaurant and a large area around it has been cleared. The pristine white linen tablecloth, the sparkling crystal glassware and silver cutlery gleam with a lavish attention to detail. Maya looks entranced.

The waiters stand ready to assist us into our chairs, pulling them out at precisely the same moment in a well-practised drill. We take our seats in unison; Maya's eyes are like saucers, the sheer elegance of the setting captivating her attention.

Maya starts laughing. 'This is amazing, Seth. Are we the only ones having lunch here today?'

I look at Seth quizzically.

'Yes, they've opened up especially for us. There's another surprise to come and I'm going to have to ask your lovely mum to indulge me. Elana, what do think?'

I frown. 'It rather depends on what I'm indulging.' I try to keep a serious face and Maya looks at me expectantly.

'It's a surprise Mum, you can't be cross. And it would be ungrateful to say *no* to a surprise.'

I pretend to give it some thought, and then nod my head, wondering what on earth Seth has planned.

Two of the waiters walk to the back wall of the restaurant, where a large white cloth is draped over something the size of a small table. Seth nods his head and they whisk away the cloth. Standing there is a full-size keyboard on a stand, with a matching stool.

Maya squeals, taking me back to when she was very small and being cool wasn't even in her vocabulary.

'Am I forgiven, Elana?' Seth asks.

'Mum, you have to say *yes*. Just say *yes*.' Maya is already half out of her seat.

'Yes.'

She jumps up, almost toppling her chair. Rushing up to Seth, Maya throws her arms around him for a brief second, then runs towards the keyboard.

I give him a look of exasperation.

'It's not even Christmas!' But I also can't hide the grateful smile as I take in Maya's excitement. Already her fingers are sliding over the keys, softly playing one of her favourite Christmas tunes.

'Seth, it's too much. You really are so kind, I don't know quite what to say. No one has ever done anything like this for Maya, before. It's overwhelming.'

I reach out and touch his hand.

'It's nothing, Elana. She enjoys her little keyboard and I'm all for encouraging musical talent. It's time she stepped it up a little. She plays beautifully.'

I sit back, watching my daughter in this atmospheric and surreal setting, which feels truly magical. Seth is right, Elana is a natural when she sits in front of a keyboard.

'Niall was in a band when he was at school; he played bass guitar and keyboard. It's something I've never spoken about to Maya, but that's where her musical interests come from – definitely not from me.'

Niall would be so proud and here I am, sharing a special moment with Seth. Suddenly my stomach turns over and when I look back at Seth he has a small box in his hand.

'I wanted to make this day special for you both. For the most part, the world isn't a bad place to be, but at times it can be a rather sad place. Loneliness can make that feel like solitary confinement and that's a real shame, because it can also be a place where miracles really can happen.' He places the box on the table in front of me and all I can do is sit here, knowing that this time it's going to break his heart.

'Seth, we've been over this and you said you understood; that being friends would be enough and reassuring me that you knew it could never work between us. I love you like the dear friend you have become, but a heart requires more than that.'

He sits forward, taking my hand in his.

'I know what I said, but I lied. I've never given up hope that I'd grow on you. Oh, I knew it was a long shot and that twenty years is a big age difference. But I want to take care of you and Maya. It makes me happy.'

I'm sitting here, facing Seth, with a lump in my throat. I don't want to hurt this wonderful man and yet my senses are still tingling from the memory of seeing Luke and Joe. My heart had leapt with joy when I saw them and saying goodbye left me feeling bereft.

'Oh Seth, you deserve so much more than that. You are a passionate man and you deserve to have that returned in equal measure. Age is nothing, I've come to realise. It's about what's in here.' I place my hand on my heart and I can see the hope that shone in his eyes a few moments ago begin to fade.

'I knew the moment that I saw you look at Luke what your answer was going to be. But I had to try one last time, Elana. I couldn't help myself. If there was even the slightest glimmer of hope that you would come to look at me as more than just a friend, it was a risk worth taking. I hope Luke realises the mistake he's made.'

My face feels like a mask.

'You didn't tell him how you feel about him, did you?'

I hang my head. 'There's nothing to tell.'

Seth curls my fingers tenderly within his hand.

'Then you are fooling yourself, Elana. Life wants you to be happy; there's nothing to fear in reaching out for it. You told me he was too young for you and yet moments ago you said that you've come to realise that age is nothing. If you were in love with me, as you are with Luke, then I know you would be saying *yes* to me now. I love you enough to let you go, but it has to be for a very good reason. Put your indecision and fear behind you now. It's time, Elana.'

I lean forward and kiss his cheek, knowing that the only way I can help Seth is to encourage him to move on. I hope what I've given him is a little self-belief in the fact that he's a man who deserves to be loved, in every sense of the word.

Chapter 55

Luke

Being a Professional

I knew Elana would eventually pick up the pieces of her life, but seeing her and Maya with that Seth guy was a shock. It threw me and I have no idea what I said to her, because all I could think was 'well, it was always going to happen, so don't pretend to be shocked'. Besides, I'm not a part of her life and it's been almost a year since I've seen her.

When Chris stepped back in, offering to whisk Anita away to a foreign climate and a better lifestyle than she had over here, as torn as she was to leave Joe behind, she couldn't say *no*. Chris makes her happy. I made no attempt at all to dissuade her, but I was also very careful not to encourage her in any way. It had to be her decision. I had nothing to lose and everything to gain. Everything.

And so life settled down into a new routine. Shortly afterwards, Dad was in and out of hospital with heart problems and ended up having triple bypass surgery. He's on the mend now and doing well, but it meant that virtually overnight I was in charge and having to run the company single-handedly. Mum was back and forth to the hospital and in between times ferrying Joe to and from nursery. I took on an older woman with secretarial experience to answer the phone, handle the general admin work and act as my assistant. In fact, Janice virtually runs the office now, leaving me to sort out the business side of things and organise the guys.

A tap on the door almost makes me jump, I was so deep in thought. Greg's head appears in view sporting his usual, lop-sided grin.

'Just to let you know that it looks like we'll be finished a day early on this job. Leeson's delivered the outstanding items on Friday. So we'll wrap it up today, barring anything unforeseen occurring.'

I look at him and blink, trying hard to shut off my thoughts and concentrate on his words. He steps inside, shutting the door behind him.

'Are you alright? You look confused.'

I nod, indicating for him to take a seat.

'I bumped into Elana James, yesterday, at the outdoor skating rink.'

'Mate, I thought all of that was behind you?'

'It was ... I mean, it is.'

He looks at me in exasperation.

'You know, Luke, you don't make things easy for yourself, do you? I know the only reason you stopped dating Lisa was because of how you felt about Elana. That was madness, mate, as – nice as she is – you admitted she'd virtually rejected you.

Lisa is still moping about, hoping you'll change your mind. Cheryl says it's a waste that you're on your own. I mean, I know guys who would fight to be in the position you're in. Cheryl says you're a catch ... not that I can see it, of course.' He starts laughing, but I know that he's concerned and wanting to lighten the moment. Greg doesn't do heavy emotion and he has this uncanny ability to float through life seemingly with ease. Fortunately, Cheryl is a good woman and exactly what he needs.

I groan inwardly. After Anita left I was raw emotionally, but all of my attention was focused on Joe and getting things set up so he had a routine. With Mum's help things were soon running smoothly. When Greg dragged me out for a drink, several months later, and Lisa suddenly reappeared, I knew his intentions were well meant. I just wished he hadn't done it. Yes, we had a few dates, but my heart wasn't in it. On the face of it, it should have worked between us, but the chemistry just wasn't there for me. She wasn't Elana and that was that. Then work took over and with being a single parent my life was pretty much full. I disciplined myself not to think of Elana, and not to wonder 'what if?' What was the point?

'Do yourself a favour, Luke, and phone her. I have no idea what was said yesterday, but I can tell that it isn't over for you, for whatever reason. Yesterday just stirred it all up, once again. Talk to her and tell her how you feel and maybe when she rejects you this time around it will finally sink in.'

There's another tap on the door and Janice pops her head around.

'I have a Mrs James on line one, wanting a quote for some

replacement windows.' Janice looks at Greg, who looks at me.

'Time I left you to it, I think. Good luck, boss.' He gives Janice a little salute on his way out and she giggles.

'You can put Mrs James through, Janice. Thank you.'

As soon as the door is shut my palms start sweating. I wipe them on my jeans and when the phone buzzes, I pick up the receiver, taking a deep breath to steady my voice.

'Elana, how can I help?'

'Morning, Luke. I should have mentioned it to you yesterday. I'm ready to go ahead with the replacement windows and wondered if you could pop round to measure up and give me a quote? I'd ideally like the work done in early spring, if that's possible.'

'We're working about four months in advance at the moment, so I think that's do-able. When is it convenient for me to call in?'

My heart is pounding, almost drowning out her reply.

'I'm here all day today and tomorrow. After that I have to go up to London for a meeting. So, the sooner the better, but anytime you can fit me in will be fine.'

Greg is right, it's time I finally put an end to this little fantasy I can't keep from creeping into my head. Maybe then I can move on.

'I'll pop around later this morning once the guys have all checked in.'

'See you later, then. Thanks, Luke.'

As I put the phone down I slink forward, letting my head bang down on the desk out of sheer desperation. Am I just really, really stupid, or is there something wrong with me? Dad would have relished the idea of going out to do a quote to help out and I could have avoided this encounter with relative ease. Elana needs her windows replaced; she's not doing this because she wants to see me. If that was the case she would have said something yesterday – suggested a coffee on neutral territory, or something.

Besides, Seth is perfect for her. The irony of the fact that he's a good couple of decades older than her isn't lost on me. But it's not the same the other way around, is it? I could instantly see that he's very protective of both Elana and Maya, which showed in his body language and the way he moved things along. He was curious about me, I saw that, but quickly appraised the situation as merely one of a matter of exchanging a few pleasantries.

You're a fool, Luke, and you know it. Get yourself to Bay Tree Cottage and see for yourself that there's nothing at all to read into this. It's another job, that's all. Maybe assign it to Ted, rather than Greg. Elana prefers not to be interrupted when she's working and Ted isn't a talker, that's for sure.

Chapter 56

Luke

A Walking, Living, Breathing Disaster

Standing in front of Bay Tree Cottage transports me back. I half expect to see Eve and Amelie walking up the drive. A lot has changed in the last year, but Bay Tree Cottage looks almost exactly the same. I can see that the outside has now been tidied up and Elana has done a lot of replanting. It looks welcoming and inviting. Just like Elana. You're an idiot, Luke. You keep telling yourself that you have moved on. Now you are a business man, turning a good profit and keeping a dozen men employed, but it doesn't mean anything, does it? You are also a single dad who is raising a young son, albeit with the help of his own parents, but you're doing a good job. It's time to be the professional you are, exude confidence and get the customer to sign on the dotted line. What are you scared of? You know Ted will do a good job and you'll have one more happy customer to add to the list. End of story.

The door opens and suddenly she's there in front of me,

once more gesturing me inside her home. 'Luke, thanks so much for coming.'

Every single thought I had when I was standing outside is dead in the water. Elana, I want to pick you up and tell the world you're mine.

'Hi, Elana. My, you've made a few changes in here.' As I slip off my shoes and step through into the dining-room section of the open-plan area, it's radically different. For one thing, there's no office area.

Elana follows my gaze.

'I work from the third bedroom, now. It's cosier and means the dining room feels much more special. Eating in the kitchen was always a little cramped.'

All of the furniture is new; nothing original remains. The floor still looks as if it's just been laid.

'Well, all credit to you, it doesn't look like the same cottage.'

It's obvious Seth enjoys the finer things in life. This is a dining room befitting those special occasions; perfect for entertaining people over a lavish dinner.

Standing here holding my briefcase, as if I'm a stranger, a random salesman on a routine visit, hits me hard. Is this what I needed to kill all hope? A sense of total disconnect as reality dawns?

'Shall I leave you to it?' Elana asks, already turning away from me and talking over her shoulder. 'I'll put the kettle on. When you're done come through to the dining room and we can discuss the options over coffee.'

She's cool, calm and collected. My nerves are jangling like wind chimes on a windy day and I head off upstairs to make a start. It takes a lot longer than normal as my mind keeps wandering and I have to keep re-measuring to make sure I don't make a mistake. The last room to do is the sitting room and Elana doesn't even look up as I walk past her, she has her head in a book.

The moment I enter the room I see it. The little music box with the bay tree on top is sitting in the centre of the mantelpiece above the fire. It's the only item on the shelf and because of the connection it seems to dominate the room. So it's a nice little piece, she's hardly going to hide it away in the cupboard just because I gave it to her. If it sparked any emotion in her at all, then she would have put it away – out of sight, out of mind.

I finish measuring up and settle myself down on the sofa to work out the various costs, depending on the type of finish Elana selects. It's easier to do that in here, unwatched, where I feel calmer and less under pressure. Incredibly, the windows have held up very well, but once the new ones are in this cottage will feel complete. Baby Girl jumps up on the sofa, to settle down next to me and I stop to smooth her beautiful fur. It's hard to believe how much she's grown. She purrs contentedly, trusting that this stranger is no threat. She's almost unrecognisable from the tiny little kitten, mewing in the corner of the utility that day, as Maya approached her in awe.

Reluctantly, I gather everything up and walk back into the dining area, standing awkwardly in front of Elana. She has already placed a second mug on the table, in the seat across from her.

'Take a seat, Luke. White, one sugar. You see, I remember.'

Her hand scoops back the wayward curls that have fallen down over her left eyebrow and suddenly a year just melts away. So much has happened in the interim and yet my feelings haven't diminished at all.

'Thanks. Um ... right. I've priced each window and door separately, in case you want to do it in a couple of hits.' I slide the quotation form across the table, tilting it so I can run my finger down the columns. 'In this box you'll see a total cost, this is for hardwood and this is for uPVC. If you want anything other than the standard white finish there will be a surcharge.'

When I finish speaking I look up at her and I can see she's staring at me and not the figures.

'Is that all you have to say? I've been sitting here for the best part of an hour, waiting, and that's it?'

I swallow hard. I skipped the presentation, thinking she wanted to get straight to the cost and now she thinks I'm a rank amateur. I dive into my briefcase, pulling out a glossy window brochure.

'Of course I'll leave you with all the information to help you make an informed choice—' My words tail off, I can see she's not at all impressed and I've blown it.

'I'm not with Seth, Luke. I never was. Unwittingly I think I've broken his heart, but he understands. He said that as soon as he saw the way I looked at you yesterday, he knew when he asked me to marry him that I would turn him down. He still asked the question, though, because he wanted to make absolutely sure. When you love someone it's what you do.'

I sit back, my stunned eyes searching her face.

'You rejected Seth, for me?'

She rolls her eyes. 'This isn't about options, Luke.' Elana pushes away the brochure with force and it slides across the table, landing on the floor. 'There is no second-best when it comes to affairs of the heart. You can't engineer *love*, that's why they call it *fatal* attraction. You find yourself attracted to someone regardless of the consequences, knowing that no matter what goes wrong in the future, you have to go with what your heart tells you. It's taken me a while to realise that. Seth is a good man, but I'm not in love with him. I let you walk out of my life for what seemed like all the right reasons at the time. I wouldn't change that, because here we are nearly a year later starting with a clean slate. There are no guarantees for anyone, but at long last I've cut all of my ties with the past. I'm ready to move on, but are you?'

When I still don't say anything, she stands abruptly, the sound of her chair scraping on the floor cutting through the silence, gratingly. My eyes follow Elana as she walks off into the kitchen, standing at the sink with her back to me.

'Luke, I think you'd better leave, now. I've made a big mistake. I'll be in touch about the windows.'

I gather everything up and walk towards the front door, my head feeling like it's going to explode. When I stop and turn, her stance is still rigid.

'I—'

'Just go.'

Chapter 57

Luke

Time to Man-up

Outside in the car the numbness begins to wear off and anger takes over as her words sink in. I turn the key and the engine kicks into life, but inside I'm screaming at myself. Silent words that fill my head. 'What are you doing? Why didn't you just tell her how you feel?'

You're jealous of Seth, heck, you're even jealous of Niall, how sick is that? What else is there left to undermine your confidence and make you feel like you aren't good enough for Elana? You're running out of excuses, Luke, and you know it. It's time to be the man you want to be, not the one you're in danger of becoming if you keep hanging onto this negative self-image. Can't you see what you are doing to yourself?

As the wheels spin off the drive, I slam a hand down onto the steering wheel with force. 'Enough.'

How do you make up for being a total idiot, when someone feels you have hurt them in the worst possible way? And how do you make a woman like Elana hold her breath as you tell her you love her? Whatever I do has to be big, and bold, and leave her in no doubt whatsoever that I've always loved her, and I always will.

At work I go through the motions, a part of me wracking my brains for ideas. Then it hits me. I pick up the phone.

'Janice, I have a few errands to run and probably won't make it back here today. If anything urgent crops up you can get me on the mobile.'

***

I've never been in a jeweller's shop on my own before and I don't think I've ever been this uncomfortable, or so self-conscious. Two of the assistants are serving other customers. At the far end of the shop an older guy in a very smart suit, whom I assume is the manager, and a young sales woman are deep in conversation. They don't appear to have noticed me. My eyes scan the cabinets and I wonder how anyone can ever make a decision when faced with this amount of choice.

'Can I help you?' The manager has strolled down to greet me, probably homing in on the fact that a part of me wants to turn and run.

'I need a ring.'

'Ah, you've come to the right place. Did you have any particular style in mind?' His tone is serious and I'm relieved to see that he isn't dismissing me as some time-waster.

'To be very honest, I have no idea what I'm looking for, but I expect I'll know it when I see it. She's a very particular lady, good taste, and I'm looking for something a little different.'

'Come this way. I'll pull a selection and we can take it from there.'

How long does it take to choose one ring? Well, the best part of an hour, it seems. Eventually all three of the sales ladies, and the manager, help me to whittle it down to a choice of two. It's the most expensive item I've ever purchased, other than the car, and it's a tough call.

'It's between the French-set, split shank eighteen-carat white-gold ring and the more traditional cushion-shaped diamond-halo style. The choice is yours, sir; only you know the lady in question.'

All eyes are on me. The square one is simple and elegant, but the French-set ring is, to my eye, more romantic. It's a statement, it's bold and, although both rings have a one-carat stone at the centre, I can actually visualise Elana wearing this.

'Well, I've made my decision and I think she's going to love this one. Thank you all so much for your help. I was really rather clueless when I walked through the door.'

'You are very welcome,' one of the ladies replies, the others nodding in agreement. 'This is a very special ring indeed and any woman would be thrilled to open a box and find it inside.'

It seems, at last, that I'm capable of making a good decision and, clearly, these ladies are impressed. As I leave the shop with it in my hand, the manager escorts me to the door.

'Good luck, but I'm sure you won't need it. I wish everyone who walked through this door was as sure of their intended, as you are, Sir. It would make our job so much easier.'

'Well, if all goes well I'll be back for the wedding ring really soon.'

He inclines his head, as I walk through the door and out into the busy street. I can do this and, what's more, I can do it with style!

Chapter 58

Elana

Never Give Up

A visit to the very grand Ellemore Publishing offices in London for a meeting is quite a trek. Mum and Dad are on holiday, savouring the warm Italian sunshine, so Carol and Philip are doing the school run today and will pop Maya home after they've given her tea. My train is due in at five p.m. so I should be home by five-thirty. A quick glance at my watch shows that it's running on time and in an hour I'll be stepping over the threshold.

It's been a good day and I'm excited about the new project. This biography is going to be a delight, as I've been a Patricia Montague fan for many years. As a newly-wed it was Patricia's cookery programme that inspired me to experiment. Her smooth voice and charisma made many a reluctant cook step up to the chopping board for the first time. Clickety-clack, clickety-clack. The rumble of the train is comforting, as if it's saying 'homeward bound, homeward bound'. The city is exciting, but when you are on your own it can make a person feel diminutive. Insignificant, even, as you become swallowed up in the vast crowds of people on the streets. I guess I'm just a country gal at heart and the pace of village life is enough for me.

Maya is doing so well at school and she's changing fast, from the shy, rather intense, little girl she was into this little person who isn't afraid to be heard. She has a level of confidence that often leaves me astounded. She is always lecturing me on what I should, and shouldn't, do. It's hard not to laugh, as more often than not she's right. With regard to Seth, she simply said that it was a shame, but I could tell that she wasn't at all surprised at my decision to turn him down. I feared she'd be disappointed as they had quickly established a real rapport. I could tell Maya enjoyed having an older man in her life; someone who could give her answers to the myriad questions floating around inside her head. When I asked her whether she was alright about it, she simply said 'It happens, Mum. You'll know when you meet the one.' How adult is that?

Clickety-clack, clickety-clack. I mustn't risk falling asleep, lulled by the swishing of the train as it speeds along. Homeward-bound.

Philip's car isn't on the drive as I pull up in front of the garage. However, the lights are on in the cottage. I open the door half-expecting to be greeted by Carol and Maya, and informed that Philip is fetching a takeaway as a treat. Instead it's very quiet, no TV or chattering to be heard. It's never quiet here, as Maya always has some sort of music going on in the background.

'Hello?' I shed my coat and slip off my shoes. Stopping to rub my left foot, which is sporting a blister from all the walking, I call out 'I'm home.'

Silence. The door to the sitting room is ajar, and as I swing it open my jaw drops. Luke and Maya are sitting side by side on the sofa. I have to swallow before I can talk.

'Surprise!' Maya jumps up and runs towards me, wrapping her arms around my waist before stepping back to look up at me with smiling eyes.

'Um ... Is everything alright? Where are Granddad and Grandma? I didn't see your vehicle out there, Luke.'

'They left a little while ago.'

Luke stands, glancing across at me nervously. 'I parked up on the top road. There wasn't any space down here when I arrived.' He looks as if he's telling a fib. There's always space.

'What's going on?' I feel breathless, as if I've just come back from a run. I'm surprised Philip and Carol would simply let Luke in and then go off home, as if he's a babysitter. I mean, they know Luke and, of course, Maya is safe with him, but he's only dropping off the receipt for the deposit for the windows. It's rather an imposition and rather out of character.

'Mum, we've been sitting here talking about the chimney.'

'The chimney?'

'You know, time to write that letter to Santa, ready for it to go up in smoke? You're the one who believes in the little bit of magic, Mum.'

I smile, raising my eyebrows at Luke in acknowledgement. They've been reminiscing about last Christmas, when Luke was here working on the cottage.

'Ah, the letters on the ledge.' I nod and we exchange smiles.

'So I've written mine and Luke wrote one, too. We thought it would be nice to light the fire tonight.'

Maya seems in the mood to really get the festivities started, despite the fact that whenever I mention Santa these days she rolls her eyes.

'But first,' Luke jumps in, 'I think you ought to read them, just in case Santa can't deliver. Remember Maya's request for the grand piano?'

Maya and Luke glance at each other and begin laughing. My heart constricts as my eyes take in every little curve of his face and the way his smile lights up his face. They're teasing me and that's the price I pay for his babysitting services. I have no choice but to play along, but I'll be honest and say that it hurts seeing the two of them conspiring, as if they are close. Life isn't fair sometimes, but then no one ever said it was meant to be.

'Okay. If I get soot on the sleeve of this blouse, you guys, I won't be happy.'

I move over to the fireplace and bend, curling my arm up under and extending my hand out to reach the ledge. Reaching out, it only takes a moment to locate the carefully folded pieces of paper.

'So I have to read these?' I hold them up in front of me, half-laughing as they both nod their heads in unison.

The first one is in Maya's handwriting and simply reads:
Just say yes!

The second makes my heart skip a beat.
Marry me?

I look up at Luke as he stands there, his eyes seeking out my own. He looks like he's holding his breath. He says nothing.

'Mum, open the music box.'

Maya nods at the little box with the bay tree on top. I wipe away a tear that begins to trickle down my cheek, my heart pounding and my legs beginning to feel distinctly shaky. When I tip the lid there's a small red box inside. I take it out and stand with it in my hand. My eyes wander and I notice there are streaks of soot on my fingers and a smudge on the cuff of my blouse.

'Open it,' Luke whispers, softly.

It's exquisite; the perfect ring, and something I would happily have chosen for myself. When I look back up at him his gaze holds mine for a few seconds, which seem to stretch out into an eternity.

'Will you marry me, Elana? Will you let me take care of you and Maya, and let Joe and me be a part of your lives? I've loved you since the very beginning. I just didn't think you could ever love me back.'

Maya hasn't moved a muscle. She's standing with her hands pressed over her mouth, then lets them slide down to her chin.

'Say *yes*, Mum, say *yes*! You know he's the one!'

'Of course it's a *yes*. I just thought you'd never get around to asking the question.'

Suddenly we all step forward at the same time and hug, a mass of arms, tears and pure joy.

'Time to put the letters back and light the fire, Mum. Make the magic happen.'

And so that's what we did. The fire grew from a gentle lap of flames licking around the logs into a welcoming and warming intensity of heat as we sealed the deal.

With Maya safely tucked up in bed, I rejoin Luke and he takes my hand, his lips brushing my cheek. As his arms circle around me he pulls my body into him and buries his head into my hair.

'At last, you're mine, really mine.' His words are but a whisper and his breath tickles as I relax into him. I feel safe and I know that I'm the luckiest woman in the world. He has no idea how wonderful and strong he is; or how much it excites me to be in his embrace.

'I love you, Luke. And I need you. I want to go to sleep in your arms and I want your face to be the first thing I see every morning when I wake up.'

He lifts me up in those strong, muscular arms of his and I fight a little smile that hovers around my lips. Every woman wants a hero and Luke has rescued me from myself.

'That's an invitation no man could refuse. Guess I'm one hell of a lucky guy to be the one you picked. And maybe it's about time I showed you just how much you've fired me up, Elana.'

I feign a look of shock as he carries me out of the sitting room, but I can't resist kissing him softly on the neck.

'Well, I hope it's worth the wait.' My words make him laugh and I put a finger to his lips to remind him that we have to keep the noise down a little.

And it was. Totally worth the wait.

This year the only thing that will be on my Christmas list

will be a *thank you* to Santa for helping to make my family, and my life, truly complete. No one is ever too old for a little Christmas magic – are they? And fate takes us where we need to go when the time is right.

Epilogue

'Hi, Daddy. I'm so happy you're back, I've missed you.'
'I've been here, my darling, but you can't always see
me.' Niall's form is merely a shadow, but it's enough to comfort
Maya.

'I like it when you visit me, Daddy. It's been a while.'

'I know, Princess. But I have a new job, now. I need to help
some people who are feeling really sad. It means that I'm
going to be very busy.'

'You won't be able to visit me any more?' Maya's bottom
lip begins to quiver.

'Hey, Princess, I need you to be my big, strong, girl. You
have Mummy and Joe, now and Luke is here to take care of
you all.'

Maya nods her head. 'Luke makes Mummy very happy,
Daddy and I love having Joe here.'

Niall smiles at her and his voice is full of love. 'I chose two
very special people to come into your lives, so you wouldn't
miss me quite so much.'

'But I can still talk to you, Daddy, can't I?'

'Yes, always, Princess.'

'Will you stay with me until I fall asleep?'

'Of course I will. And I want you to know how very proud of you I am, my darling.'

'Love you a million, trillion and one, Daddy. Forever, and ever.'

In the stillness of the night Niall remains at his daughter's bedside until Maya's soft little snores are all that break the silence. He takes one last look around the room. Love radiates out from his heart, filling the space, and a sense of peace and well-being envelops him. It's time to finally let go. Elana and Maya are ready to move on and his job is done.

'Love you a million, trillion and two, Princess. Always will.'

Acknowledgements

When you are a writer you sit at home in front of the PC with only your characters to keep you company. It's wonderful, of course, but sometimes you find yourself craving company, or a listening ear. In the words of the celebrated English poet, John Donne, 'No man is an island'.

I couldn't do what I do if it wasn't for the people who keep me on track, keep me sane and are kind enough to be there during the highs and the lows.

I have to begin by thanking my superb editor, Charlotte Ledger. Working with her is always a delight and although her prods are gentle, she has me scurrying away to add an extra chapter or two, or make those tweaks that will take my story to another level. For me, that relationship is very special and it has made me grow in ways I can't even begin to explain.

The wider HarperImpulse/Harper Collins team do a tremendous job and it really helps to have that sterling support in such a fast-changing and fast-paced environment. Of course, beyond that is the wonderful team of HarperImpulse supporters – the readers and reviewers who are there to shout about the newest releases and help get the word out. You are all stars!

When it comes to personal, writerly support and sharing the angst as a new book baby is born, I send hugs to author friends Mandy Baggot, Janice Horton, Julie Ryan and Sheryl Browne, in particular. You guys provide a wonderful listening ear and words of wisdom, for which I'm eternally grateful! But beyond that is a community of online friends whose Tweets and FB shares demonstrate their very generous spirit.

Then there is the wonderful band of book bloggers and readers who have supported me since the start of my career. In no particular order: Shona, Noemie, Debbie, Anniek, Suze, Nikki, Nicky, Charlotte, Jo, Susan, AJ, Heidi, Kate, Shaz, Tracey, Kaisha, Barbara, Michele, Katie, Beverley, Rachel, Jane, Georgina, Ali, Susan, Cathy ... to name a few. But to each and every one I send my heart-felt gratitude for every review or recommendation, whether written, or by word of mouth.

Finally, my husband, Lawrence, who puts up with my irregular hours which means I can often be found in my PJs late in the afternoon, because I'm on a writing binge. Or jumping out of bed in the early hours of the morning and disturbing him, because an idea wakes me from my sleep. He understands that writing is my guilty pleasure and indulges me, because that what love is all about!

And, last but not least, to all the readers whose names I will never know. Thank you for choosing my book and stepping into the lives of the characters who made Bay Tree Cottage seem very real to me. I hope you enjoyed your visit and that it left you with that little feel-good glow.

Printed by RR Donnelley at Glasgow, UK